READY, STEADY, DIG!

BY

ROSALIND WINTER

Published in 2008 by YouWriteOn.com

Copyright © Rosalind Winter
First Edition

The author asserts the moral right under the Copyright, Designs and Patents Act 1988 to be identified as the author of this work.

All Rights reserved. No part of this publication may be reproduced, stored in a retrieval system, or transmitted, in any form or by any means, without the prior written consent of the author, nor be otherwise circulated in any form of binding or cover other than that in which it is published and without a similar condition being imposed on the subsequent purchaser.

Published by YouWriteOn.com

FOR TIM

1951 – 1990

*NUNC SAMEN INTEREA HAEC PRISCO QUAE MORE PARENTUM
TRADITIA SUNT TRISTI MUNERE AD INFERIAS,
ACCIPE SORORE MULTUM MANANTIA FLETU;
ATQUE IN PERPETUUM, FRATER, AVE ATQUE VALE*

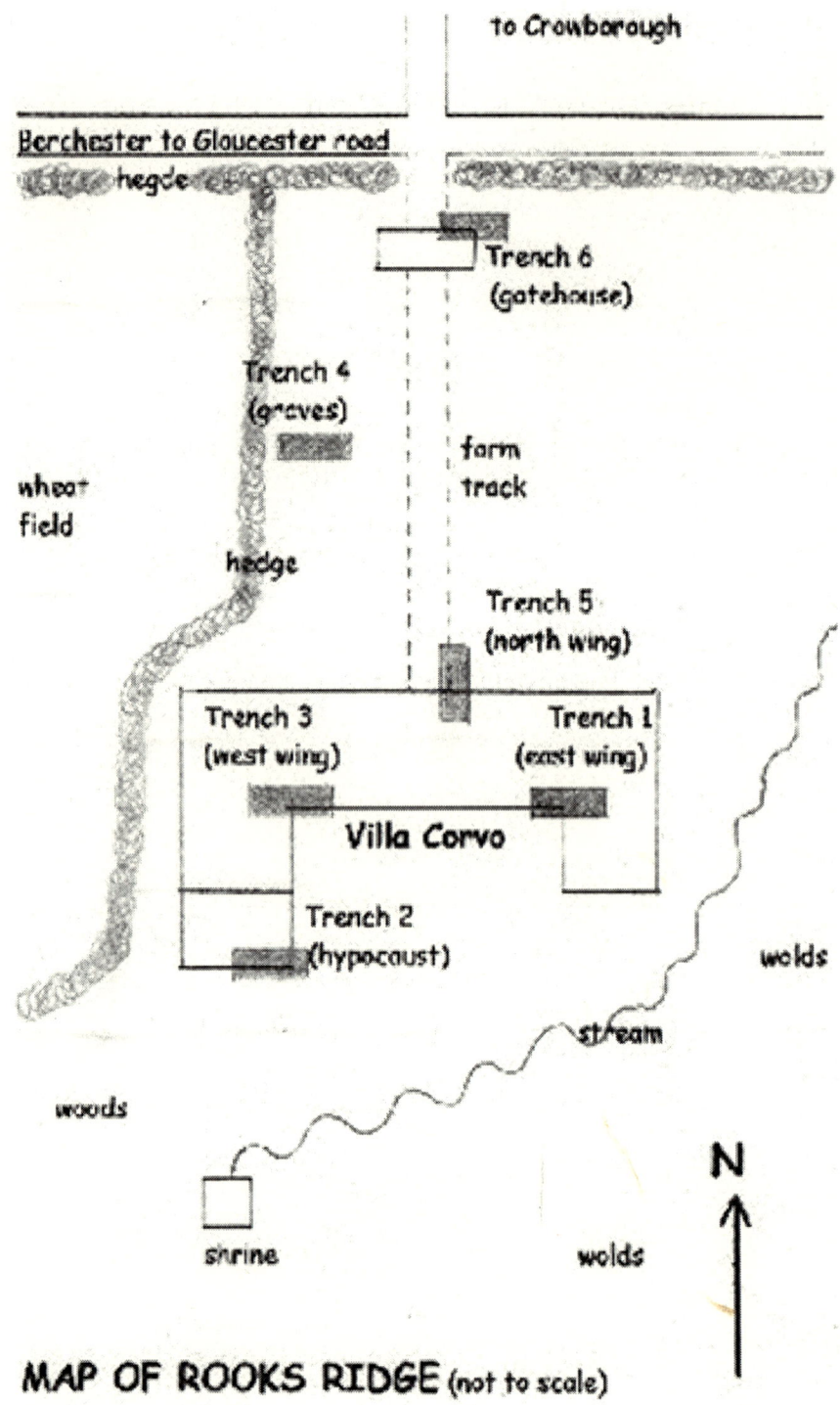

Lares (pronounced *Lah-reeze* or *Lair-eeze*) The little household gods of the ancient Roman world. Their origins are disputed: they probably started out as spirits of the farmlands and guardians of crossroads and boundaries. From there they were taken into the house, where they were worshipped as the spirits of deceased ancestors, and were joined by the Penates (q.v.), to form a single group of household guardians. Each family would honour its own Lares and Penates in the form of little statues of metal, clay or stone, which were kept beside the hearth, often in a stone shrine known as a Lararium (plural *Lararia*). The Lares presided over every aspect of the home and especially of the kitchen (there was even a Lar of the Broom), while the Penates had charge of the household's food supplies.

- extract from *The Rooks Ridge Classical Dictionary,* edited by Ronald Horton MA (Lond.)

PROLOGUE
Rome, A.D. 25

Chip chip chip. Tap tap. Chip chip. Tap tap tap.

All the while as he chiselled away in the dusty sunlight, the stonemason whispered softly under his breath. They were words that he barely understood, but he knew that they had to be said. They had to be said *to make it work.* He didn't know exactly what happened, or how. He only knew that he had to whisper the words as he chiselled away at the soft yellow-grey sandstone.

Chip chip. Tap tap tap. Chip chip.

On the surface of the stone, tiny grains of sand fell away, and the shape of a head began to emerge, while inside the stone tiny grains of sand moved and shuffled and re-arranged themselves into new patterns, according to the stonemason's whispered words, until after a while Somebody began to wonder - *Who am I ...?*

Chip. Tap tap. Chip chip.

More sand grains fell away, and now the stonemason held a little man-shaped figurine, no more than six inches high, and more sand grains re-arranged themselves inside the stone, and Somebody thought - *What am I ...? Where am I ...?*

The stonemason put down his chisel, wetted his hands, and scooped out some coarse-grained grit from a pouch at his belt. Slowly, carefully, muttering what he knew were the most important words of all, he began to shape the features, rasping away at the sandstone with his strong, calloused fingers, coated in abrasive grit, shifting a grain or two at a time from the roughly-shaped face, until there began to emerge a broad clear brow with thick curly hair springing back, a small snub nose, round cheeks and full lips that settled into a half-smile, and a strong chin with a little cleft in it. And as the stonemason worked and whispered the words, Somebody thought - *Yes! I am Petro ... I am Petro the Lar ... and this is Home!*

It was done. The stonemason relaxed with a long sigh of relief, and set the little statue on top of the Lararium. Inside the stone box, eleven other stone figurines nudged each other and exchanged speculative glances. Someone new?

'Finished, Master,' said the stonemason, looking up at a sturdy, round-faced man with thick curly black hair springing back from a broad clear brow. Marcus Verus Pugnax Corvo smiled, and rubbed his strong cleft chin.

'Excellent,' he said. 'Splendid workmanship. I shall perform the dedication immediately.'

Time passed, suns rose and set, winters came and went, and Marcus Verus Pugnax Corvo faded from the memory of his household and his family, but not from the memory of his twelve Lares. The Lares continued to serve and guard his household and his family, even when Marcus was long gone, all through the years and the many moves from Rome, to Masilia, to Londinium, to Berium Castra.

Four hundred years on from the making of Petro, the family moved once more, to a brand new villa in the wild green wolds of west Britannia, ten miles from Berium. They were Roman miles, of course, only ten thousand paces, but still a long way from the safety of the town. Too far, perhaps? So when the legions began to withdraw from Britannia to protect the mother city of Rome, and rumours of barbarian invaders chilled the hearts of country-dwellers, Caius Verus Pugnax Corvo took the decision to leave the villa and move his family back to the greater security of Berium Castra. It was to be a short-term measure, just until the danger had passed, so he buried the bulk of his treasures, with six of his Lares to guard them.

'Guard and protect these precious treasures of our household, O Lares, little gods of hearth and home. Let no strangers come a-nigh them, let no wicked hands defile them,' said Caius, in his most solemn and portentous voice. His wife, his children and his slaves coughed and shuffled restlessly in the cold morning air, impatient to be off, but Caius was not to be hurried. 'Stay faithfully and guard this our home and these our treasures, I conjure and command you, by Jupiter, Father of the Gods, by Janus, god of the threshold, by Portumnus, god of the entrance, by Cardea, goddess of the hinges, by Forculus, god of the door-leaves, by Limentinus, god of the lintel, by Culina, goddess of the kitchen, by Lanx, goddess of the platters, by Catillus and Catinus, gods of the little dishes, by Olla, goddess of the pots and the jars, by Cultrus, god of the cutlery, by Mola, goddess of the grindstone, by Scopus, god of the broom, by Peniculus, god of the mop, by Focus, god of the fireplace, by Caminus, god of the chimney, by Vesta, great goddess of the hearth, and by every god and goddess of this land, I charge you never to cease your sleepless guard, until the sun dies and the moon fails, or until the Family Verus Pugnax Corvo returns unto its own.'

At last the stone cap fell into place over the mouth of the treasure pit, and the assembled crowd of family and slaves let out a collective sigh of relief as it was carefully mortared in place. The scraping of the trowel was just loud enough to drown the sound of a gloomy little voice from down below.

'Well, lads, that's us told.'

CHAPTER I
Somewhere in the Cotswolds, May 1998

'Petro! Hey, Shorty! C'mere!'

The summons comes from a tiny, a *very* tiny man, dressed in browny-green homespun. At a glance he is the archetypal elderly Cotswold labourer; but if you do more than just glance at him, something about him makes your eyes ache. He *shimmers*. And suddenly you see that he isn't a tiny man at all: he is a huge man, big as the hills, tall as the heavens, and the browny-green is leaves and grass and earth and stone, and in his blue-grey eyes is the whole infinite, cloud-dappled, lark-haunted Cotswold sky. Then, if you dare to look again - yup, you were right the first time, he is just six inches tall.

Anyone perceiving the wisdom in those little, enormous eyes might guess that he is a genius, and they would be right. Well, in a way. He is a *Genius Loci*, a Spirit of Place, and here in the heart of *his* place he has all the strength and power and knowledge of the landscape itself.

Definitely not someone to mess with. Not here, anyway.

'Hey, Petro! Don't mess with me, I know you're in there! Get yourself out here right now!'

'Okay, okay, keep your turf on,' comes a muffled response from somewhere that is clearly below ground. There are scuffling sounds. 'I'm trying to get through, it's those dratted rabbits again, they've brought half the tunnel down.'

'Well, get a move on, you're needed up here,' says the Genius Loci impatiently. 'There's one of Your Lot in trouble.'

The scuffling sounds stop, and there is a shocked silence.

'What do you mean, one of My Lot?'

'What do you think I mean?' demands the Genius Loci in a voice that is getting increasingly irritable. 'Your Lot. Them. *The Family*.'

'Jupiter's cafetiere!' the underground Petro responds. (He prides himself on being a modern Lar, and cafetieres strike him as one of the more exciting innovations in the world of kitchen equipment. Back in the old days, a Lar only had a few crude, miserable implements to swear by, like pickle forks). 'One of *Our*

Lot?' he exclaims. 'But that's amazing! There hasn't been one of them here for years and years. We thought they'd all gone. I mean, we knew there must still be some around somewhere, otherwise we Lares would all have turned back into stone, but –'

'Look, are you going to get yourself out of that hole and come and give me a hand? Or are you going to stay down there chatting and playing mud-pies while one of Your Lot's in trouble?' says the Genius Loci, his mounting irritability now manifesting itself in a faint shaking of nearby leaves and branches, although there is no other sign of the lightest breeze.

There is a cautious silence.

'Come where, exactly?' asks Petro rather breathlessly, from beneath a slowly growing mound of topsoil. 'You know we Lares can't get very far from Home without coming over all peculiar.'

'Of course I know that. Miserable creatures, you Lares, a good long hike in the fresh air and sunshine wouldn't do you a mite of harm,' says the Genius Loci.

'You know perfectly well that it would,' says Petro firmly. 'That's the point. Here We Are, Here We Stay. And if we don't, we –

'Come over all peculiar, yes, all right, all right, I know. But it's not far,' says the Genius Loci, in tones of grudging encouragement. 'She's just down from the ridge. I'm surprised you couldn't tell she was there.'

'Wherever she is, she can't be that close,' says Petro. 'I'm not getting anything at all - at least - at least - *Wow! Juno's electric garlic press!* You're absolutely right! That's just got to be one of The Family! Hang on, hang on, I'm nearly there -'

The mound of topsoil suddenly breaks open, and a small head pokes out. You can see at a glance that the little figure that emerges is made of stone, but if you do more than just glance, you can see his black curls bobbing as he shakes his head to clear his hair of sandy soil, and you can see the fabric of his stone tunic move as he flaps it free of the clinging dirt. Just thinking about it makes your brain hurt.

'You're right,' says Petro, looking towards the edge of the plateau on which they are standing. 'She's over there, yes?' He points to the west, where the ground drops away sharply. 'No, I suppose it's not that far,' he says rather doubtfully. 'Well, maybe it is a bit - but it's still on our land, isn't it, so I'm sure I should be able to -'

'*Your* land?'

'The Family's land, I mean,' says Petro hastily. 'And yours, of course. So why don't you help her?' he adds. 'What do you need me for? Not that I don't want to help, of course, it's just that it *is* a little bit far for me. Mind you, I should be all right, so long as I'm with one of the Family. I think.'

'Wimp,' says the Genius Loci. 'Anyway, you know perfectly well why I can't do anything. We genii never reveal ourselves: people get upset. As I understand it, they can see quite clearly that we are about six inches high and at least a thousand feet tall, and for some reason it bothers them. Now you, anyone can see that you're just a skinny little runt, no threat to anything bigger than a rabbit.'

'Rabbits can be quite scary,' says Petro with dignity, 'especially when they're defending their young.' The Genius Loci rolls his eyes, and the sky above goes momentarily *fuzzy.*

'Oh all right, all right,' says Petro. 'Just show me the way.'

The Genius Loci strides off. The Lar follows him to the edge of the plateau, where he pauses, and looks down. A few yards below him lies a small figure, a young girl no more than twelve years old, very pale and quite, quite still.

'She's not dead, is she?' asks Genius Loci. 'I can't tell from here, and I ought not to get any closer.'

'No,' says Petro. 'She's not dead, or I wouldn't be here. But she's not - she's not - *well.*'

'Oh for the love of Lucius, of course she's not *well,*' says the Genius Loci impatiently. 'If she was well she wouldn't be lying there like that, and her left arm would have one joint, not two.'

'Ah, yes,' says Petro. 'I see. She's broken her arm. And fainted from the pain, I expect.' He thinks about it. 'You know, it's not really me that she needs, it's Lapidilla,' he says. Nearby leaves and branches rustle irritably. 'Oh all right, all right. I'll - I'll -'

'Do something useful?'

'Er, yes,' says Petro, sidling rather nervously closer to the inert form. 'Er, hello there? Can you hear me?'

Big brown eyes open, spot Petro, and open wider. Much wider.

'Hello,' says Petro again. 'I'm here to help you.'

'Oh good,' says the girl faintly. 'I'm glad that's what you're here for.' They both think about it for a bit. 'What exactly are you going to do to help?' she asks.

Petro could swear the leaves and branches are grinning, and he hears a very faint sound like *That's got you stumped, Shorty.'* He ignores the Genius Loci, and straightens his tunic in a businesslike way.

'Well, let's see,' he says. 'First of all I could do something about that arm.'

'Don't touch it!' squeals the girl. 'It hurts!'

'I'm not surprised,' says Petro. 'It's broken.'

'You're a fairy, right?' says the girl. 'Does that mean you can mend it by magic?'

'Well, not exactly mend it,' says Petro, 'and definitely not by magic. But I can certainly make it better. I mean, better than it is now. I can't make it well, but I can make it better. If you see what I mean. And no, I'm not a fairy.' He winces as he says it. He'd thought that people had stopped believing in fairies around about 1450, except for a few rather peculiar Victorian Men of Science, but clearly he was wrong.

'So what are you?' The girl sits up slowly, carefully cradling her broken arm, and looks at him intently. 'You're made of stone, aren't you? Only you can't be, because you're moving and talking. But you are.'

'That's right,' says Petro. 'I'm made of stone. I'm a Lar. Actually, I'm one of your Lares. There's six of us who were left behind here, and I'm one of them. Me. I'm Petro. Petro the Lar. Your Lar.' He tails off at the girl's look of polite incomprehension. 'You don't know what a Lar is, do you?' he asks.

The girl shakes her head. Black curls bounce and her small snub nose wrinkles.

Jupiter's apple-corer! thinks Petro. *She's the living image of Vera Alauda. Looking at her is like going back sixteen hundred years. Dear, sweet, sad Vera Alauda.* Stone tears glint briefly in his eyes.

'What's your name?' he asks. 'Domina,' he adds politely. She smiles.

'I know 'domina',' she announces with some pride. 'It's Latin for lady. I've just started Latin. Is 'Lar' Latin as well?'

'That's right,' says Petro, mildly surprised.

'It's probably in Chapter 4, or somewhere like that,' says the girl. 'I'm only on Chapter 2, that's the second declension, you know, dominus, domine, dominum. It's quite easy.'

'Um, yes,' says Petro, 'I suppose it is. And your name is - ?' he prompts.

'Vera,' she replies. 'Vera Rookwood.'

'Domina Vera,' says Petro. *No surprises there, he thinks. All the Family's girls are Vera, or Hilda, or Marcia, or - well, they would be, wouldn't they? They are the Verae Pugnaces Corvones, whether they know it or not. And Rookwood, of course ... now there's a Corvo surname if ever there was one!*

'So anyway,' says Vera, 'what's a Lar, and why have I got one?'

'We're household gods,' says Petro. 'We guard the Family and the Household, for ever and ever, or until we turn to stone, or someone tells us to stop. Someone in the Family, of course. Whichever is the sooner,' he adds, feeling that more is called for.

'The household?'

'Yes, the villa and everything in it,' Petro replies. 'Your villa.'

Vera looks at him, bewildered. 'But we haven't got a villa,' she says. 'We've got a council house. Number Six, Harnstone Close, Crowborough.'

'Oh, I don't mean where you *live*,' says Petro. 'At least not where you live now. I mean your home. Your Family's home. The Villa Corvo.' He gestures at the ridge above their heads. 'It's up there, just over the ridge.'

'There isn't a villa up there,' says Vera firmly. 'At least not if a villa is what I think it is, you know, mosaics and hypocausts and things. And bath-houses. It's just fields up there. I know it is. Well, it was,' she adds cautiously, 'when I last looked, which was about an hour ago, I think. Did I faint?'

'Yes,' says Petro.

'I don't know how long for, I mean it might have been more than an hour, or less, but anyway I know there was no villa there when I last looked,' says Vera. 'And if there was one now, I'd be able to see the roof at least from here.'

9

'It's under the ground,' explains Petro. 'At least, what's left of it.'

'You mean, like archaeology?'

'Well, a bit,' agrees Petro. 'That's what they call grave-robbing these days, isn't it?'

'Grave-robbing? Are there are graves too?' asks Vera.

'Of course,' says Petro. 'The Family's graves are all along the road.'

'There isn't a road,' says Vera. 'Do you mean the farm track?'

'Yes, that's right, it's just a farm track now, of course. It used to be the road that served the villa,' says Petro. 'A Roman road.'

'It is very straight,' Vera concedes. 'All Roman roads were straight, I know that.'

'This one goes straight to Crowborough. It's a farm track now, until you get to the bottom of the hill, and then it turns into a proper road again,' says Petro, feeling that they are straying rather a long way from the point, whatever that had been.

'So there's this villa,' says Vera, 'or there was, and it's where my family lived when it was a villa?'

'And since. The site has been re-used many times over the years,' says Petro, remembering some of them with a shudder. Heorot! The noise! The *quaffing!* Even the gladiator barracks had been more peaceful. 'There's not very much to see on the surface now, just a few stones and bumps in the ground, but we Lares are all still there, down in the foundations. We live in the hypocaust mainly, in the west wing under the old bath-house. Rabbits keep digging tunnels down to us, it's quite useful when we need to get above ground. Not that we do very often, it's not as if we can actually go anywhere, at least, not without one of the Family.'

'Haven't you ever been anywhere?' Vera asks curiously.

'Oh yes,' says Petro, rather wistfully. 'I was made in Rome, and after that the Family moved around all over the place. They were in lots of places in Italy, and Gaul, and Britannia, until they settled here. Then they went away to Berium Castra - I think it's called Berchester now - and they left us behind, and we're still here. It's our job to look after - ' he hesitates '- things, until they come back.'

'What things?' asks Vera, who doesn't miss much. 'Hidden treasure?'

'Wouldn't you like me to fix that arm?' asks Petro, changing the subject firmly. Vera moves her broken left arm gingerly, and decides to save up the more important questions for later.

'Yes please,' she says. 'What are you going to do?'

'Well, it sort of works like this,' says Petro, and stares very hard at the broken limb. *'Bracchium sana,'* he says. 'Is that any better?'

Vera touches her left arm cautiously with her right hand.

'It is a bit,' she says. 'Thank you. It doesn't really hurt any more, but it's still a funny shape.'

'I'm afraid you're going to need someone to set the bone,' says Petro apologetically. 'We Lares don't have that sort of skill, or power. Especially not this far from the villa.'

'You said it was just over the ridge,' says Vera.

'Well, that's a long way if you're a Lar,' says Petro. 'In fact, I'm not feeling too good just now. I really would like to get back up there. Do you think you could get a bit closer, if I give you a hand?' Vera looks sceptically at Petro's tiny fists. 'I mean, like this.' He concentrates hard, and says *'Adiuva.'*

Vera gets very carefully to her feet, and begins to move unsteadily up towards the ridge. Petro follows her, anxiously.

'Not bad, Shorty,' whispers a bramble bush, or something deep within its leaves.

CHAPTER II

Up on the plateau, deep under ground in the remains of the hypocaust, a small rough-haired terrier is getting irritable, or rather more irritable, irritability being the default state of terriers everywhere.

'Seen any rabbits, then?' demands the terrier of the two small, man-shaped figurines who are watching him from behind one of the crumbling brick pillars. Only the fact that they are man-shaped deters him from biting them, biting things being the habitual reaction of terriers to almost everything. Odd, he thinks, they don't smell of man. They smell of stone. He shrugs off the thought. There are far more important things to think about just now, like rabbits, and also (although this he is trying to ignore) the very real possibility that he may be stuck.

'Rabbits? Rabbits?' says the smaller of the two figurines, whose name is Mopsus. 'Dunno, Dog, what's a rabbit?'

'You know,' says the terrier. 'Little furry beggars, long ears, twitchy noses, too cute for their own good.'

'No, that's hares,' says Mopsus firmly. 'There's no rabbits here. We're Romans, we are, we've never heard of rabbits, have we, Grumio? Rabbits didn't come in until the Normans.' There is a small pause. 'I shouldn't have said that, should I?'

The larger figurine rolls his eyes.

'So where's these non-Roman rabbits, then?' asks the terrier, in a way that is definitely menacing, and includes a swift glimpse of small white teeth.

'I don't know why you're bothering to cover up for them, Mopsus,' says the larger of the two figurines, whose name is Grumio. 'Noisy little beggars, parties every blooming night, and they breed like, well, rabbits.'

'I like them,' says Mopsus in a small voice. 'The dog's right, they are cute.' Grumio rolls his eyes again.

'So?' says the terrier. 'Where are they, then? I know they live here, I can smell them.'

'They're out,' says Grumio. He doesn't like the rabbits much, but he doesn't like the terrier either. Not liking things is Grumio's default state. The terrier bares his teeth again, and growls.

'Leave a message?' suggests Mopsus in a placating voice.

'You sure they're out?' demands the terrier, trying to see past the two Lares into the depths of the hypocaust, where a faint scratching and scuffling can be heard that could easily be one or more rabbits panicking in a confined space.

'Ho yes,' says Grumio firmly. 'We're household gods, we are. We'd know.'

'Right then,' says the terrier, trying to turn round. 'I'll be off now, come back later maybe.' He tries a bit harder to turn, and finds himself firmly wedged between two of the crumbling hypocaust pillars. 'Ah, couldn't give us a hand here, could you?'

Mopsus and Grumio look at the terrier and look at each other.

'Stuck, are you?' says Grumio unnecessarily. 'Not sure how to help you there. You could try Janus, I suppose.'

'Janus?'

'God of doorways,' explains Mopsus.

'A quick invocation might do the trick,' says Grumio. 'Mind you, I don't know if he turns out for dogs. Probably not,' he says, noting with some satisfaction that the terrier is starting to look distinctly panicky. 'That'll teach you to come digging where you're not wanted,' he adds. 'And you've brought half the tunnel down, that's a real pain, that is. Our Petro's Up Top, and he'll have a load of earth to shift when he wants to get back again.'

The terrier gives up on the two Lares, and starts to bark.

CHAPTER III

Up on the ridge is a wide flat plateau, with a number of humps and bumps in the short turf that to a trained eye could easily be the remains of a Roman villa. The Cotswold escarpment rises to the east and south, and to the north and west the slope drops steeply down.

Running almost due north, a broad farm track plunges straight down the slope from the plateau to meet the main road from Berchester to Gloucester. Where the track meets the road it becomes a road itself, running for another arrow-straight half a mile to the little town of Crowborough in the valley bottom. A thick hedge of hazel and hawthorn follows the track down to the road, and on the west of the hedge is a small field of wheat. The hills to the south are densely wooded, but everywhere else, as far as the eye can see, is the short, sweet turf of the open wolds, sprinkled with harebells and scabious, wild thyme and trefoil, and a myriad other tiny downland flowers, and close-cropped by sheep and the rabbits who have made their warren up on the western side of the plateau.

Vera and Petro reach the top of the slope, from which Vera can just see her house on the edge of Crowborough. It is a place and a view that she loves and never tires of, even now when her broken arm is starting to throb again, and she knows that sooner or later she will have to make her way back home unaided.

Suddenly there is the sound of hysterical barking from somewhere below ground.

'That's Rags!' says Vera sharply, stopping abruptly at the top of the slope. 'I'm sure that's Rags.'

'Rags?' says Petro. 'It sounds more like a dog to me - a small terrier, maybe, or -'

'Yes, yes, he's a terrier, he's my Step-Dad's terrier!' says Vera. 'I remember now, I was supposed to be looking after him, and he ran off after a rabbit, and I was afraid he'd get stuck down a rabbit hole.'

The subterranean barking continues unabated.

'It sounds as if he's got stuck down a rabbit hole,' says Petro.

15

'And I ran after him, and I fell over something, and that's how I broke my arm,' says Vera, starting to sound tearful. 'Poor little Rags, supposing he can't breathe down there?'

'It sounds to me as if he can breathe just fine,' says Petro, raising his voice to make himself heard above the canine decibels.

'But he might run out of air before we can rescue him!' says Vera. 'Can't you do something?'

'Well -' Petro thinks about it, insofar as he can hear himself think. 'I could try - *Tace!*'

The result is instant silence, but the effect is not as satisfactory.

'You've killed him!' shrieks Vera, snatching up Petro with her good hand and shaking him madly. 'You've killed Rags!'

'Stop stop stop!' yells Petro. 'Put me down! Put me *down!* The dog's fine, I tell you!'

'He isn't barking,' says Vera suspiciously, but at least she stops shaking him. 'He normally never stops. How can you say he's fine? He's dead, I know he's dead, and my Step-Dad will kill me!'

'He's not dead, I've just shut him up,' says Petro firmly. 'I don't suppose it will last for long, I'm not very good at dogs, but it should hold for a few minutes at least. I suppose you want me to go and get him out for you?'

'Yes please,' says Vera meekly. She puts the Lar down gently on the grass. 'Be careful, he bites things.'

'What things?'

'Well, most things,' says Vera, 'and I don't want him to bite you.'

'Thank you, Domina.'

'I mean, you're made of stone, he could hurt his teeth.'

'And we wouldn't want that,' says Petro politely. 'Hang on up here, and I'll go and see what's what.' He bows hastily, and plunges into the small mound of loose topsoil from which he had earlier emerged. There are muffled sounds of coughing and spluttering, and Petro's head surfaces briefly.

'The dratted dog's brought the tunnel down,' he says. 'This may take some time.' His head disappears once more below the ground.

'Hurry! Oh, hurry!' urges Vera.

'Vera! Is that you, Vee? Who are you talking to, and where's Rags?' says a new voice, and Vera turns to see her Stepfather struggling up the slope towards her.

'There you are!' he says. 'Rags, where's Rags?'

'Darrell!' says Vera, torn between relief and apprehension. 'I broke my arm. Rags is down there - down in - down in - a rabbit hole,' she adds, realising that *down in the Roman villa* will require more explanation than she wants to attempt at this moment. Her arm is really hurting again now, and her Stepfather has a face like thunder, or more like thunder than usual. 'He ran away after a rabbit, and I think he's got stuck.'

'I told you to look after him!'

'I did, I tried, but he saw a rabbit,' says Vera, wondering whether bursting into tears at this point would be helpful, but deciding against it.

'Blasted dog,' says Darrell. 'I'll have to get a spade.' He turns abruptly, and sets off down the slope again at high speed.

'I broke my arm!' says Vera faintly, but with little expectation of any response. In her Stepfather's world, a child with a broken arm has nothing on a trapped dog, especially a champion ratter like Rags.

'Has he gone?' asks Petro's voice from a little below ground level. 'Who was he?'

'Darrell. He's my Step-Dad,' says Vera. 'He's gone to get a spade. Have you managed to find Rags yet?'

'Sorry, no, I just can't get through that way,' says Petro. 'A spade? You mean he's going to dig?'

'Well, yes,' says Vera. Petro heaves himself out of the ground.

'I'll try one of the other entrances,' he says. 'We have to get the wretched dog out before he comes back, we can't have him digging around here. Try to stop him, will you? Can't you tell him you've broken your arm?'

'I did,' says Vera sadly.

'And - ?'

'He's gone to get a spade.'

Petro regards her with new concern. She looks so like sweet, sad Vera Alauda, trying not to cry and having every reason in the world.

'I'll get the wretched dog out, don't you worry,' he says, trying to sound more confident than he really feels. 'And I'll see if I can get Lapidilla to come out and have a look at that arm for you,' he adds.

'Who's Lapidilla?' asks Vera.

'She's another Lar,' answers Petro. 'She'll be really excited to meet you, Domina Vera.' Vera smiles wanly. 'She's better than me at healing,' continues Petro. 'We Lares all have our own characteristics or special skills, and hers is healing. You'll like her. Just wait there.'

Petro scuttles off towards the hedge, and disappears between the roots of a hazel, where the rabbits have created one of many entrances to their warren in the villa foundations. Vera gives him a little wave as he vanishes, and sniffs hard to stop the tears which are threatening to come.

CHAPTER IV

Darrell Grindley is only thirty, but a regular substantial intake of beer and cigarettes is already slowing him down. However, with Rags' safety at stake he manages to make it back to the plateau in far less time than Vera might have hoped or expected. He is carrying a spade, and he is not alone. Concern for Rags' predicament has prompted him to enlist the help of two of his drinking buddies from next door, Arthur Lupin and his younger brother Orson, known as Big Mac. Big Mac has brought a pickaxe with him, and Arthur has a game bag, in case of rabbits.

'Right, out of the way, Vee,' says Darrell, and there is a renewed storm of hysterical subterranean barking as Rags recognises His Master's Voice.

'Yeah, let the dog see the rabbit,' says Arthur, chortling.

'Dog's down there,' says Big Mac, who is Big just about everywhere except his brain. It is widely believed that Big Mac's brain cells have had to learn semaphore in order to communicate with each other, and last time a doctor reluctantly looked in his ears, she was temporarily blinded by the daylight. Big Mac raises the pickaxe and brings it down with a resounding thump.

'Ouch!' says the Genius Loci, taken unawares by this sudden assault on his territory. He peers down from the woolly white softness of a passing cloud on which he has been quietly relaxing. He scowls at the little group on the plateau; the sky goes suddenly dark, and large drops of rain begin to fall in a highly localised, and some might say rather spiteful, pattern. The Genius Loci grins, and settles back again on his cloud, which has now turned distinctly grey and threatening.

'That's all we need, rain,' says Darrell crossly. Big Mac continues to wield his pickaxe for a few minutes, then he stands back to let Darrell in with the spade. Vera watches apprehensively as Darrell shovels away at earth which is rapidly turning to mud in the increasing downpour. She is getting cold, her arm hurts more and more, and she wants to go home, but the thought of Petro and the hidden villa detains her. Suddenly Darrell's spade breaks through into an underground cavity, and the sound of Rags' barking goes up several notches in volume. Darrell kneels down and peers into the hole.

'He's here!' he says. 'I think he's stuck.' Darrell gradually enlarges the hole, working with his hands now, and drops onto his belly to reach in. Rags yelps as Darrel manages to grab him by one of his back legs and pulls, but it's no good, he's still firmly stuck. Darrell lets go reluctantly and pushes himself to his feet again.

'We'll have to dig some more,' he says, looking at Arthur. Arthur has no intention of doing any hard work, something he tends to avoid at all costs, and he hands the spade back to Darrell. More digging enlarges the hole still further, and now Rags can be seen from above, wedged tightly between two crumbling pillars of brick.

'Blimey,' says Arthur, peering down into the hole. 'Blimey, Dazza, that's a hippy-corpse.'

Unlikely as it might seem to anyone who knows him, Arthur Lupin once watched a whole hour-long episode of a popular TV archaeology programme called *Ready Steady Dig!* This extraordinary event took place one Sunday afternoon following a particularly heavy lunch that included even more beer than usual, when he had mislaid the TV remote and lost the use of his legs through severe idleness.

Having once watched *Ready Steady Dig!* has given Arthur a reputation amongst his cronies as something of an intellectual, and it also prompted him to buy a metal detector in the hope of instant riches from the ground. However, so far he has not been able to bring himself to read the Manual, an activity that he regards as sissy, preferring instead the tried and tested method of pressing all the buttons very hard at random, then kicking the machine and swearing at it. This has not worked, and he is intending to take it back to the shop some day and complain.

Darrell and Big Mac regard him in bewilderment.

'Hypocaust,' says Vera.

'Yeah, that's what I said,' says Arthur. 'Them old Romans used to have their baths in them.'

'Over them,' says Vera, her painful arm temporarily forgotten in the rare opportunity to show off. 'They were part of the underfloor heating system of Roman villas. We did it in Latin.'

'S'ackly,' says Arthur. 'Dazza, mate, your dog's been an' gone an' found a Roman viller.'

Darrell looks at Arthur, and looks back at Rags, who is wriggling frantically and whose frenzied barking is reaching a crescendo.

'Well, he's still stuck,' says Darrell. 'Gimme the pick, Big Mac, I'll have to get one of them pillars down.'

'No!' cries Vera. 'You mustn't damage it.'

'No,' agrees Arthur importantly. 'That's our Hairy Tidge there, mate. You can't bash it with a pick, you has to exhumate it.'

'Heritage,' says Vera. 'Excavate.'

'Oh yeah, and how does that go?' demands Darrell, hefting the pickaxe.

'You has to use trowels,' says Arthur sagely. 'Little pointy trowels, and paintbrushes.'

'Paintbrushes! I don't want to decorate the blasted place, I want to get our Rags out of there!' says Darrell.

'You sure about the paintbrushes?' asks Big Mac, who didn't see the TV programme. 'You won't shift much with a paintbrush.'

'That's the *point*,' says Arthur authoritatively. 'You has to do it reeelly slow, so's you don't damage nothing. There could be, you know, treasure and stuff, you don't want to damage that.'

Darrell and Big Mac regard Arthur dubiously. Rags falls silent as the three men consider the situation. The rain falls steadily, but none of them notices. The word *treasure* glitters in the air between them.

'You could go and get your metal detector thing,' says Darrell slowly.

'Dunt work,' says Arthur. 'I meant to take it back to the shop.'

'We could still give it a go,' insists Darrell. 'I got to get Rags out first, then we'll give it a go.' He reaches down into the hole again, and starts to excavate around the dog with his hands. The sluicing rain helps, and pretty soon Rags is free and above ground again, and expressing his relief by racing round and round in circles, yapping hysterically.

'Go and get your detector,' says Darrell.

'What, in this weather?' says Arthur. They look at the louring sky. The Genius Loci has no intention of letting up just yet. He enjoys a good downpour once in a while, and besides, he has taken rather a dislike to Darrell and his mates.

'OK then, when it clears up a bit,' agrees Darrell. 'I got to get Rags home anyway, he might get a chill.'

'I broke my arm,' says Vera, without much hope of any helpful response.

'Oh yeah,' says Darrell, 'and our Vee has broke her arm. We best get down home, have a few beers, maybe, come back when it stops raining.'

He scoops Rags up into his arms, and strides off down the hill, Arthur and Big Mac following with the spade, the pickaxe and the game bag. Vera waits in vain for some assistance, then stumbles damply in their wake.

CHAPTER V

Early morning on the following day sees Vera creeping quietly out of Number Six, Harnstone Close, Crowborough, heading for the villa on the ridge above the town. It is a glorious dawn, the air fresh and blindingly clear after the Genius Loci's fit of temper, which finally wore off just after one o' clock in the morning.

By that time Darrell, who had been forced to spend most of the evening in A&E with Vera and her Mum, was far too exhausted to think of excavations. Next door, at Number Seven, Harnstone Close, Arthur had eventually resorted to the Manual (*Important: Please read the whole of this booklet carefully before attempting to operate the machine*) and had finally managed to get his metal detector working, but by that time Big Mac was sound asleep and snoring mightily. Big Mac had spent the evening down at the Pig and Whistle, where, unbeknownst to Darrell and Arthur, he had regaled the public bar at great length with the whole story of the afternoon's events.

Arthur had seriously considered a solitary expedition to the ridge with his metal detector (a little voice in his head was whispering insistently *No need to share*); but he had been put off by vivid memories of the *Ready Steady Dig!* programme, which had featured a particularly well-stocked Romano-British grave-site, with Artist's Impressions. Telling himself that metal detecting in the dark, the very *very* dark night, would probably be a waste of time, he nevertheless went so far as to step outside the front door, impelled by almost irresistible greed. The sudden harsh scream of a fox sent him scuttling back indoors again, and now he too is sleeping, and dreaming of mighty hoards of glittering coin with maybe a golden torque or two to impress Maureen, the barmaid down at the Pig and Whistle. Thus Vera has the day to herself, so far at least, and as it is only 6am she calculates that Darrell and his cronies will not be pitching up for many hours yet, Darrell not being an early riser, and his mates even less so.

The grass sparkles with dew, birds sing in the hedgerows, and the air is filled with the sweet green warmth of a myriad growing things. Vera looks up at the ridge, and on upwards at the high sheltering eastern wolds where the sun is beginning to rise, and as her eyes dazzle she sees, just for a moment, dark against the hillside, the outline of a big stone house, its red roof tiles glittering with dew, and she hears distant voices, faint but somehow familiar.

'Welcome back, Vera Alauda!'

Then the vision is gone, and Vera feels a sharp pang of loss and loneliness, and an inexplicable hint of fear.

A solitary blackbird pours out his sweet, sad morning song, and a magpie chatters suddenly in a tree. Now there is a smell of smoke in the air, and a feeling of menace that comes from - yes, from the high wolds, from the east.

'Run! Run!'

And somehow Vera knows that deadly danger came here once, out of the rising sun, plunging down from the eastern hills in a horror of smoke and flame and the flash of bright swords. She shivers in the morning light, and looks nervously towards the dawn, but there is no fire, no flame, although the smell of smoke still lingers on the air, and the blackbird sings as if his heart is breaking.

'They come with swords!'

Vera falls to her knees, shaking with unaccountable terror, and the bright day grows cold and grey around her.

'Run, Alauda, run!'

And the day goes dark.

'Domina Vera!' Petro's anxious voice rouses Vera from - a faint? a trance? She doesn't know, she can't remember. She is crouching on her knees, shivering violently, and her face is wet with tears.

'Petro!' she says, and there he is, and this time he is not alone. With him is another Lar, a slender young woman, watching her with solemn concern.

'This is Lapidilla,' says Petro. The female Lar bows, and touches her brow in what Vera somehow knows is a formal gesture of respect.

'You are safe, Domina,' says Lapidilla gravely. 'The danger passed, long, long ago, but the memory of that day is still here, deep in the grass where the blood ran red.'

'Whose blood?' asks Vera softly. 'Was it my family's?'

'We do not speak of it,' says Lapidilla. 'But always we remember, whenever the blackbird sings that particular song, and the magpie calls out his warning, and the dew is heavy as it is today, and the sun rises just so in the morning. It was a beautiful dawn, and a sad twilight, but it was long, long ago.'

'Yes yes yes,' says a fussy little voice, and Vera looks round to see a third Lar bustling towards her over the short grass. 'Yes,' he says again impatiently, 'it was all very sad, but that was then and this is now.'

'Can't argue with that,' says Petro, and Vera has the distinct impression that he doesn't much like the newcomer, who is tall (for a Lar), quite a bit older than Petro and Lapidilla, and rather thin and sharp-looking. Vera suspects she won't like him very much either: there is something about him that makes her think of her Maths teacher, and that is not a promising start to any relationship.

'And we were all fond of Vera Alauda, in our way,' the third Lar continues briskly. 'Even the magpie tried to warn her, but it was too late, and there's nothing we can do about it now.'

Lapidilla looks at him with solemn, reproachful eyes. 'Yes there is, Adro,' she says quietly. 'We can *remember*.'

Petro pats her on the shoulder.

'Exactly,' he says. 'We're Lares. Remembering is what we do.'

'Yes yes yes,' says the third Lar again. 'But today there's more important - I mean, there's *other* things to do.' Petro gives him a dark look, and Lapidilla turns away. 'There's the new mistress to welcome fittingly,' the third Lar continues firmly, 'and all the flooded tunnels to mop out, if you need something else to get on with.' He turns to face Vera, gives a sweeping bow, and says, *'Salve,* Domina Vera. We your faithful Lares welcome you to Villa Corvo.'

'Er, thank you,' says Vera. 'What's your name?'

'Adrogantio at your service, Domina,' says the Lar, and bows again. Petro sniggers.

'I told you we all have our different characteristics,' he says obscurely. The third Lar glares at Petro, and Vera makes a mental note to look up *adrogantio* in her Latin dictionary as soon as she gets home.

'Did you say there's been a flood?' she asks.

'I'm afraid so,' Petro replies. 'The Genius Loci had a bit of a hissy fit, and it didn't stop raining until well after midnight.'

'The Genius - ?'

'How is your arm, Domina Vera?' asks Lapidilla, interrupting with a look of grave concern. 'Petro told us it was broken. Has it been properly tended?'

Vera holds out her plastered left arm. 'Yes, thank you, we went to A&E last night. That's at the hospital.' The Lares look blank. 'It's a place where people go to get well. Or not, sometimes. Do you like my plaster?'

Lapidilla examines it with professional interest.

'A splint of stone!' she exclaims wonderingly. 'Yes, that is *very* fine. I have never seen that before. We use willow splints and lambswool and linen, and willow bark for the pain.'

'They gave me lots of Junior Calpol,' says Vera. 'I think it must have made me a bit woozy. I thought I could hear voices, and I smelled smoke.'

'Yes, the smoke and the burning are still there, deep in the stones and the long grass,' says Lapidilla sadly, 'and sometimes, too, the voices echo down the years.'

'It's the dratted blackbirds,' says Adrogantio. 'They will keep singing about it. *Sorrow, sorrow, sorrow...* And that magpie's no better, harping on all the time. *Danger! Danger!* What earthly use is that to her now, poor sweet lady? What use was it then?'

'She should never have tried to come back,' says Lapidilla softly. 'Our dear Vera Alauda.'

'Well, at least they remember,' says Petro. 'We -'

A loud burst of mildly tuneless singing interrupts Petro, and he winces. Vera searches for the source of the sound, and sees a young woman dancing towards them over the grass. Her small bare feet seem to skim the ground, and she leaves no footprints in the dew. She is just a little taller than Vera, slender as a reed, with long flowing curls of shimmering gold, into which, regrettably, large quantities of foliage and flowers have been artfully entwined.

'*Salve!* Welcome!' she trills. 'I am Stillaria! nymph of the stream! and its valley!' She approaches in a waft of floating draperies that are mostly green, but with quite a lot of pink. Somehow Vera knows that this is a girl who really, really likes pink, and sings a lot, and uses far more exclamation marks than any rational being can possibly need.

'Her name's Stillaria, so we call her Drippy for short,' says Petro quietly. 'She can be a bit, well -'

'Yes, I can see,' says Vera, as the nymph does a little dance, humming tunelessly and waving quite a lot of filmy handkerchiefs around. She ends up in front of Vera, and a small bunch of violets appears in her hands. She offers them with the air of one bestowing an infinitely precious gift.

'Er, thank you,' says Vera. 'I'll put them in water as soon as I get home.'

'May they last for ever!' cries Stillaria.

'Bet they won't,' says Petro. 'They're already wilting.' Vera decides to go with the flow, and call her Drippy too. She knows in her heart that this name will not be too difficult to remember.

'The trees! and the grass! and my pretty, pretty flowers! all welcome you!' cries Drippy, waving her arms about to indicate variously a clump of hazel, the groundcover, and a few dandelions in the immediate vicinity. 'And all the birds of the air! and the bright butterflies! and my busy, busy bees!'

'Slugs and snails, too, don't forget them,' says Petro. Adrogantio sniggers. 'And you left out frogs. Don't forget the frogs.'

'Toads,' says Adrogantio. 'Snakes. Bats.'

'Stop teasing her,' says Lapidilla reproachfully. 'She can't help being enthusiastic. It's her *job*. Hello, Dri - Stillaria. How nice of you to come and welcome Domina Vera, but I expect you have lots of *other* things to do today.'

'Songs to sing, flowers to sniff,' suggests Petro. 'We're really busy right now, we need to talk to Domina Vera about an important matter.'

'Like what!' asks Drippy.

'The villa,' says Petro. 'It's been discovered, and we don't think that's likely to be very good news.'

'Oh, you mean by those horrible men! yesterday!' cries Drippy. 'I saw them! with their pickaxe! and their spade! hurting my poor poor grasses!'

'Yes, the Genius Loci wasn't too thrilled about them either,' agrees Petro. 'So just trot off now, will you, there's a good nymph, and leave us to get on with discussing what we can do about it. Go and tend a bosky dell, or something.'

'I go! I go! May the sun shine ever brightly upon the hour of our meeting! Farewell, farewell for now!' The nymph waves a filmy handkerchief, and dances lightly away over the dewy grass.

'Sorry about that,' says Petro. 'She can be a bit much, especially this early in the morning.'

'I can see that she might be,' says Vera cautiously. 'But she seems very nice.'

'All nymphs are a bit daft,' confides Petro. 'It's in their nature.'

'But she does do a lovely job with the valley,' says Adrogantio judiciously. 'Not a flower out of place when she's been through it. Not a leaf. Not a twig.'

'And the stream,' adds Lapidilla. 'She keeps it really nice. Always pretty, always babbling away.'

'A bit like her, really,' says Petro.

'And of course, her shrine always was a picture,' says Adrogantio.

'Where is it?' asks Vera. 'I should like to see it.'

'Up there, on the hill to the south,' says Petro. 'There's a spring there, where the stream rises, and the shrine is over the spring. The Family made it, but of course the place was sacred long before they came. Drippy's been around here for ever.'

'It was such a pretty place,' says Lapidilla. 'I remember there were always flowers, even in the winter, all around the little pool where the spring came up out of the ground. The pool was lined with stone, and the water was so clear and always so cool, even on the hottest days, and yet in winter it never froze over. The Family used to take us up there, whenever there was a death, and the household had to be purified. They would make the sacrificial offerings for the dead, and wash us in the spring, and carry back spring-water to scatter all around the house.'

'I used to enjoy going up there,' says Petro wistfully. 'I wish I could see it again.'

'Can't you?' asks Vera gently. He shakes his head sadly.

'It's much too far for us Lares to go,' he says.

'I could take you,' says Vera. 'I'd like to do that.' The three little figures beam at her. 'Should I take an offering, do you think?' she asks diffidently.

'Drippy would like that. I don't suppose anyone's made an offering there for centuries. If you need any ideas for what to take her, she loves flowers,' says Petro. 'Especially pink ones.'

'It would have to be when the old man's not around,' says Adrogantio. 'I think he still goes up there a lot.'

'What old man?' asks Vera.

'We don't know who he is,' answers Petro, 'but we often see him, walking up the bank of the stream towards the path that leads to the shrine. Drippy says that years and years ago, he came there once with a little urn full of ashes, and scattered them in the pool. So she made a wild rose grow there for him, and the next time he came, he saw it and smiled.'

'That was kind of her,' says Vera.

'Oh, she's got a kind heart,' agrees Petro. 'If only she weren't so soppy.'

'And it was good of her to come and welcome Domina Vera,' says Lapidilla.

'Nosy, more like,' says Adrogantio.

'You can't blame a nymph for being curious, Adro,' says Petro. 'They're all like that. Anyway, come and meet the others, Domina: they're really eager to welcome you.'

Vera intercepts a sceptical glance from Adrogantio to his fellow Lar.

'What?' she asks. Petro looks sheepish.

'Well, all right,' he says reluctantly, 'Mopsus is very, very shy, that's why he didn't come out with us to meet you. And Grumio's still in a bit of a strop about the dog, and the hole in the ceiling. Mind you, he's almost always in a strop about something or other, so don't mind him. And Cibus is sulking because he's our provisions Lar - well he's not so much a Lar, he's really one of the Penates, they're the ones in charge of food supplies - and there ought to be a welcoming feast for you, but he can't do it. All there is to eat around here is green stuff, and Drippy won't let him have that, even for you, and rabbits, of course, and we told him he's not to touch them, because Mopsus would cry. He's really daft about rabbits, is Mopsus.'

'He's daft about everything, if you ask me,' says Adrogantio. 'Worst thing the Normans ever did, bringing in the rabbits,' he adds. 'Mopsus is bad enough about hares, but at least they don't actually live with us.'

'Mopsus is very sensitive,' Lapidilla translates. 'You mustn't be offended if he doesn't say anything, Domina - as Petro says, he's rather shy.'

'I look forward to meeting them all,' says Vera, quite bravely, she feels, in the circumstances.

Adrogantio leads the way to the spot where Darrell dug up the hypocaust. Three more little stone men are standing there in the damp gloom down below. Mopsus is unmistakable: he just has to be the one hiding behind the other two and trying to look as if he isn't there at all. He is very young and very skinny, with long wispy hair and a prominent Adam's apple that bobs nervously as Vera approaches. He looks as if he may burst into tears at any moment, or run away, or both. The one she guesses is Grumio is shorter, fatter and older; he doesn't look too pleased with life, and Vera has the impression that this mood is habitual. This is not her impression of the third member of the trio, although currently he looks almost as cross as Grumio. He is a clever-looking, sharp-faced Lar, a little older than Petro, and as confident as Mopsus is shy: he looks as if he thoroughly enjoys life, and there is curiosity and mischief in his eyes.

'Good morning, Lares,' says Vera. 'I am so glad to meet you all, Grumio, Cibus, Mopsus.'

The three little figures all bow to Vera and touch their brows, Cibus with grin and a particularly sweeping flourish.

'Very well,' says Adrogantio, 'Now let us proceed to business. Domina Vera, those men who were here yesterday - are they likely to come back?'

'Not exactly,' says Vera. 'They're *certain* to come back. And Arthur, that's the short skinny one, he's got a metal detector.'

'A what?' demands Adrogantio, as the Lares all exchange puzzled looks.

'What's a metal detector?' asks Petro. 'What does it do?'

'It detects metal,' says Vera. 'I mean, it can find metal under the ground. From above the ground. You use it to search for treasure.'

The Lares exchange horrified looks.

'So there is treasure here?' says Vera. 'That's what you were left here to guard?'

Adrogantio nods.

'There is much coin, in gold and in silver,' he says. 'Also jewels and plate, brooches and rings. Your respected ancestor, Caius Verus Pugnax Corvo, left them for us to look after when he took his loved ones away to safety in Berium Castra, after he heard that the barbarians were coming. He never guessed that they would stay.'

'Caius never came back,' says Petro. 'We do not know what became of him, but we know that the Corvo line has gone on, down through the years. You are the latest, Domina Vera, you and your family.'

'So the treasure belongs to us, to me and my family?' asks Vera cautiously.

'To you and all of your blood kin,' says Adrogantio. 'That man who came yesterday with the spade - is he kin to you?'

'He's my Stepfather,' answers Vera. 'No, he's not a blood relation.'

'But soon he will come back, looking for your treasure,' says Adrogantio. 'And from what Petro tells me, I do not think he will give it to you. So - how are we to stop him?'

CHAPTER VI

It is impossible to overestimate the carrying qualities of even a very quiet voice in a public bar, when it announces 'My bruvver's mate's dog found this hippo-crust up on Rooks Ridge, he says it was just like he saw on the telly on that *Ready Steady Dig!* an' he says it's gotta be a roaming viller, what they used ter bury treasure in, like, you know, gold and jools and stuff.'

Big Mac's voice was by no means quiet, and the story carried fast and far.

It carried first to Maureen, barmaid of the Pig and Whistle, who instantly grasped one important element.

'The telly! We could all be on the telly!' she exclaimed in great excitement. 'Wonder if anyone's told the telly people yet?' Maureen then diverged from the general course of the River Rumour, into a tributary known as *What am I Going to Wear?* and softly grounded on the warm shoals of 'Our Doreen's got this great new crop-top that she might give me a lend of for if I get on the telly, it's a sort of a turkwarze blue with all sparkly bits.'

Big Mac's voice carried a different element of the story further, to a small group, one might almost say a huddle, of three serious-looking middle-aged men called Mr Black, Mr Grey and Mr White, who were sitting around a table in the darkest corner of the public bar. These were just the sort of men that you bought something off of, when you claimed to have bought something off of a man in a pub, Officer, but I'm afraid I didn't get his name and I don't think I would know him if I saw him again. Men like these tend to flinch at a word like 'telly,' because it makes them think of closed-circuit surveillance, which they regard as a gross infringement of their human rights to do whatever it is they do whenever they think no one is watching. On the other hand, words like 'treasure' and 'gold and jools and stuff' do not cause them to flinch, but to stiffen almost imperceptibly and regard each other speculatively out of the corners of their eyes. One of them had a stub of pencil and a small notebook. He licked the end of the pencil, and carefully wrote down *'Rks Rdge - £££?'*

In a remarkably short time, the news of the afternoon's discovery had also crossed the social divide between the public and the saloon bar, by way of the Landlord, who knew a good drinking rumour when he heard it, and was more than happy to encourage in-depth discussion of the matter, with all the additional sales opportunities that would undoubtedly arise as a result. He judiciously replenished the bowls of free peanuts on the bar, and prepared himself to lob the conversational ball back into play whenever this should prove necessary.

Mrs Landlord had rather greater vision than her husband, and was keenly aware that while the locals might discuss the matter at great length, to the enhancement of that evening's takings at the Pig and Whistle, a word to the press would undoubtedly extend both the audience and the profits. Just minutes after Big Mac's announcement, Mrs Landlord was picking up the telephone and composing a detailed message for the answerfone of Jim Southerton, senior reporter at the Crowborough Herald.

Meanwhile in the saloon bar of the Pig and Whistle the story soon attracted the attention of Mr Decimus Gibbon, History Teacher at Crowborough High School, and from there it was but a short leap to the office of his old university friend, Mr Ronald Horton, now County Archaeologist for Bersetshire.

The story moved on from the saloon bar, and soon it reached the ears of Mr Cummins and Mr Gowings, who were holding an impromptu meeting of the Crowborough Allotments Committee in the snug. Mr Cummins had once found an old coin whilst harvesting his Maris Pipers, and had taken it to the Berchester museum, where it had been identified as a silver penny nearly 350 years old. Mr Cummins had poetry in his soul, and the thought of having discovered, having *actually handled*, something as old as that had sparked a new interest in digging that did not relate solely to vegetable produce. Mr Cummins had got the archaeology bug, and these days he watched *Ready Steady Dig!* with the enthusiasm of a connoisseur and the condescension of a gifted amateur towards a bunch of mere professionals. For many years it had been Mr Cummins' secret dream that one day he would unearth something even more exciting than a 350 year old silver penny on his allotment; and while the reported Roman villa was not actually there, it was at least in Crowborough, it was at least *local*. Mr Cummins' eyes shone with excitement as he enlisted the help of Mr Gowings to Take Matters Further. This involved the rapid adjournment of the Allotments Committee meeting to the bedroom of Mr Gowings' grandson Stuart, where they forced Stuart to abandon his game of *Killer Robot III,* and transport them instead to bonze.com, official website of *Ready Steady Dig!*

Thus it is that the following morning, while Darrell, Arthur and Big Mac are still soundly sleeping, the Lares Conspiracy's plans for tackling the Darrell threat - *'Sabotage the metal detector!'* (Petro) *'Tell our Mum!'* (Vera) *'Set the dogs on them!'* (Adrogantio) *'What dogs?'* (Lapidilla) *'Poison them!'* (Cibus) *'Bash them over the head!'* (Grumio) *'Hide!'* (Mopsus) - are disrupted in a major way by the arrival at the villa site of, variously, Mr Ronald Horton the County Archaeologist; Trystram Wentworth, Director of *Ready Steady Dig!* and two researchers called Trinni and Troy; Mr Cummins and Mr Gowings on their bicycles; Jim Southerton the reporter and his photographer, Spike; three middle-aged men with a tendency to lurk and pay close attention to potential cover; and Maureen, Doreen and a number of other ladies of a certain age, all wearing highly impractical clothing and footwear, come to see if any people off the telly are here yet.

Oh, and a little old man called Hob.

CHAPTER VII

Mr Horton is appalled. He has been first to reach what already he thinks of as The Crowborough Villa Site, but not by much, and now people are converging, lots of people, all chattering and clamouring until he can barely hear himself think.

The Bersetshire County Archaeologist is an unimposing figure of a man, with a permanently anxious expression. Small, thin and thirtyish, with fair hair and wide, worried blue eyes behind round gold-rimmed spectacles, life has never been very kind to Mr Horton, and it shows. Bersetshire has very little money to spend on actual archaeology these days, so most of his time is spent behind a desk at County Hall, where he deals with letters and telephone calls, and in his spare time works on an obscure monograph that he hopes will one day Make His Name, although he knows in his heart that this is unlikely. There is not much of a Name to be made from mid 8th century local pottery, no matter how meticulously catalogued and described, and he is nothing if not meticulous. But Mr Horton loves mid 8th century local pottery for its own sake, and at this moment he wishes fervently that he were back in his office with nothing more threatening to deal with.

'Keep back! Keep back!' he cries, with an attempt at authority, waving his arms to ward off the approaching throng, but no one takes any notice except Maureen and Doreen and their chums, and all they do is giggle at him. 'This is a protected site!'

'By whom?' asks Jim Southerton the reporter, who is tall, dark, and almost as handsome as he thinks he is. He opens a notebook and extracts a pen from his top pocket.

'By me!' cries Mr Horton boldly.

'And you are ...?'

'Ronald Horton, MA (Lond.),' says Mr Horton. 'County Archaeologist!'

'Age?' asks Jim.

'Thirty-one,' replies Mr Horton, slightly non-plussed. 'What has my age got to do with anything?'

'Don't ask me,' says Jim. 'Our readers like to know, I can't think why. Now, can you confirm that this is an internationally important discovery that will change our understanding of Romano-British Archaeology for ever?'

'No,' says Mr Horton.

'No?'

'No,' repeats Mr Horton. 'How can I? I haven't even had a proper look at it yet.'

'So go on, then,' says Jim. 'What's stopping you?'

'You are! You and all these people!' cries Mr Horton angrily. 'They shouldn't be here! This could be an important site -'

'Ah,' says Jim, pouncing. 'So it is important! And will it change-'

'No, it won't change anything!' retorts Mr Horton crossly. 'It would be far more likely to confirm lots of things that we already know about the Romano-British period. Only it won't get a chance to.'

'Why not?' demands Jim.

'Because we don't have the funding,' says Mr Horton. 'We can't possibly afford to open up a new site, especially one that could be as big as this.'

'So it is big?' asks the reporter. 'How big, Mr Horton? Hundreds of acres? Thousands?'

'I don't *know*!' says Mr Horton. 'If it is a villa, it could be quite extensive, but that's immaterial. We barely have the funds for a couple of test pits, let alone a major excavation.'

'Excuse me,' another voice breaks in. 'Perhaps I could be of some assistance there.'

Mr Horton turns to face a slender, elegant man of about thirty-five, dressed in what even he can guess are designer jeans and matching jacket, a man with softly waving blond hair glimmering with artfully placed highlights, and a floppy silk cravat that seems to serve no useful function except to declare that the wearer is the sort of person who habitually wears floppy silk cravats, probably a different one every day.

'*Timeo Danaos*,' says Jim Southerton darkly.

'Good morning,' says the slender, elegant man. 'Trystram Wentworth, Director, Independent British Broadcasting Corporation. These are my colleagues, Trinni and Troy.' He waves a hand at two exquisite young people standing a deferential foot or so behind him, a small, red-headed man and a tall, willowy brunette.

'Troy,' says the exquisite young man. He leaps forward and grasps Mr Horton's hand, briefly but firmly. '*Ready Steady Dig!*'

'No!' shrieks Mr Horton. 'Don't touch *anything*!'

'He means the programme,' says the exquisite young woman. 'I'm Trinni. We are researchers for *Ready Steady Dig!*'

Mr Horton goes visibly pale. He watches *Ready Steady Dig!* every Sunday afternoon, with the horrified fascination of tiny trembling minnow observing the purposeful approach of a gaping pike. They use *JCBs,* for heaven's sake! They gouge and scrape away at the earth until they smash something ancient, precious, unique and irreplaceable, like mid 8th century local pottery; and then they send the JCB away and get out their little trowels and make a huge point of doing things *carefully*. The cameras film them, doing things carefully, over and over again. Usually they manage not to show the freshly broken edges of the initial finds, but Mr Horton can see them in his mind's eye, and it hurts him to his archaeological soul. That's not how they conducted digs when he was a student. That's not how he conducts the very few digs that he has the funding for. That's TV archaeology, and he loathes it with a passion.

The reporter Jim Southerton sees at least some of this in his face.

'I think you just got your funding,' he says. 'You poor devil.'

Mr Horton draws himself up to his full height of five foot seven.

'No,' he announces defiantly. 'Never! These people have no more idea of how to conduct an archaeological excavation than - than - a blind mole! They will come here over my dead body!'

'They could practise burying that and digging it up again,' says Jim. 'I wouldn't put it past them. And I don't see how you are going to stop them.'

'I am the County Archaeologist!' cries Mr Horton.

'Exactly. I don't see how you are going to stop them.'

Trystram Wentworth gives them both a tight little smile. 'We shall need the *landowner's* permission, of course,' he says, and the implication *And not yours, or anybody else's* comes over loud and clear. 'So who is the landowner? Does anyone know?'

'Yes,' says Mr Gowings, stepping forward. He is Chairman of the Crowborough Allotments Association, and knows everyone in

Crowborough and its environs, at least everyone who has any connection to The Soil. 'The landowner is - ' he hesitates, ' - er - Mr - er - Hob.'

He steps aside, and indicates the little old man called Hob, who has been watching events from a distance. Now he shuffles forward to the front of the group gathered around Mr Horton. He is wearing a disreputable overcoat with no shirt, and baggy black trousers tucked into the tops of a pair of serious-looking work boots. One feels that if he had a cloth cap, he would probably doff it. He fixes Trystram with eyes of a bright, sharp blue.

'Ahhhhh -' he says.

'*You're* the landowner?' asks Trystram, doubtfully. Can this shabby old scarecrow really be a man of property? Hob's eyes twinkle wickedly as he clocks Trystram's expression of mingled astonishment and distaste.

'Arrrrrr,' he replies. Jim Southerton gives him a surprised look, but says nothing.

'Splendid!' cries Trystram, seeing a chance to trim a major element of his budget. 'If you will let me have your name and address, I shall ask our Legal and Financial Department to be in touch with you immediately. They will offer you what we call a *Fa-ci-lit-ies Fee*.' Trystram pronounces this very slowly and clearly. 'This could be as much as - as - one hundred pounds!'

This does not get quite the reaction he expects.

'Arrrrrr?' says Hob thoughtfully. 'A thousand pound?'

'No, no, a hundred -' Trystram hesitates. After all, he does have five thousand budgeted for this. 'Yes, yes, I meant to say a thousand pounds, of course.'

'No,' says Hob, shaking his head slowly. He turns away.

'But, but, Mr -!'

'- Hob,' supplies Jim Southerton helpfully. 'He's a well-known local character.'

'Mr Hob! Mr Hob!' cries Trystram, as the old man begins to make his way slowly and carefully down the hill.

'I should go after him, if I were you,' says Jim cheerfully. 'I'm betting he'll settle at about five thousand.'

'But how could a scruffy, ignorant old beggar like that possibly know what we normally pay?'

'Ah,' says Jim. 'Thought so, you cheapskate. Believe me, he'll know. And you'll end up paying him the lot. At the very least.'

A seriously irritated Trystram Wentworth trots off down the hill in the wake of the determined old man. Jim catches the eye of Mr Gowings, who is looking, for some reason, rather bewildered. Jim winks at him.

'Nice to see a poor, scruffy, ignorant old beggar like Hob getting a bit of luck for a change,' he says, straight-faced. 'Maybe he'll be able to afford to get his tackety boots re-soled before the winter comes.'

Mr Gowings gives a reluctant snort of amusement.

'Maybe,' he says. 'Or even re-roof his broken-down old hovel, do you think?'

'Could be, could be,' agrees Jim, and they exchange conspiratorial grins.

Part-way down the slope, it can be seen that Trystram has caught up with Hob. They confer for some time, and Trystram waves his arms about a lot. Then Hob continues his steady downhill march, and Trystram climbs back up to Rooks Ridge. The look on his face suggests that Jim's financial estimate has been painfully accurate.

'Five and a half thou, take it or leave it, the scrawny old so and so,' says Trystram crossly. 'But we simply can't lose this one. It's just perfect for the programme.'

'Yes,' says a dispirited Mr Horton. 'That's exactly what I'm afraid of.'

'Well done, Trystram!' says the exquisite Trinni loyally. 'You did include the field over there, didn't you?' She indicates about five acres of young wheat on the western slope beyond the hedge.

'Of course,' says Trystram sharply. 'The old boy said it was his, and we can soon strip off the crop.'

'Strip off the crop!' cries Mr Gowings in horror. 'That's perfectly good wheat growing there!'

'Wheat, is it? Not a problem,' says Trystram, his mood improving now that he is clearly upsetting someone else almost as much as Hob has upset him.

'But that's sheer vandalism!' protests Mr Gowings. 'Destroying a perfectly good food crop!' He looks pointedly at Jim

Southerton. 'I hope you're getting all this down for your paper, young man.'

Jim shrugs.

'I doubt our readers would be very interested, Mr Gowings,' he says. 'I don't think many of them eat wheat.'

'Don't eat -? Well, of course they do!' says Mr Gowings. 'They eat bread, don't they?'

'Exactly,' says Jim. 'They eat bread. How many of our readers do you suppose know where their bread comes from, let alone care?'

Mr Gowings shakes his head sadly.

'Vandalism,' he says again. 'I don't suppose there's a hope of stopping it.'

'None at all,' agrees Jim. 'I bet they want it for their Field Walkers' Challenge.'

Mr Horton gives a hollow moan.

'Their what?' asks Mr Gowings, determined to know the worst, the better to stoke up the fires of his indignation.

'They plough up a field, and they have teams of amateur field walkers in colour-coordinated tracksuits, and they give them an hour to pick up whatever archaeological treasures they can find within their allotted square,' explains Jim. 'Although I believe they mostly find pebbles.'

Mr Horton gives another faint moan of protest.

'The finds are all properly recorded,' says Troy defensively.

'Oh yes?' says Mr Horton. 'And what would you know or care about that?'

'They have to be,' confirms Trinni. 'For the prizes.'

'Prizes!' hisses Mr Horton. 'Archaeology isn't about prizes, it's about scholarship!'

'And for the chance to go on to the Finals,' continues Trinni, 'where they get to compete against all the other winning teams from the series. It's a very popular part of the show.'

'The *show*!' wails Mr Horton.

Jim Southerton takes him by the elbow in a kindly gesture of support.

'It's no good, you know,' he says. 'They're going to do it, whatever you say. Why not make the best of it, and sign up as a consultant to the programme?' He fixes Trystram with a hard stare. 'I'm sure there's got to be plenty of funding for that?'

'Er, yes,' says Trystram. 'We should be delighted to have you on board, Mr Um-'

'Horton,' says Mr Horton coldly. 'Precisely what authority would a consultant have over the mechanics of the dig?'

'None whatsoever, I should think,' says Jim, before Trystram can get a word in. 'But at least you get to see exactly what they're grubbing up, I mean excavating. You might be able to - as it were - guide them in the right direction. I mean, someone's got to decide where the trenches go. And where they don't go.'

'Yes!' says Mr Horton with a faint glimmer of hope. 'I could do that, I suppose.'

'You could try,' says Jim. 'And then afterwards you could give me an in-depth interview for the paper about how they trashed the site.' Mr Horton moans again, and Trystram glares. 'I'll give you my agent's name,' says Jim. 'She'll make sure you at least get a reasonable fee.'

Trystram's glare becomes icy.

'Five hundred a day plus expenses for three days,' he says coldly. 'And that's not negotiable.'

'I'll take it,' says Mr Horton. 'Provided,' he adds, with a spark of spirit, 'that you can categorically assure me that the appointment will never appear on my cv.'

Trystram shrugs, and turns away to confer with Troy and Trinni, who are being besieged by Maureen, Doreen and their friends, who want to sign up to take part in the Field Walkers' Challenge.

'And what would you like to call your team?' asks Trinni.

'Werl,' says Maureen thoughtfully. 'We most of us comes from Old Street, so we thought we could be The Old Street Walkers.'

Jim Southerton stuffs his fist in his mouth, and decides that this may be a good time to leave. Days don't get a lot better than this, and it would be a shame to spoil it. Especially when it can be immeasurably improved by a drink and an in-depth interview with Hob on the way back to the office.

CHAPTER VIII

Old Hob makes his slow and careful way through a rose-hung, lichen-covered wooden wicket gate, and down a moss-encrusted path of crazy paving. He extracts a very large key from one of the pockets of his disreputable overcoat, and unlocks the front door of his tiny, almost unbearably picturesque cottage.

Once inside, he eases off his enormous boots, hangs up the disreputable overcoat, and reaches down to stroke the creature that approaches to greet him.

No, it is not a lurcher, not a whippet, not even an ugly but engaging mongrel: it is a pure white Persian cat. In his gleaming state-of-the-art kitchen, Hob pours himself a gin and tonic, adds a slice of lime and a small nugget of ice, and lights up a black Sobranie. He shuffles into his elegant minimalist sitting room and stretches himself out comfortably on a white leather lounger. Through tiny windows of an ancient near-opacity, the sun shines in on a glass and chrome coffee table, a heavy onyx ashtray, an enormous flat-screen plasma TV, and a single photograph in a silver frame of a young woman dressed in the fashion of fifty years ago. She is not beautiful, nor even particularly pretty, but she has a very sweet expression, and in one hand she carries a spray of tiny white roses. There is nothing else in the room except a richly glowing Persian rug of intricate design that partly covers the gleaming oak floor boards.

The long-haired cat springs up and settles himself neatly on Hob's lap, shedding a few silky hairs on his black tracksuit. Out of one pocket Hob draws a slim silver mobile, flips it open and presses a single key.

'Ahhhh, Chief Constable, a very good morning to you,' he says. 'Ravenscroft-Corbie-Hob here. A little of your time, if you please.'

Jim Southerton the reporter makes his way through the rose-hung, lichen-covered wooden wicket gate and down the moss-encrusted path of crazy paving.

'Anyone home?' he calls out, and pushes open the door of the tiny, almost unbearably picturesque cottage.

'Come in, come in, my boy. Join me in a g and t?' asks Sir Oriole Ravenscroft-Corbie-Hob, who insists on being called Hob, for, as he says, who wouldn't with a daft set of names like his?

'And here's me expecting to find you supping a pint of Winkles Old Peculiar out of a jam-jar,' says Jim demurely. 'So how are you keeping, Uncle?'

'Pretty well, pretty well, my boy,' says Hob, handing his nephew a glass. 'All the better for that bit of nonsense up on Rooks Ridge. You know, I often wondered if those old stones and bumps in the grass might be something of interest.'

'It's a pity you didn't call in the professionals before now,' says Jim. 'Or even Mr Cummins.' Hob snorts in mild derision. 'Now that those TV people have got their teeth into it, there's no chance of a proper dig.'

'Never wanted one,' says Hob. 'And now I'm going to get an improper one. No doubt there'll be some good stories in it for you, my boy? And a bit of fun for me, I hope. Not to mention five and a half thousand pounds for the church organ fund.'

'Good stories? Yes, I think so,' says Jim. 'Did you notice ...?'

'The presence of those three fine upstanding citizens Mr Black, Mr Grey and Mr White? Yes, I've just been on the 'phone to Bunny about them.'

'Bunny?'

'The Chief Constable to you, my boy,' says Hob. 'Good man, Bunny Holloway. I was at school with his father.'

'*Bunny?*' says Jim again, this time with unholy glee. 'All these years a reporter, and I never knew the Chief Constable was called Bunny.'

'Well, I don't suppose he is very often, unless you happen to have been at school with his father,' admits Hob. 'Nice lad, I always thought. Now, don't you go teasing him, young James. I know you.'

'How could I resist?' says Jim. 'How could anyone?'

'Try,' says Hob severely. 'Try very hard, if you know what's good for you, my boy. By the way,' he adds, 'I hope that delinquent paparazzo of yours got some good shots of the Messrs Monochrome casing the joint?'

46

'Of course,' answers Jim. 'And I've left him up there taking a few more. I'll be sure to let Bunny have a set for his cohorts. I've also told him to wait until everyone's gone, and take a comprehensive series of views of exactly what the place looks like now, before all the fun starts.'

'Excellent,' says Hob. 'Well done, my boy. Something else interesting,' he adds thoughtfully. 'Did you notice the little Rookwood girl?'

'Rookwood? No, I don't know that name,' says Jim.

'She's a local girl,' says Hob. 'Her father was Jack Rookwood, corporal in the Bersetshire Yeomanry, killed in Northern Ireland a few years back. Then her mother took up with that wastrel Darrell Grindley, and had the bad sense to marry him. Don't tell me you've never come across Darrell Grindley in your line of work?'

'Oh lord, yes, I know Dazza Grindley,' says Jim. 'Got his own coffee mug down at the Magistrates' Court.'

'Very likely,' says Hob. 'Anyway, his step-daughter's a nice little thing. Her name's Vera, I believe. She was up there today. Odd.'

'What's odd about one of the village kids being up there?' asks Jim.

'What was odd,' replies Hob, 'is that she was hiding.' They think about this for a while, without reaching any conclusions.

'Talking of good stories,' says Jim, and he tells Hob about Maureen and her team of field walkers. Hob chuckles.

'No, no, my boy, that won't do,' he says eventually. 'Can't have the television people making fools of them. Doesn't Doreen Massey live at Knight's Cross?'

'No idea, Uncle, I don't know her.'

'Well, she does. You go back up there right now, and suggest that they call themselves The Ladies of the Knight instead.'

CHAPTER IX

Back at the villa on the ridge, Vera watches from behind the shelter of the hedge as the site gradually starts to clear. The newspaper photographer with the black spiky hair lingers longest, photographing everyone and everything with great attention. It is now nearly three o' clock, and as he at last turns to leave, Darrell, Arthur and Big Mac finally show up, completely unaware of the morning's dramas. Spike takes a few shots of the trio as they toil up the slope towards him, carrying Arthur's metal detector, a spade and a large sack.

Arthur sees him first.

'Ere, oo're you?' he demands.

'Spike Sharp, Crowborough Herald,' answers Spike. 'And who are you?'

The trio look at each other, and look around uneasily. They do not reply to Spike's question. Spike stares fixedly at the metal detector, and raises his eyebrows at the spade.

'Got permission to be here, have you?' he asks casually, edging around so that he is now down-slope from them all. They are giving off an air of half-hearted menace, but Spike is not too worried: he reckons he can easily outrun these clowns should the need arise.

'Don't need no permission,' says Darrell aggressively.

'You sure about that?' asks Spike.

'Push off,' says Big Mac.

'Why was you taking photos?' demands Arthur uneasily.

'Lovely views up here,' replies Spike, edging a little further down the hill, and easing his mobile from one of his jacket pockets. 'Do you know you need the landowner's permission to use a metal detector on private land?'

Darrell says something rude about the landowner's permission. Spike shrugs. He doesn't want these idiots to trash the site, but he knows he can't stop them. He can see that they know it too.

'Push off,' says Big Mac again, advancing until he looms over Spike as only Big Mac can loom. Spike backs off a little further down the hill.

'I'm going, I'm going,' he says, and turns. Then he turns back, grinning broadly. 'I'm going,' he repeats. 'But they're not.'

The trio follows the line of Spike's pointing finger, and Arthur drops the metal detector as if it were red hot. Advancing up the hill towards them are two uniformed police constables. Bunny the Chief Constable has clearly been quicker off the mark than anyone might reasonably have expected.

'Everything's safe for now,' whispers Vera to the Lares, from her hiding place within the hazel hedge. 'The police have arrived. They must be going to stay for a while. They've brought sandwiches.'

'Police?' says Petro doubtfully. 'Is that like the Praetorian Guard? Or the City Watch?'

'A bit, I think,' replies Vera. 'They uphold the Law.'

'Not very much like, then,' says Grumio.

'What kind of sandwiches?' asks Cibus, with professional interest.

'I can't tell from here,' says Vera. 'Look here, how is it that you all obviously know what sandwiches are, but not policemen? And you've never heard of A&E, or hospitals? And for that matter, how come you all speak English?'

'We're household gods,' says Adrogantio. 'We're omniscient. That means we know everything.'

'Well, not quite,' says Petro. 'The Lares' place in the household is mainly in the kitchen, so we're not so much omniscient as kitcheniscient. We know everything about kitchens, and since people speak English in kitchens now, not Latin, we know English. And of course we know sandwiches. I must say, I think peanut butter sounds absolutely wonderful. And some of your modern devices... Combination microwaves! Electric carving knives! Cling film! And woks! I wish I could see a wok,' he adds, rather wistfully. 'I know in theory what they look like, of course, and what they do, but it would be really good to actually see one.'

'We haven't got a wok,' says Vera. 'If we had, I'd bring it to show you. I could bring you some cling film, if you like.'

'Thank you, Domina Vera,' says Petro politely. 'But it's not quite the same.'

'No, it's completely different,' says Adrogantio rather impatiently. 'Now please, can we get to the point?'

'Sorry,' says Petro. 'Domina Vera, are those policemen here to protect the villa from being dug up?'

'That's right, but they won't stay here for ever, and anyway they're only here to stop people digging who aren't allowed to, like my Step-Dad and his friends. Those television people will be back before long, and they are allowed.'

'What's television?' asks Petro.

'You ought to know about television,' says Vera. 'Lots of people have them in their kitchens.'

'Really? But do they belong there?' asks Petro. 'I mean, are they actually kitchen equipment?'

'No, I suppose not,' admits Vera. 'They really belong in the living room, but a lot of people have them in their kitchens as well these days, and in their bedrooms, too. They're known as TVs for short. A TV looks a bit like a microwave oven, only you watch moving pictures on where the oven door would be. Some of those people today, they're going to dig up the villa, and make pictures about it to show on television, so that people all over the country will be able to see what's happening.' A sudden thought strikes her. 'Hold on, surely you ought to know about TV *dinners?*'

'You mean you can *eat* them?' demands Petro. 'Now I'm really confused.'

'No,' says Vera patiently, and explains TV dinners. Cibus looks appalled.

'You mean people sit watching pictures while they're eating their dinner? Whatever happened to conversation?'

'I don't think people do it much any more,' says Vera sadly. Certainly not in our house, she thinks.

'Anyway,' says Adrogantio loudly. 'We don't want these television people digging up the villa, so how do we stop them?'

Nobody has anything to suggest.

'We ought to worry about Darrell and his friends first,' Vera points out. 'They'll be back up here as soon as the police have gone.'

'Not if they were ill,' says Cibus thoughtfully. 'If Drippy would let us have a few herbs, do you think you could …?'

'Well, I could,' says Vera doubtfully. 'But I don't think I ought to. What sort of herbs?'

'Deadly nightshade?' suggests Cibus. 'That ought to work on the television people too.'

'No!' says Lapidilla firmly.

'But even if I could get Darrell and his friends to eat some, I don't see how I could get at the television people's food,' says Vera. 'I mean, I expect they will bring their own commissary wagon.'

'Commissary …?'

'It's like a mobile kitchen,' explains Vera. 'They bring it with them.'

'A kitchen!' exclaims Petro joyfully. '*Now* we're cooking on gas!'

The meeting breaks up with Lapidilla still vetoing the deadly nightshade proposal, rather to Vera's relief. She does not like her Stepfather, but she doesn't not like him quite that much. Going a long way round to avoid being seen by the two policemen, Vera makes her way home very thoughtfully, and without coming to any useful conclusions.

CHAPTER X

Weeks pass. Vera spends a great deal of time at the villa. Every fine evening and weekend she takes her homework up there, and as a result her school marks improve immeasurably. Petro helps her with her Latin, and Adrogantio with her Geometry, although Maths is a closed book to him (as a Roman, the whole concept of zero is completely beyond him). Cibus proves to be a whiz at Home Economics, while Drippy the nymph is roped in to help with a project on the local ecology.

History is more problematic. The Lares know everything anyone could ever wish to know about the development of kitchens and kitchen equipment through the ages; but of events in the outside world they have very little idea. Adrogantio explains that the villa site has not been continuously occupied, although over and over again throughout the years, members of the Family have somehow made their way there and settled, sometimes briefly, sometimes for longer periods of time. From these episodes they know about the Norman Conquest, when the invaders created domestic rabbit warrens to provide food for the table: before then, Adrogantio tells Vera, there were no rabbits in England. They know about the Peasants' Revolt and the Black Death, when Vera's ancestor Rooke of Crowborough fled from the town and built a rough shelter on the villa site, where he isolated his family and saved them from the dreadful pestilence, and in the process gave his name to Rooks Ridge. And they know quite a lot about episodes such as the Gunpowder Plot and the Civil War, which were subjects of eager gossip by the people occupying the villa site in those times. There are gaps, however, in their knowledge, some of which Vera herself can fill in for them. Petro in particular is thrilled to hear that Prince Charles was eventually able to return from France and claim his executed father's throne. Adrograntio looks down his nose at this news: Vera can tell he was a Roundhead sympathiser without even having to ask.

While she is up at the villa site, Vera finds that she often runs into Hob, and her school ecology project provides a convenient excuse for her regular presence there to the sharp old man. ('Ecology! Ha! When I was your age, we called it Nature Study. Seen that blackbird's nest in those hazels, have you, young lady? And there's a pair of skylarks nesting in the wheat, but I haven't found that one yet, they're clever little things, skylarks').

At home, things are less happy. Vera's Mum has got wind of the metal detector, and keeps a beady eye on Darrell's activities whenever he's not down at the Job Centre trying his best to avoid finding gainful employment. Between Vera's Mum and the irregular visits to the villa site of Hob and the police, Darrell and his cronies have no chance to further their practical archaeological activities, and in consequence Darrell is in a permanent black mood.

Vera pesters her Mum unsuccessfully to buy a wok, and smuggles a jar of peanut butter up to the villa. This makes Petro very happy, although Cibus the gourmand feels that it would be much better with some crunchy bits left in. When Vera tells him that crunchy peanut butter is indeed an available option, his admiration for the twentieth century knows no bounds. Lapidilla is thrilled with a gift of sticking plaster, and Adrogantio is rendered speechless by a pocket calculator. Grumio is harder to please until Vera persuades him to talk about his work in the old days. It turns out that he was Lar of the chimney: a box of matches gets an apparently tepid response, but Vera can tell that he is impressed. Finding a present for Mopsus is easiest of all: two small blue plaster rabbits called Mr Hoppy and Mrs Flopsy, which Vera once won at the local fun fair, bring joyful tears to his eyes. He re-names them Saliendillius and Micandillia, and spends many a happy hour trying to get them to talk to him.

Vera talks to the Lares a great deal, but especially to Petro. At home there is no one she can really communicate with, except on the most basic of levels, her half-brother and sister being too young for any serious companionship.

'Petro, tell me about Vera Alauda,' she says, one soft, quiet evening when they are alone in the dusk, watching tiny bats flitting up and down the hedgerow after moths.

Petro hesitates, and sighs.

'Our little Lark,' he says softly. 'Alauda is lark in the Roman tongue. She sang like a lark, and she loved this place, she loved the very air, the wide skies and the high wolds. When she was a child she used to say she wished she could fly like a lark, up, up into the blue. Poor sweet lady, she died down here, down in the long grass by the hedge. You can still see the drops of her blood in the berries of the hawthorn.'

'Oh Petro - and you loved her so much!'

'We all did. She was the darling of the house, but the last time we ever saw her alive, her heart was broken. She was fifteen, you see, and the time had come to send her away to the city to be married. She went away weeping to her cage in the city. If only she had stayed there.'

'She came back?'

'Yes,' says Petro sadly. 'She ran away, she ran home here to her beloved hills and skies. The Family had gone by then, but we guess she didn't know that. Only a few slaves were left here to mind the house and the livestock, and afterwards they told us what happened. They loved her too, and when they saw her coming they called out a welcome to her. And then the barbarians came, down from the hills in the east. The slaves all ran away. There was nothing they could do.'

'So she died alone?' asks Vera.

'Not quite alone,' says Petro. 'She had Fidelio.'

'Who was Fidelio?'

'He was one of us,' says Petro. 'He was a Lar. He was the newest of us, and she was the first child born to the house after he was made. From her very first breath, she had his whole heart. We Lares rarely reveal ourselves to anyone, even in the Family, but Fidelio was her constant companion. When she was a child he talked to her and played with her, and as she grew up she confided in him all her hopes and her fears and her dreams. She took him with her when they sent her away to the city, and she brought him back with her when she came home to her death.'

'So what happened to him?' asks Vera. 'Where is he now?'

'He still here,' says Petro. 'But he is stone. Since she died, he has never moved, never spoken. He never will again. Adro says he was badly made. Me, I think he was made too well.'

CHAPTER XI

Early one fine sunny morning at the end of July, the staff of *Ready Steady Dig!* arrive at Crowborough and set up their administrative centre in St Peter's Church Hall. Workstations, computers and telephones are soon in place, and then come the people: half a dozen young men and women to be based at the Church Hall, and twenty students to carry out the excavation itself, supervised by a team of five senior archaeologists, led by Professor Irwin Jones. The camera crews go straight up to Rooks Ridge with all their equipment, as do an advance party of geophysics specialists to make an initial survey of the site.

Mr Horton the County Archaeologist, who has turned up punctually at 8am, surveys his fellow professionals with a jaundiced eye, but he has to admit that they seem pleasant enough, for men and women who have, in his view, sold out to the media.

Unsurprisingly, these quislings hold rather different views from Mr Horton's. To them, TV archaeology means that millions of people now know, and care, about their heritage; and millions of pounds have been poured into the investigation of sites that would otherwise still languish under the turf at best, or at worst become prey for unchecked treasure-seekers. Yes, a few corners are cut, because TV demands quick results; yes, the programme's premise that a site can yield up its secrets in 'only two days' is one that makes them wince; yes, they frequently experience irritation, apprehension, and nostalgia for the old days when time was of no account; but there are compensations. Unlike their non-media colleagues, harassed and confined by budgetary restrictions, they have unlimited access to ruinously expensive field equipment and laboratory tests, state of the art computers, a large team of diggers and an efficient administrative staff who take care of their every need. They also get invited to some very good parties. So there are compensations; but, they all agree, the presence on the moral high ground of a supercilious, self-righteous little tit like Mr Ronald Horton MA is not one of them.

Professor Jones, who leads the team, and who earns at least ten times as much in a year from *Ready Steady Dig!* as he does from his prestigious but cash-strapped university, adopts his usual tactic to neutralise the interloper: at the very first opportunity he introduces him to Bony Jay.

Bony Jay is the celebrity presenter of *Ready Steady Dig!* Formerly a minor rock star and now a moderately successful chat show host, Bony's role on the programme is to represent the ignorant masses, and he does it very well, being a great deal more ignorant than most about matters archaeological. He is a small, stocky, energetic man in his late forties, with black curly hair that regrettably he allows to grow into a pigtail at the back. He adopted the nickname 'Bony' several years ago when he signed up for the second series of the programme, on account of the archaeological finds that had most interested and excited the majority of the viewing public in the first series. Years later he persists in trying to foist similar nicknames onto the archaeologists. Professor Jones, who unfortunately comes from the small town of Muncie, Indiana, is particularly vulnerable in this respect, and he has let it be widely known that any student of his who dares to approach his office humming a certain obnoxious theme tune is likely to find himself on the wrong end of the ancient Viking throwing-axe that adorns his desk. Nor are Bony's attempts to lighten the programme's atmosphere with jolly nicknames very well received by the four other men and women of the archaeological team, who already feel that they are compromising their dignity and their academic standing by taking part in *Ready Steady Dig!* Relations between Bony and the professionals are consequently distinctly cool.

However, he does have a way with people, and thus the archaeologists grudgingly admit that he has his uses, for example in dealing with the likes of Mr Horton. Very few people can resist when a genuine celebrity makes a huge fuss of them, and Mr Horton is certainly not among their number. Besides, Mr Horton is fundamentally a good-natured man, which means that he can't withstand anyone who is actively nice to him.

'Why don't we go straight on up to the site, Ron?' asks Bony, and adds cunningly 'You can show me around, tell me all about it. Bring me up to speed.'

In spite of the fact that Bony has called him 'Ron,' a contraction of his name which he detests, this is irresistible to Mr Horton, especially as the other archaeologists are all now standing with their backs to him, huddled around a computer which they are obviously not going to let him anywhere near. Besides, he has not been able to visit the site since he first saw it, and he welcomes the chance to get back up there again before his colleagues have seen it at all, and perhaps lay down a few ground rules with this man who must, he feels, have great influence on the shaping of the programme. In this he is of course completely wrong, but then what Mr Horton knows about the making of television programmes could be written in magic marker on one of the very smallest shards in his precious collection of mid 8th century local pottery.

Bony ushers him to a splendid, glossy-white Range Rover and drives him up to Rooks Ridge. At the foot of the slope, just off the main road, a large marquee is already in place, together with a massive generator, a JCB, two sets of Portaloos, a caravan with 'Mr Jay's Dressing Room' on the door (Bony insists on his own dressing room), and a commissary wagon, into which the weekend's food supplies are already being loaded. Bony parks up, and they get out to survey the site.

Mr Horton scampers happily around, pointing out the hypocaust pillars in the hole made by Darrell and Big Mac, and sketching out for Bony what he believes may be the general ground plan of the villa: three wings in a U shape, on the east, north and west, with the farm track forming the access road, running straight down from the centre point of the north wing to join up with the modern roadway. He speculates at considerable length on the probable existence of a gatehouse somewhere on the track between the villa and the road, although no sign of such a structure can now be seen. Bony listens with half an ear, and wonders how soon he will be able to interrupt the flow to propose a cup of coffee.

Mr Horton stops abruptly in mid-speculation, and stares in awe as a team of students begins to quarter the site with ground-penetrating radar and other geophysical wonders to which he can never hope to afford access in his ordinary working life. A plough is already ripping up the wheat in the five acre field to the west of Rooks Ridge, to the distress of a number of sitting hares and nesting skylarks, which explode into life as the monster machine bears down upon them. Almost reluctantly, Mr Horton realises just how excited he is. After all, when this bunch of clowns has left in two days' time, the site will be all his, and, while he won't be able to afford to do very much, he feels sure that one of the county's local amateur archaeology groups can be persuaded to devote some time to continuing a project that has actually been featured on television. So he will have free manpower, and he will have access to all the geophysics and the lab results, something that he can never normally afford; and he will be in charge! This is heady stuff. A happy man against all his expectations, Mr Horton descends from the ridge to take coffee with Bony Jay.

Deep under the villa, the Lares are all prostrated with migraine, a side-effect of the ground penetrating radar that would probably surprise its manufacturer. They have done their best to camouflage the treasure pit, but they are powerless against the wonders of modern science. Sooner or later, a big pit with a stone lid, filled with several kilograms of assorted metal objects, is going to show up as a major anomaly in the Cotswold soil.

And a few hundred yards away, all along the farm track that was once the access road to the villa, the Family's graves, too, are about to reveal themselves to the geophysicists; as is a single, solitary grave, hastily dug long ago under cover of night by a frightened group of mourning slaves.

CHAPTER XII

By the time Jim Southerton the reporter arrives on site at 10.30am to cover the weekend's events, filming is already under way as the JCB starts to rip out the dig's first trench. This is to be placed over what appears from the geophysics to be the eastern wing of the villa, in order to establish its extent, while a second trench is being opened without mechanical assistance over the hypocaust at the south end of the opposite wing. After some argument with the Director, Trystram Wentworth, who as usual wants to get things moving as quickly as possible, Professor Jones has banned the use of the JCB at Trench Two, on account of the presence of the rabbit warren, which has made the ground there very unstable.

Mr Horton is surprised but relieved: at least one part of the site will be properly excavated, rather than pulverised, into giving up its secrets. He regards Professor Jones with new approval; Trystram Wentworth sulks, but he knows when he is beaten. Professor Jones is a mild-mannered, unassertive man, but he generally succeeds in getting his own way, largely because he is very big and he looks like a dangerous lunatic.

Deep-set eyes of a piercing blue peer out from a face like a clearing in a jungle. Masses of wild black hair and beard are streaked with purest white, at the brow, sideburns and chin. His students all call him Badger, although they do this very, very quietly. Professor Jones' excessive and striking facial hair is television gold, of course, as are his jumpers. Professor Jones was a teenager in the 1960s, and his aesthetic sensibilities got stuck on Op Art. The walls of his apartment are covered in the dreadful stuff, and so are his woollies. An elderly aunt called Jane, who is a prolific knitter, turns out for him garment after intricate garment adorned with eye-boggling graduated geometric shapes in black on white, or possibly white on black - only Aunt Jane knows which. Looking at Professor Jones is thus quite hard on the eyes, but it does make it easy for the camera to home in on him, so Trystram has made no effort to persuade him into more subdued and dignified attire. Besides, the viewers love the jumpers, and a Mad Professor on the team is a prize that any TV documentary producer would eat his Granny for. Mr Horton, no snappy dresser himself, just thinks that Professor Jones looks rather odd, but he can't quite pin down why.

As the pace of the excavations begins to pick up, the Lares have retreated as deep as they can into the maze of burrows under the hypocaust in the south end of the west wing, and most of the rabbits have retreated with them. Every now and again, one of the rabbits panics and makes a bid for the open air, startling the archaeologists and thrilling the cameramen, who film them avidly. Trystram Wentworth knows that they will enthral the viewers too, certainly a great deal more than anything the archaeologists have managed to find so far, this being the usual detritus of broken shards of brownish grey pottery and old animal bones.

At one end of the large marquee, three students with toothbrushes and washing up bowls are already cleaning the so far uninspiring finds, while at the other end Trinni is assembling her teams for the Field Walkers' Challenge. Mr Cummins has persuaded Mr Gowings to join him under the soubriquet of The Allotmenteers, and they are reluctantly donning the compulsory uniform of matching tracksuits. Maureen, Doreen and their friends are making heavy weather of deciding which colour to go for: Maureen favours the oh-der-neel, while Doreen is convinced that the shartrooze will bring out the colour of her eyes. Two other teams have decided that the Challenge could provide a valuable opportunity to reconnoitre the site and pick up useful information: Darrell, Arthur and Big Mac are ready to go in tracksuits of a fetching lime green, while Mr Black, Mr Grey and Mr White have opted, perhaps predictably, for the black. Several teams of pupils from Crowborough High School, supervised by Mr Horton's friend, Mr Gibbon the History Master, are also taking the Field Walkers' Challenge, as are the Women's Institute, the Mothers' Union, the Over-Sixties, the staff of the Goat and Compass, the Scouts, the Guides, the TA, the British Legion, the Ramblers, the Cricket Club and the Bell-Ringers - in fact just about everybody from the neighbourhood of Crowborough who fancies being on the telly.

Jim Southerton the reporter and his photographer Spike are currently scrounging coffee from Mrs Hamble, who rules supreme over the commissary wagon. There she regularly converts perfectly good and wholesome ingredients into a series of unappetising dishes that everybody nonetheless eats, for the sole reason that there is nothing else available. Mrs Hamble is currently preparing a very nasty looking quiche for lunch, while Spike flirts with her and Jim encourages her to gossip.

Up on the plateau, Bony Jay, Professor Jones and the four senior archaeologists are also drinking coffee as they discuss the latest geophysics results, while Petro, unable to bear any longer the subterranean effects of the ground-penetrating radar, has crept and dodged his way out from the hypocaust to hide beneath the landrover on whose bonnet the computer print-outs have been spread.

'So we're agreed on the north end of the west wing for Trench Three, and I guess this is the obvious target for Trench Four,' Professor Jones declares, indicating an interestingly patterned section of the print-outs. 'These markings here, all along the trackway: they look as if they could be graves. So where exactly, do you reckon? Here, maybe, across the slope, so that we can take in the west end of the first of the group, and the east end of the single one off by itself near the hedge? We can always extend the trench later if we find that they are graves, and then we can open them both right up.'

There is general agreement to this proposal, and Professor Jones trots off to confer with the driver of the JCB. Petro is stunned. Not content with digging up the villa, these people are going to desecrate the Family's graves! It is more than he can bear. Throwing caution to the winds, he abandons the shelter of the landrover, races back to the hedge and plunges into the rabbit hole where the other Lares are anxiously waiting for him.

'They're going to dig up the graves!' he wails. 'Starting with Septimus Verus and Vera Alauda!'

The Lares are appalled.

'Can't we distract them somehow?' cries Lapidilla, wringing her hands in anguish.

'Deadly nightshade, that would distract them,' says Cibus, who is something of a one-track Lar.

'No,' says Lapidilla for what feels like the hundredth time. 'We can't harm them. Surely there must be something else we can do?'

'What about a curse?' suggests Adrogantio. 'I don't mean one of the really big, powerful ones, obviously -'

'Since when could Lares do any curses, let alone big powerful ones?' demands Petro.

'I can,' Cibus announces boldly. Petro gives him a sceptical look.

'Such as?'

'Well, for a start, I can do milk. I can make it turn. And eggs, maybe.'

'Turn into what?' asks Petro.

'Sour milk,' says Cibus. 'That's an easy one.'

'And the eggs?'

'You'll see,' says Cibus. 'Watch this!' He stares down the slope in the general direction of the commissary wagon, and narrows his eyes purposefully. *'Acesce lac!'* he shouts. *'Ovum exclude!'*

'Bleeeeagh!' says Bony Jay, and sprays a mouthful of coffee all over the geophysics results. 'The milk's off!'

From under the ground, a faint sound of sniggering can just be heard.

Seconds later a shrill scream from the commissary wagon stops everyone in their tracks. The cameramen swing around like pointers and set off at a run, but Trystram Wentworth arrives first and leaps up the steps to the kitchen area, closely followed by Bony Jay.

'It's a monster! A monster! It's got all claws and spikes!' shrieks Mrs Hamble, in a voice that could shatter crystal. 'And a beak!'

'It's a chick,' says Jim Southerton.

'It's got spikes!'

'Feathers,' says Jim. 'Wet feathers.'

'Looks like spikes to me,' says Trystram, backing away.

'It's just a chick,' says Jim.

'But where did it come from?' asks Bony Jay.

'Egg,' says Jim. He points to two half eggshells lying on the worktop.

'It's a monster!' shrieks Mrs Hamble again. Cups and plates rattle on their shelves.

'That's no ordinary bird!' says Trystram.

'It's a hen,' says Jim. 'A baby chicken. That's pretty ordinary.'

'Not in a TV commissary wagon,' says Bony Jay. 'I mean, *fresh* food?'

'There's today's story for you, then, Jim,' says Spike. 'IBBC Television tries to poison its staff by serving real food. Can we get one of the school kids from the Field Walkers' Challenge to hold it while I get a few shots for the paper?'

CHAPTER XIII

In spite of Cibus' successful diversion, all too soon the JCB is on its way from the west end of the villa, where it has just ripped open Trench Three, and down the farm track-way to begin on Trench Four. Professor Jones and Mr Horton gallop in its wake, and stand poised to scrutinise the bared soil for the first sign of artefacts or bones. The great yellow scoop descends over the graves of Septimus Verus Pugnax Corvo and Vera Alauda, as the Lares, all thoughts of concealment abandoned in their distress, look helplessly on from the mouth of a rabbit burrow under the hedge.

At the third scoop, Mr Horton gives a wild cry and leaps perilously into the shallow trench, only narrowly avoiding decapitation. The driver swears and backs his monster machine away.

'Stop, stop stop!' screams Mr Horton, and falls to his knees, scrabbling at the ravaged soil with his bare hands. He extracts what looks like a large, curved, greenish-coloured stone, and a beatific smile transforms his homely features.

'Man-made?' asks Professor Jones, joining him in the trench with a wary glance at the JCB.

'Yes, yes!' cries Mr Horton in rapture. He spits on the potsherd, wipes it with his sleeve, and holds it up for inspection and approval. 'It's Berumware!'

'You don't say! Mid 8th century local stuff?' says Professor Jones, impressed. 'Are you sure?'

Mr Horton nods, drunk with ecstasy. "It's my field. I'm writing a monograph.'

'Get that digger outa here,' orders Professor Jones, as Trystram Wentworth bustles up, closely followed by Bony Jay.

'What's happening?' asks Trystram. 'Why has the digger stopped? Surely Roman graves must be deeper than this?'

In silent rapture, Mr Horton shows him the nondescript potsherd, cupping it in his two grubby hands like a precious offering.

'It's just possible we could have an early Anglo-Saxon occupation layer,' says Professor Jones.

'But we're looking for Roman!' objects Bony. Professor Jones gives him a withering glance.

'We are archaeologists,' he says carefully. 'We are not looking for Roman. We are investigating whatever is here.'

'And what's here,' says Mr Horton, still glowing with joy, 'could be a really important new Anglo-Saxon site!'

Trystram's face falls. Anglo-Saxon! They have had Anglo-Saxon on the programme before, and it was a ratings disaster. The Anglo-Saxons built in wood, not stone, which meant that all his cameramen had to film were some faint discolorations in the soil which the archaeologists insisted were post-holes, but which were so faint that even they couldn't always agree on exactly which were and which weren't. This had not exactly made for good television. Even the finds were dismal: Trystram recalls a few bits of crude, poorly-finished mud-coloured pot, some animal bones and oyster shells, and a single lump of badly corroded metal that turned out to be an early key. The archaeologists found this very exciting. The viewers did not.

'How soon to get through it?' Trystram demands. Professor Jones and Mr Horton exchange speaking glances.

'I can't say,' replies Professor Jones. 'This could be a single errant piece, or it could be occupation debris. If we close down Trench One in the east wing as soon as it's been cleaned up and recorded, and bring in a double team down here, we could maybe clarify things in - let's say - ' he flinches a little at Trystram's expression '- by the end of the day.'

Mr Horton begins to protest - the end of the year, more like, he thinks - but Professor Jones hushes him with a sharp kick on the shin.

'Just let us get on with it, Trystram,' he says. 'This could be major.'

Trystram knows from long experience how far Professor Jones can be pushed. He turns away and yells up at the ridge. 'Get some extra students down here *now!*'

'Smart work with that pot, Horton,' says Professor Jones very quietly, and Mr Horton glows. Maybe these TV archaeologists aren't such bad chaps after all.

From the mouth of the rabbit burrow, the Lares watch the JCB trundle off, and exchange puzzled glances.

'They've found something,' says Petro. 'But it can't be the graves, not that close to the surface.'

'It looks to me like a bit of broken pot,' says Adrogantio, narrowing his eyes as Mr Horton holds up his treasure to display it. 'Sort of a greenish colour.'

Petro thinks about it.

'Wasn't it just down there that our Unferth and that great lunk from Geatsburh …?'

'You know, I do believe it was,' replies Adrogantio, recalling one of the more dramatic post-Roman interludes at Rooks Ridge. 'The pair of them were bickering even worse than usual, and Unferth smashed a pot over his head. I'm sure it was one of those greeny-coloured ones we used to get from Breca of Hrafnsburh.'

'Whose head?' asks Cibus.

'You must remember,' says Petro impatiently. 'That great hairy oaf who came here with his band of unwashed thugs to sort out poor old Hrothgar's monster problem. Now, whatever was his name …?'

'Beowulf,' says Lapidilla.

CHAPTER XIV

Professor Jones leaves a glowing Mr Horton to get Trench Four properly under way, and heads back up to the villa to supervise the progress of Trench Three over the west wing of the villa. As well as the clear outlines of the villa's western walls, the geophysics has shown up an intriguing anomaly, and he hopes to get down on to it before the light begins to go in a few hours' time. The senior geophysicist has hazarded a guess at metal, but if so it's a lot of metal, and the possibilities are exciting.

Whatever it is, Professor Jones can see that it lies below the Roman floor level, and there is so far no sign of later disturbance, which gives him reason to hope that it is not some buried modern artefact. He has had his disappointments in that area, an old hub-cap in a mediaeval monastery being perhaps the most embarrassing; but this, he hopes and believes, is contemporary with the building. As the students trowel away at the demolition rubble, Professor Jones is nearly as impatient as Trystram Wentworth to rip out the stones and broken roof tiles and get down to it.

From yet another rabbit hole, the Lares watch, dismayed. First the archaeologists pinpointed the Family's graves, and now they have managed to home straight in on the treasure pit, and there are barely six inches of rubble and earth to move before they reach what is clearly their goal.

Some considerable delay does occur when clear signs of extensive burning show up in the demolition layer, and, after a briefing from Professor Jones, Bony Jay does a piece to camera explaining that the villa did not fall into gradual decay over the years following the Roman period, but was apparently destroyed in a single catastrophic fire around the middle of the fifth century.

Vincent, the programme's resident artist, is brought in, and creates a dramatic depiction of a blazing building and a horde of grimacing blond barbarians. In the foreground he finds himself for some reason including the slender figure of a young woman, who looks remarkably like the dark curly-haired girl he noticed earlier during the Field Walkers' Challenge.

Over in the five acre field, Vera straightens up and decants her latest collection of pebbles and potsherds into her school team's finds tray, and for the hundredth time looks anxiously up at Rooks Ridge. Joining the Field Walkers' Challenge was the only way that she, as a member of the public, could get anywhere near the site today; and she feels that she has to be near.

Trinni blows a whistle to signal the end of the competition, and the teams all troop back to the marquee to hand over their finds to what Darrell keeps calling the archaeologits. Darrell's head is aching from last night's beer, and he is hot, tired and cross, and he and his cronies have wasted half a morning in back-breaking work that has not advanced them in the slightest towards their ultimate goal. Mr Black, Mr Grey and Mr White feel somewhat the same, but they have been keeping their eyes and ears open, and they now have a very good idea of the layout of the site, and of the more promising locations for nocturnal in-depth study.

The sorting of finds begins, with much jettisoning of stones, pebbles and the like. The winning entry will be judged on weight, rather than on the more debateable element of quality, so as usual all of the participants have picked up from their allotted squares every single mineral item they can find that might conceivably be man-made. According to the rules of the competition, Professor Jones' opinion will be final in case of any disputed item; but none of the staff has ever had the nerve to ask him for his opinion, out of a very real fear that he might give it. Professor Jones is not a fan of the Field Walkers' Challenge, although he tolerates it because it doesn't actually do any harm and it keeps Trystram happy.

A heap of discarded rubble soon surrounds the archaeologists, and the Field Walkers stand around drinking black coffee and keeping an eagle-eye to be sure that nothing is discarded that could possibly contribute towards their totals. Notes are made, and the finds are handed over for cleaning and weighing and further scrutiny. It seems to be quite a good haul: a couple of nice flints, a few bits of possibly Iron Age pot, masses of Roman kitchenware and some good pieces of embossed Samian, a fifth century roof tile still with its maker's thumb-print impressed in the clay, three silver coins and three of base metal, a few bits of probable Anglo-Saxon and mediaeval stuff, a musket ball that could be from the Civil War, a large quantity of broken clay pipes, and a number of marbles from the necks of Victorian ginger beer bottles.

At last the winning team is announced, and an ecstatic Maureen gabbles her acceptance speech, thanking everyone she can think of and breaking down in happy tears at the end. Bony presents her with a handsome trophy based upon the *Ready Steady Dig!* logo of a grinning skull over crossed trowels, in heavy crystal. The ensuing polite applause almost - but not quite - drowns out a sudden yell of excitement from Trench Three.

In the west wing of the villa, the lid of the treasure pit now lies exposed, and the Lares watch in dumb dismay as Professor Jones prepares it for lifting. Bony Jay speculates wildly to camera, and Vincent the resident artist can barely keep up with his imaginings. But these are nothing to what is actually revealed when the stone lid finally rises and is carefully set aside. Gold does not tarnish, even after sixteen hundred years in the ground, and this is unmistakeably gold.

Professor Jones stares at the mass of gleaming treasure, and says something he has been longing for the opportunity to say ever since his very first archaeological dig:

'I have looked upon the face of Agamemnon!'

CHAPTER XV

While Trystram Wentworth is passionately demanding the immediate disinterment of the entire find, Professor Jones talks on his mobile 'phone to his eminent colleague, Professor Smith, who specialises in the jewellery and coinage of the late Romano-British period. Professor Smith insists that the finds must be left untouched and in situ, and promises to make all speed to the site. Professor Jones breaks it to Trystram that he will not arrive until the following morning, and the Director throws a magnificent tantrum.

What can be seen of the treasure without moving anything is photographed and filmed from every possible angle, and Professor Jones supervises the creation of a provisional inventory. Part of the rims of two enormous round platters, apparently of solid gold, are carefully measured and approximate diameters are calculated at just over twelve inches. Also visible is the cover and neck of what appears to be a big silver wine flask, and filling all the space between these three large pieces there are gold coins, silver coins, brooches, bracelets, rings. It is impossible to see the depth of the treasure pit, but the size of the platters mean that it must be over a foot deep at the very least. Everyone gazes in deep shock at what has to be one of the largest treasure hoards ever found on British soil. Minds boggle almost audibly, and fingers itch.

Trystram is desperate to see the whole lot dug up immediately, and alternately threatens and cajoles, but this is to no avail: the most that Professor Jones will allow is the temporary removal of a single large gold coin, which everyone examines with awe, before getting back on his mobile and notifying the Coroner's office of the situation.

Trystram tries to object to what he sees as unnecessary haste, which will inevitably bring bureaucracy down upon them in one of its most time-consuming forms, but Professor Jones is adamant: the law relating to finds of precious metal is one that even television cannot be allowed to ignore. The Coroner must be notified immediately, and that is that. Professor Jones closes his mobile, carefully supervises the covering of the treasure pit with a protective tarpaulin, and then walks calmly back to Trench Four to catch up on Mr Horton's activities there.

The Lares huddle together in one of the rabbit burrows that connect up with the hypocaust and consider the disaster. The treasure has been found, and in the morning it will be taken away beyond their reach. They have less than twenty-four hours to come up with a plan that will enable them to keep faith with the Family and continue the task they were enjoined to do and have carried out now for sixteen hundred years. None of them says it, but they are all thinking the same thing: if the treasure is gone for ever, then so is their reason for still being here, and they know that they must all turn back into stone, like poor, sad Fidelio.

There is a more immediate problem facing them too. Soon they will have to find a new hiding place for themselves deeper within the rabbit warren, for work is continuing on Trench Two, and soon the whole of the hypocaust will be exposed.

'In fact I think we'd better get moving now,' says Petro. 'Get your stuff together - Mopsus, I'll take Micandillia and you carry Saliendillius. Got your sticking plaster, Lapidilla? Matches, Grumio?' Fortunately Vera took away the peanut butter jar when the contents were finished, and also the pocket calculator, which she needs for her school work: both of these would have been very difficult for the Lares to move. For a moment, Petro is tempted to leave one of the modern artefacts for the archaeologists to puzzle over, but common sense prevails. Anything that might arouse suspicion about the site is surely to be avoided. So it is with dismay that he notices, as he picks up the former Mrs Flopsy, that one of her ears is missing.

'Mopsus!' he exclaims. 'Surely Micandillia had two ears when Domina Vera gave her to you?'

Mopsus lets out a wail of anguish, and tears spring to his eyes. 'She's hurt! She's hurt!'

'Oh don't be so daft,' says Grumio. 'It's not *alive*. It's just a plaster model, for goodness sake.'

Mopsus begins to cry at these harsh words, and Lapidilla tries both to hush him and to comfort him simultaneously.

'The ear must have snapped off while we were moving around, trying to watch what was going on,' says Petro anxiously. 'It could be in one of the rabbit burrows - but what if it's in the hypocaust?'

All the Lares except Mopsus exchange worried looks. 'You all go on, get yourselves and your stuff out of here,' says Petro. 'I'll stay and look for it.'

'But if you should be seen!' cries Lapidilla.

'Don't worry,' says Petro. 'If they do spot me - well, all they'll see is a stone statue, just another find. They'll take me down to that big tent, and then as soon as it gets dark and they've all gone, I can make my way back up here again.'

There is really no other option. Five Lares retreat into the warren, and Petro makes his way cautiously down a rabbit burrow towards the hypocaust.

Petro inches forward to the spot where the burrow opens into the hypocaust. Only a couple of feet or so to his left, one of the student diggers is gently trowelling away at the loose earth. A sudden voice from above startles him.

'Hello there, how's it going?' asks Jim Southerton, from where he is standing just above Petro's head. Only inches of soil lie between his feet and the Lar's hiding place.

'Careful on the edge of the trench there,' replies the student. 'It's a bit crumbly - there's rabbit holes everywhere. We keep hitting cavities in the ground.'

'Less digging for you, then,' says Jim. 'It must be hard work in this weather.'

'Rain's worse,' says the student philosophically. 'At least we're all getting a good tan.'

'So how do you think the dig is going?' asks Jim. 'By the way, what's your name?'

'Simon Jackson.'

'Age?'

'Twenty-one. Why do newspapers always want to know how old people are?'

'It's a mystery to me,' says Jim. 'What's that you're working on there?'

'Not sure,' says Simon, sitting back on his heels and scratching his head. 'It looks to me like a scrap of plaster, but it's very white - almost as if it's new, or newly broken.'

'And did you?' asks Jim.

'Definitely not,' says Simon firmly. 'It was already on the surface like this when I got here, and I haven't even touched it yet, let alone broken it. I'm just making sure I can lift it without damaging it, and then we'll see.'

Jim settles down to watch as Simon scrapes a little more earth away, leaving his find on its own small pyramid of supporting soil. Then he inserts the tip of his trowel, and carefully lifts the small white fragment. He turns it over, and frowns in surprise. The unbroken side is bright blue.

'What on earth is it?' asks Jim.

'I've no idea,' admits the student. 'It looks modern to me, but what do I know? Time to call in the expert,' he says, and signals to Professor Jones, who is talking to Bony a little way down the hill.

Professor Jones examines the find with some bewilderment.

'This hasn't been cleaned up yet?' he asks.

'No, Professor, it was like that when I found it,' says Simon, rather defensively. 'It was right on the surface, with the white side up.'

'Must be something about the soil, ' says Professor Jones. 'All that gold and silver looks amazingly clean, too - almost as if someone's been polishing it. Gold doesn't tarnish, of course, but you wouldn't expect silver to look like that after all those years in the ground.' He continues to examine the little piece of plaster, turning it over and over in his hands.

'What on earth is it?' asks Bony, looking over Professor Jones' shoulder. 'It looks like a rabbit's ear.'

Below his feet, Petro winces.

'Hare's ear, maybe,' says Professor Jones absently. 'Rabbits didn't come in until the Normans.' He thinks about it. 'I'm going to get this straight to the marquee, and then go on to the Church Hall and have a look at a few references,' he says, and walks off down the hill.

'Hares were magical creatures, weren't they?' asks Bony, who is a bit of a New Ager in many ways. Simon the student shrugs.

'No idea,' he says. 'I don't do magic, just science.'

'Tell me about it,' says Jim to Bony. Celebrities' dotty beliefs are always good for a feature story when news is scarce.

He steps towards Bony and the ground gives way, and his left foot plunges into the rabbit hole where Petro is crouching.

'Careful!' yells Simon, catching Jim as he falls headlong into the trench. 'I said to mind where you're putting your feet!'

Jim winces and leans down to rub his ankle. As he does so, a tiny voice whispers *'Petrificato!'* from somewhere near his foot.

'Who said that?' he says.

'What?'

'I'm sure someone said something like -' Jim breaks off, and reaches out to the heap of loose soil that his fall has created on the floor of the trench. 'Here, what's this?' And he pulls out a small sandstone figurine.

Bony can tell that this is something special, even if it were not for the fact that Simon Jackson is gaping like a stranded codfish. Jim dusts the clinging soil away from his find, and marvels at the realism of the tiny features. He holds the figurine up for Bony to see.

'Here,' he says. 'It's a little stone man. Don't you think he looks a bit like you?

CHAPTER XVI

As night falls on the first day of the dig, work comes to a halt all over the site. The students pitch their tents along the hedge that borders the main Berchester to Gloucester road, and collect their evening rations from a still-shaken Mrs Hamble before she locks up the commissary wagon for the night. Mr Horton heads for a modest Bed and Breakfast just outside Crowborough, while the archaeologists and television personnel retire to their rather more luxurious hotel in the town - all except Bony Jay, who wanders aimlessly around the site, wistfully thinking that just one of those massive gold coins could solve all his current financial problems at a stroke. In spite of the exorbitant fee that he extracts from the Independent British Broadcasting Corporation for his role on *Ready Steady Dig!* Bony is constantly in debt, owing mainly to three ex-wives and one current one. This is why he always insists on having a Dressing Room on site: he saves on his hotel allowance by sleeping in it.

It is only just dark and far too early yet for bed, so Bony makes his way to the large marquee, and wanders over to the workstation of Vincent, the programme's resident artist. Idly he flips through Vincent's drawings, which are always good, and usually a lot more exciting than anything the archaeologists manage to dig up. One drawing in particular catches his eye: Victor's impression of the destruction of the villa. Bony chuckles. One of the advancing barbarians bears a remarkable resemblance to a blond Professor Jones. Then he looks again. The young woman in the foreground, helplessly watching the advancing tide of death: she looks just like his sister, Verity. Odd, thinks Bony, when did Vinnie ever meet my sister? He is pondering this question when he is startled by a tiny sound coming from somewhere very close by.

Something in the Washed Finds Tray from Trench 2 is moving.

Bony knows that this cannot be the case, but his ears are telling him otherwise. This is something that should not happen to a TV presenter, especially after the cameras have gone for the day.

'Er, hello?' says Bony.

Something in the Washed Finds Tray from Trench 2 is now definitely not moving. It is so not moving that you can *hear* it. It

81

is the sort of silence that something makes when it is keeping very, very quiet.

'I know you're there somewhere,' says Bony, craning to see over the Finds Table, and then stooping to look underneath it. 'I heard you, whoever you are. I know I did. You moved. Who are you? Where are you? What do you want?'

'Well,' says a very tiny voice that somehow isn't the least hard to hear. 'Getting all this junk off me would be good for starters.'

Bony inches forward. In the Washed Finds Tray, shards of pottery are moving convulsively. There is something underneath them, and it isn't more pottery.

Bony tentatively lifts what he knows is a small piece of Samian ware. He is good at Samian. It is the only stuff that isn't the same colour as all the other stuff, ie greyish blackish brown. Samian is red. He can do Samian. He moves another piece of pottery, glancing nervously towards the entrance to the marquee in case of sudden archaeologists. The archaeologists do not like him to touch Finds. They shout at him, and threaten to write to the Governors of the IBBC.

No archaeologists appear to be imminent, so Bony shifts yet more bits of broken Roman tableware. The remaining mass of greyish blackish brown in the Finds Tray continues to move.

'Come on, come on, can't you just tip the lot out?' says the very tiny but clearly audible voice. 'Tip it on the table, can't you?'

'But these are Finds!' says Bony, shocked.

'Finds my foot,' says the tiny voice. 'They're junk, man. They're broken pots. I broke this one myself. They're rubbish.'

Bony cracks. He lifts up one side of the tray, and tilts it. A rush of greyish blackish brown shards of pottery, together with a fair bit of muddy water, pours out onto the table, and with it the small sandstone figurine that he saw Jim Southerton unearth that afternoon in Trench 2.

'What are you doing in there?' asks Bony, only faintly aware that there are many other, more fundamental questions that perhaps he should be asking at this particular moment, such as 'Why am I talking to a small sandstone figurine?' and 'Have I finally gone completely insane?'

'I fell in,' says Petro, getting to his feet and dusting himself off, or rather mudding himself off. 'I was just looking for something, and I fell in.'

'But where did you *come* from?'

'That tray over there,' says Petro, pointing to one which is marked *Professor Jones to see - urgentest* in big black letters. 'You must remember me, I saw you up there at the villa. Some bloke trod on me, then he dug me up, and this other bloke put me in a tray, and someone else brought me down here and handed me over to this chit of a girl with a bowl of water and a toothbrush. You ever had some chit of a girl scrub you all over with a toothbrush?'

'Urk,' says Bony, trying not to think about it.

'Then she puts me in that tray over there, says Professor Jones is down at the Church Hall and no-one's to touch me until he comes back to have a look at me, and off she goes,' says Petro. 'So who's this Professor Jones, then? Not the long-haired bearded weirdie in the crazy black and white tunic? We had a door porter once who looked just like him. Used to frighten half the visitors to into fits, and the rest nearly died laughing. Celtic, he was. That would be, what, about twelve hundred years or so back.'

'How long did you say?' asks Bony feebly.

'Twelve hundred, you know, MCC.'

'Cricket? What's cricket got to do with anything?'

'*Cricket?* Ah,' says Petro. 'I think we've got a bit of a language problem here. Cricket...? That's some sort of a game, yes? Played by virgins, all dressed in white?'

'Well -'

'Or are they mourners? Or maybe they just like white? Sorry, you have to expect a few linguistic misunderstandings, I'm not really omniscient except when it comes to kitchen stuff, but if it's really important I'm sure I'll grasp it.'

'It's not important,' says Bony weakly. 'Forget about the cricket. I wish I could,' he adds gloomily. Memories of the last Test Match are still causing him some pain.

'I tell you what,' says Petro suddenly. 'There's something very, very odd going on here.'

'No really?' says the TV presenter talking to the little sandstone figurine. 'Do you think so?'

'Yes,' says Petro slowly. 'How come I'm talking to you?'

'Well, I was hoping you could tell me that,' says Bony. 'It's never happened to me before, talking to a statue, at least not without smoking something illegal first.'

'And how come you can see me moving?' asks Petro. 'That ought to mean ...' He breaks off, and looks hard at Bony for the first time. Small man, black curly hair, that distinctive cleft in the chin... '*Jupiter's pasty crimper*!' he exclaims. 'What's your name? Domine,' he adds.

'You mean you don't know who I am?' demands Bony, who is not used to going unrecognised, except, he has to admit, by small sandstone figurines. 'I'm Bony Jay!'

This does not get the usual response. Petro frowns at him.

'Jay ... Jay. Well, I suppose - I mean, really Jay?' he asks.

'Actually its stands for Jared,' says Bony. 'My parents were Non-Conformists, but I don't talk about that.'

'*Jared*? And *Bony*?'

'Bony's a nickname. Because of the archaeology, you know. The bones.' Bony sees that Petro is not satisfied with this explanation, and adds 'I was born Jared Trueman.'

Petro beams at him.

'Trueman!' he exclaims. 'Yes, that sounds all right. And Jared means 'descendant,' doesn't it? And Jay, of course ... Well, well, well. Another one! I had a feeling Domina Vera wasn't the only one around.'

Petro stands up straight, then gives a sweeping bow.

'*Salve, Domine,*' he says. 'Welcome home.'

CHAPTER XVII

Once Petro has explained about the continuing existence of The Family, and his conclusion that Bony must be a direct descendent of Caius Verus Pugnax Corvo, it takes the cash-strapped TV presenter about two seconds to grasp the most important consequence of these revelations.

'So that gold and silver and stuff up in Trench Three - *it all belongs to me!*'

'Well, not exactly,' replies Petro, in a rather disapproving voice. 'The treasure belongs equally to every direct descendant in the male line of Caius Verus Pugnax Corvo. That includes Domina Vera, and her paternal uncles and cousins if she has any. And I have an idea that there may be someone else around too, but I haven't quite been able to put my finger on who it might be. We've had a lot of other things to think about lately,' he says apologetically. 'But I'm sure it will come to me sooner or later.'

'Don't bother racking your brains on my account,' says Bony. 'I don't want to share that treasure with any more people than I have to. Do uncles and cousins really count?'

'Yes,' says Petro firmly. 'Everyone born with a Corvo surname counts - that means sons, and children of sons, but not children of daughters. And anyway: we both know that the treasure is partly yours: but how do you think you are ever going to prove it?'

The little bubble of hope bursts, and Bony sits down, looking as depressed as he feels. Somehow he knows that the explanation that his names mean 'descendant' [of] 'bird of the genus *Corvidae*' + 'True'(man) is not likely to cut much ice at the Coroner's Inquest into the disposal of the hoard.

'Look here,' he says desperately, 'surely I could have just one gold coin? That's all I need, I'm not greedy, just one piece would solve all my problems. And you could go and get it for me - no one would see you, not if I took you back up to the villa after dark, and put you down somewhere where you could crawl under the tarpaulin that they've put over the treasure pit.'

Petro thinks about this tempting offer. He is desperate to get back to the villa: the Lares have a plan to rescue the treasure, but with so much to shift before dawn, and especially with the two heavy plates and the wine jug, it is going to take all of them to carry it through. Besides, it's a very long way to the villa from the marquee, for a Lar, at least. And after all, it wouldn't be the first time that the Lares have disbursed a little of the Corvo treasure to members of the Family in need. It is theirs, after all, even if they can never prove it to anyone's satisfaction but the Lares'.

'I'll do it,' he says. 'But first you have to help me find something.'

'Anything!' says Bony, thrilled to have got his way so easily. 'What is it?'

'A small blue plaster rabbit's ear,' answers Petro. 'Our Mopsus lost it, and we need to get it back.'

'Rabbits aren't Roman,' says Bony, who can be a quick learner when it comes to matters archaeological. 'Rabbits didn't come in until the Normans.'

'That's exactly the point,' says Petro. 'Shall we start looking?'

A frustrating hour later, Bony is at last climbing up to the treasure pit on Rooks Ridge, surreptitiously carrying Petro, who is in turn carrying the blue plaster rabbit's ear, which they eventually tracked down in a clear plastic envelope with a very big question mark on it in black felt-tip pen.

To guard the treasure overnight, Trystram Wentworth has hired three burly security guards from Berchester, Andy, Bill and their supervisor, Charlie, and by now they are comfortably settled beside the tarpaulin that covers the treasure pit, well-equipped with night-scopes, two-way radios, discreet but businesslike coshes, a thermos of tea, and a packet of sandwiches apiece. The Coroner's Office, Constable Whicker, who is also staying on Rooks Ridge for the night, sits a little way apart from the security men. He feels it would be inappropriate to fraternise, but he silently admires the night-scopes and the two-way radios, disapproves of the coshes, and envies them their tea and sandwiches

Constable Whicker has not come here prepared to stay the night. When the message arrived at the Coroner's Office in Berchester that reportable artefacts had been unearthed at an archaeological dig in Crowborough, Constable Whicker assumed that the call was a mere formality. It never occurred to him that the find would comprise many hundreds of thousands of pounds worth of Romano-British gold and silver; nor that the archaeologists would insist that it must remain in situ until morning. Now that he's seen it, Constable Whicker doesn't feel that he can go home and leave it to the security guards. It's not exactly that he doesn't trust Andy, Bill and Charlie; it's just that he is an honest man, and he knows in his heart of hearts that, without an independent witness to keep an eye on him, he wouldn't even trust himself not to pocket one or two pieces from this vast collection that no-one has fully inventoried yet.

Bony sits down and chats to them all for a little while, doing his gracious celebrity act to excellent effect. Gratifyingly, Charlie and Constable Whicker turn out to be regular viewers of his chat show, while Andy and Bill were great fans of his music back in his rock star days. It is a very long time since Bony has felt so appreciated. He knows he is a big celebrity, but it often seems to him that the archaeologists don't, or if they do, they simply don't care. This is incomprehensible to Bony, to whom fame is meat and drink, the whole stuff of life. He loves the *Ready Steady Dig!* fans, probably at least as much as they love him; the archaeologists, bafflingly, find them embarrassing. When people ask Professor Jones for an autograph, he looks round to see who they're talking to; Bony, by contrast, always has a special pen for the purpose, and a stock of portrait photographs to hand out. He even keeps a magic marker near to hand at all times, for those fans - and there are a surprising number of them - who want him to sign his name on spades, trowels and the like. Bony often wonders what happens to all these implements, and he has been gratified to find them turning up occasionally on eBay. Whenever this happens, he follows the bidding with great interest, and has to resist the temptation to join in himself and boost the prices.

Constable Whicker and the three security guards do not ask him to sign any such implements, but they seem to be hugely appreciative of the photographs which he gives them, and Bony is enjoying himself so much in this warmth bath of adulation that eventually Petro has to kick him sharply in the ribs to remind him of just what he's here for. When Charlie offers him a mug of tea, he manages without much difficulty to place Petro on the ground behind him as he takes it. Then he sits back and stretches out his legs casually so that his feet touch the very edge of the tarpaulin that covers the treasure pit, in the hope that this will enable Petro to creep around him unseen and duck underneath the heavy canvas.

Bony watches surreptitiously from the corner of his eye, while distracting his companions with show business anecdotes, of which he has a large number. It works: Bony sighs with relief as a tiny flicker of movement at the edge of the tarpaulin indicates that Petro has made it. All he has to do now is make his way to the treasure pit in the centre, and back out again with a coin. Petro has assured Bony that this will be easily accomplished once the moon sets, which will happen at around one o'clock in the morning, and he has promised to bring the coin to the entrance of one of the rabbit burrows in the hedge, where Bony can collect it next morning. A happy man, Bony brings the conversation to a conclusion, says goodnight, and strolls away down the slope to his caravan and his bed, while Andy, Bill, Charlie and Constable Whicker settle back to their vigil.

CHAPTER XVIII

As Bony sets off down the hill to his bed, Darrell, Arthur and Big Mac watch him from the meagre cover of a clump of bushes at the foot of Rooks Ridge. They are debating in furious whispers as to their best course of action for securing the treasure, but so far they haven't thought of anything other than a direct frontal assault. Even Big Mac is not stupid enough to think that this has much chance of success against four men on their guard, who will certainly have mobile 'phones, and who are within easy hailing distance of immediate reinforcements in the shape of twenty or more students and Bony Jay.

Hidden in a clump of trees just off the Berchester to Gloucester road, not far from the site entrance, Mr Black, Mr Grey and Mr White sit in an anonymous-looking saloon car with false number-plates, patiently waiting for the right moment, which they intend will occur just after 3am.

From the lee of the hedge, at the mouth of one of the many rabbit holes on the western side of the plateau, Adrogantio, Lapidilla, Grumio, Mopsus and Cibus are watching the security men and the Coroner's Officer, and waiting and hoping for Petro to get back from the marquee and rejoin them. Like Mr Black, Mr Grey and Mr White, and unlike Darrell, Arthur and Big Mac, the Lares have a plan. It is a desperate plan to be sure, but it is the best they have been able to come up with; and it will need all six of them if it is to have any chance of succeeding.

'It moved,' says Andy suddenly, round about one o' clock in the morning. 'The tarp, it moved.'

'Nonsense,' says Charlie uneasily. Could someone be trying to tunnel up to the treasure pit from below? There are, after all, an awful lot of experienced earth-movers around the place. Constable Whicker comes closer and regards the edge of the tarpaulin warily.

'I tell you, it moved,' Andy insists. Andy, Bill, Charlie and Constable Whicker all watch intently for some minutes. Nothing stirs.

'There, see? It must have been the wind,' says Charlie, but it is a completely windless night, and the tarpaulin is a heavy one. Consequently he is rather relieved when Andy announces 'I'm going to have a look, boss.'

Andy carefully peels back the far corner of the heavy fabric, where he is still convinced that he saw a tiny but definite movement. He gives a start of surprise.

'Here, there's a little stone man,' he says. They all look at Petro, who has turned himself to stone only just in time.

'No one told us there was a statue to guard, did they?' asks Bill.

'Nope,' says Andy. 'Just a heap of gold, wasn't it?'

'Don't worry about it, lads,' says Constable Whicker. 'Just leave him where he is. Unless you're afraid that a little stone man is going to run off with one of those gold coins!' He chortles merrily, and draws the tarpaulin back again over the treasure pit.

The first fire engine comes racing through Crowborough at 3.30am. At the excavation site, chaos reigns. The commissary wagon is blazing merrily, and the occasional sharp explosion suggests that Mrs Hamble's store of cooking gas cylinders will need restocking in the morning. Having called the Fire Brigade, Andy and Bill are now doing their best with fire extinguishers which they have found in the large marquee. They are not wasting their efforts on the massive blaze, but instead concentrate on dousing the vulnerable canvas. Charlie meanwhile drives the JCB to a safe distance from the flames, and Constable Whicker rouses the startled students from their tents and herds them away from the danger. Bony Jay rushes around the place, pigtail flying, wringing his hands and saying 'What can I do? What can I do?' He has never been good in a crisis.

Charlie parks the JCB and dismounts. He glances back up to the ridge, and lets out a howl of rage and dismay.

'Andy! Bill! It's all a diversion, lads! There's men up on the ridge! Get back up there now!' He pulls out his cosh and sets off at a run. Andy and Bill drop their fire extinguishers and follow their boss.

Darrell, Arthur and Big Mac are so absorbed in investigating the treasure pit that they do not even see the security guards approaching. With a banshee yell, Charlie brings Darrell down in a neat rugby tackle, Andy takes Arthur without much of a struggle, and Bill attempts what ten men would normally find a challenge: he tries to detain Big Mac. Big Mac shakes him off with barely an effort, and lumbers down the slope, straight into the arms of Constable Whicker.

After a brief and painful interlude, Constable Whicker picks himself up, pulls out a handkerchief which he presses to his bleeding nose, and watches as Big Mac vanishes from sight in the direction of Crowborough. He staggers back up the slope and collapses next to Bill, who is groaning and clutching his belly, where one of Big Mac's boots has made what will prove to be a lasting impression. Charlie and Andy secure their two captives with professional-looking handcuffs, and Charlie pulls out his mobile 'phone.

Within minutes a large contingent of Bunny's Finest has arrived to remove the two prisoners and track down Big Mac (which will not prove difficult - he has gone home to bed). The Fire Brigade is doing sterling work on the blazing commissary wagon, and a local GP, who has been awoken by the sirens and has come to see what is going on, leads Bill and Constable Whicker away to the large marquee for first aid.

Left alone beside the treasure pit, Charlie and Andy exchange apprehensive glances. They can see that the tarpaulin has been disturbed, and neither of them wants to be first to look underneath it. Obviously they interrupted Darrell and co before they could get away with any significant amount of loot, and even if they have managed to pocket a few small bits and pieces, the imminent police shake-down will soon recover that; but what if they have caused any damage? Charlie has strict instructions from Trystram Wentworth and Professor Jones that no one is so much as to look at the golden hoard, let alone touch anything, and he prides himself on always carrying out his clients' instructions to the letter; but at last they can bear it no longer. Charlie pulls back the tarpaulin and gazes down into the treasure pit. He takes a deep breath.

'When they asked us to guard a massive hoard of gold and silver coins, jewellery and plate, Andy,' he says flatly, 'do you suppose that they meant what looks like two old thruppenny bits?'

'No, Charlie,' says Andy. 'I have to say that I don't.'

'Only that's all that's here, Andy,' says Charlie.

'And that little stone man's gone too,' says Andy, patting his boss sympathetically on the back.

CHAPTER XIX

Anguish abounds next morning when the archaeologists and television crew arrive at the site. No-one is allowed in: the policeman guarding the gate to the farm track directs everybody back in to Crowborough, to what was the *Ready Steady Dig!* Administrative Centre at St Peter's Church Hall, and is now the CID Incident Room as well.

Bony Jay and the student diggers are already there, having been evacuated from the villa site by the police in the early dawn, and an excitable gaggle of ladies from the WI is plying them with tea and coffee from two enormous urns. None of the students has had more that a couple of hours' sleep on the wooden floor of the Church Hall, and Professor Jones can see at a glance that the chances of getting any serious work out of any of them today are going to be slim. This turns out to be irrelevant. A hollow-eyed Trystram Wentworth breaks the news that he has just been given by Detective Chief Inspector Maurice Morris of Berchester CID: no one is going to be allowed back to work on the site today. The whole place is now officially a crime scene.

When everyone is finally clutching a plastic cup of tea or coffee, Chief Inspector Morris steps up onto the stage at the end of the hall and demands their attention. To a shocked silence, he outlines the events of the night, the burning of the commissary wagon and the theft of the contents of the treasure pit.

'Ladies and gentlemen,' he says impressively. 'We have a problem.' This statement is greeted with a chorus of derisive laughter, which he ignores. 'Three suspects were apprehended last night,' he continues, 'two of them actually beside the treasure pit on Rooks Ridge. The third man got away from the Ridge, but we caught up with him at his home not long afterwards. The problem we have is this: the treasure is gone, yet neither of the two men apprehended on the spot had so much as a silver penny on his person, nor did the third man when we arrested him, and there was no sign of any of it at his house either. Admittedly he could just conceivably have got away with the missing artefacts and dumped them somewhere before we got him - but Constable Whicker is certain he was not carrying anything when he ran off.'

'How can he be sure of that?' demands Jim Southerton. The Landlady of the Pig and Whistle had 'phoned him at 3.30am to alert him to the fire engines racing through Crowborough, and he had lost no time in getting to the villa site.

'Because the man grabbed him with both hands by the throat,' says Chief Inspector Morris simply. 'That was just before he nutted him. Constable Whicker says the man did not drop anything before that, and he did not pick up anything afterwards.'

'It could all have been concealed on his person,' persists Jim.

'Impossible,' says Professor Jones. 'The pit is over a foot deep, and it was full to the brim with metal objects, including two enormous plates and a big jug. If he had all the contents hidden in his clothes, he could barely have moved, let alone run.'

'He was a big strong man,' says Bony. 'I saw him clearly, although I'm afraid he was just too far away for me to tackle him.' *As if* thinks everyone in the hall.

'He is indeed big and strong,' agrees Chief Inspector Morris. 'But Constable Whicker assures me that when he ran, he did not *clank*.'

'So where has all the stuff gone?' asks Jim. 'Can you be sure that it has actually been taken off the site?'

This question produces howls of outrage. Chief Inspector Morris raises his hand for silence.

'No,' he says baldly. 'We are currently conducting an intensive search of the entire area. If it is indeed still there, rest assured that we shall find it. However, the three security men and Constable Whicker were all with the treasure from the moment Professor Jones and Mr Wentworth left them for the night. They can vouch for each other. The only other person seen to go anywhere near the treasure before the fire started was Mr Jay.'

All eyes swivel to Bony, who cringes.

'I never touched the stuff!' he cries. Jim Southerton is looking at him in a distinctly predatory way, and he imagines the headlines. This is a nightmare. 'The security men, and that policeman! They can tell you I never touched it!'

'They have indeed confirmed that,' says Chief Inspector Morris. 'I did not intend to suggest otherwise.' *But it did me good to see you squirm,* he thinks. He is a frustrated and an angry man this morning, and it does make him feel just a little better to see one at least of these idiots suffering too. They actually left hundreds of thousands of pounds worth of gold and silver sitting up there on Rooks Ridge overnight, with only three civilians and one elderly policeman to guard it! And this after letting half the population of Crowborough know it was there! Chief Inspector Morris is not looking forward to the enormous task of interviewing every single member of the Field Walkers' Challenge teams, all of whom knew about the discovery, on top of all the student diggers, the camera crew and the archaeologists, plus anyone else that any of them might have mentioned it to in the course of the day. He could be here until Christmas just taking preliminary statements from that lot. Chief Inspector Morris glares down at his audience.

'I think I can say that we have clearly established that the only period when the treasure was not being watched was from the moment the fire was spotted at 3.15am until the security guards and Constable Whicker returned to the ridge no more than fifteen minutes later.'

'Surely that just isn't time?' says Jim.

'There's the problem," says Chief Inspector Morris. "The three men we arrested all claim that the treasure pit was empty when they got to it. I don't feel particularly inclined to take their word for that, but the fact remains that if they did take the stuff, then they did it and hid it in less than fifteen minutes."

"Impossible," says Professor Jones.

'Exactly,' says Chief Inspector Morris. 'They were obviously there with the intention of stealing it - but I don't believe they actually did.'

'So are you going to hold on to them?' asks Jim.

'For now,' answers Chief Inspector Morris. 'They're all talking to their solicitor at the moment.'

'Even if they didn't steal the treasure, do you think they're the ones who set the fire?' asks Jim. 'I imagine you're assuming that it was arson?'

'I don't really think there's much doubt about that,' replies Chief Inspector Morris. 'Obviously we're waiting for the Fire Investigators' report, but I shall be very surprised if the fire was accidental. That's another thing that makes me think those muppets we've got in custody weren't the only villains around on

Rooks Ridge last night. I don't think they have enough brains between the three of them to set a fire like that.'

The TV crew and the archaeologists spend a restless, frustrating and largely unproductive day at the Church Hall, but at least their computers and the raw geophysics material are there, and Chief Inspector Morris eventually allows Professor Jones and Mr Horton to go up to the marquee, under strict supervision, to fetch the all finds. As a result, a certain amount of useful work can be done, and Bony Jay bores the TV crew by doing several long pieces to camera on the dramatic events of the night, lightly skipping over his own less than heroic role.

Trystram Wentworth spends some time in a deep depression, until it occurs to him that even if they can't finish the dig, he still has the makings of a programme, and almost certainly a far more interesting one than a routine episode of *Ready Steady Dig!* Arson and major theft should be pretty good for the ratings. It's just a pity his camera crews weren't there to record the actual fire. Some imaginative drawings by Vincent the artist-in-residence would seem to be the only option, until three of the student diggers, led by Simon Jackson, approach him with apparent diffidence to show him what they filmed on their mobile 'phones. *Glory Halleluiah!* thinks Trystram. He can see at once that this is wonderful stuff: hand-held, shaky, indistinct, these clips alone are worth a BAFTA.

'You - ah - haven't shown these to the police yet, have you?' asks Trystram, heart in mouth. The students shake their heads.

'No, we haven't been interviewed yet,' replies Simon Jackson, who seems to have appointed himself spokesman for the trio. Trystram's heart bounds with joy in the morning.

'I'm sure they wouldn't be very interested,' he says casually. 'Especially not when they're so busy -'

'I'm sure they would,' says Simon, who is nobody's fool. 'So we thought we'd show them to you first, so that you can take copies. Only once the police get wind of them, you'll be lucky ever to see them again.'

'That was very good of you,' says Trystram, who has an uneasy feeling that he is missing something here. 'I'll just get one of my people to take a look at them, and I'm sure you'll have them back in an hour or so.' *Not if I can help it,* he thinks.

'Certainly, ' says Simon. 'We thought £2,500 apiece?'

Trystram glares at him, and silently deplores the avarice of youth, and its sound business sense. 'You've been talking to that reporter, haven't you?' he says darkly.

Simon grins at him. 'First thing I thought of,' he says cheerfully. 'I met him yesterday when he fell into my trench. Nice guy. He's already offered us £250 each for three stills to go in his rag.' He beams at Trystram. 'Oh, did you want exclusive? That'll be £5,000 each, only could you let me know straight away? I'm expecting a call-back from Sky News any minute.'

The Fire Investigators' provisional report soon arrives. Whoever started the fire in the commissary wagon did so by cutting a hole in the glass of one of the windows and pouring in petrol, followed by a match or other source of fire. The hole in the glass is perfectly round, clearly cut by an expert.

Chief Inspector Morris thinks about his three prisoners, and none of them strikes him as likely to be an expert in glass-cutting. He could see any one of them throwing a brick through the window to get access to the commissary wagon - but a careful, meticulous job like this? And if they did do it, where's the glass-cutter? No, every additional piece of evidence that he receives goes further and further towards convincing Chief Inspector Morris that Darrell, Arthur and Big Mac are not the men he is looking for. Which is a huge shame, of course, because at the moment they're the only ones he's got.

All things considered, Chief Inspector Maurice Morris is having a really, really bad day, and it just goes on getting worse. At half past eleven, a letter is delivered to him at the Church Hall from the office of Mr Unwin, Duty Solicitor, on behalf of his clients, Mr Darrell Grindley, Mr Arthur Lupin and Mr Orson Lupin, alias Big Mac.

'My clients state that they are all keen amateur ornithologists. At 3.25 this morning, they climbed up to Rooks Ridge to find a good position from which to witness the Dawn Chorus. My clients

were so completely absorbed in this task that they did not observe that the commissary wagon was on fire.

'On reaching Rooks Ridge, my client Mr Darrell Grindley tripped over the corner of a tarpaulin, badly injuring his ankle (see separate document representing Compensation Claim No. 1 against IBBC Television). Fearing that others might suffer a similar mishap, my client Mr Arthur Lupin rolled up the tarpaulin, seriously straining his back in the performance of this public-spirited act (see separate document representing Compensation Claim No. 2 against IBBC Television).

'My clients allege that they were then attacked from behind by three men. Believing that they were being mugged, my clients attempted to fight off their attackers, and Mr Darrell Grindley and Mr Arthur Lupin sustained significant injuries (see separate document representing Compensation Claim No. 3 against Bee-Safe Security Consultants of Berchester).

'Mr Orson Lupin took the decision to leave the scene to seek help. On his way down the hill he encountered a fourth man, now identified as the Coroner's Office, Constable Whicker, who viciously struck my client with his nose, causing him severe bruising to his forehead (see separate document representing Compensation Claim No. 4 against H.M. Coroner).

'In addition to compensation for the physical injuries thus sustained by my clients during the course of the incident, my clients will also be seeking damages for the severe mental and emotional trauma which they experienced as a result of the unprovoked attacks on them and the subsequent unjustified detention in a police cell of Mr Darrell Grindley and Mr Arthur Lupin, and the arrest at his home at 5am of Mr Orson Lupin (see separate document representing Compensation Claim No. 5 against Bersetshire Constabulary), which also meant that they missed the Dawn Chorus, which was a particularly fine one that morning (see attached statement to that effect from Mr Ernest Leslie Mildenhall, Senior Assistant Warden at Crowborough for the Royal Society for the Protection of Birds).'

Detective Chief Inspector Morris is at least 99.9% certain that Darrell, Arthur and Big Mac did not steal the treasure, although he is just as certain that they had intended to. But he knows when he is on a hiding to nothing. The Crown Prosecution Service won't touch this one.

    He lets them go.

CHAPTER XX

Meanwhile Professor Jones is on a mission to hunt down Simon Jackson, who has some explaining to do.

'There are finds missing,' he announces, when he finally tracks down the student digger in the centre of a group of admiring and envious friends. 'And they were both from the trench you were working on yesterday.'

'Sir?' says Simon, descending from the heights of financial euphoria. Professor Jones' expression looks like seriously bad news.

'That odd piece of plaster with the blue glaze,' says Professor Jones. 'And the reporter from Crowborough Herald has just told me that there was a little stone statue. He wanted to know what I thought about it.'

'I gave the plaster thing to you, sir,' Simon reminds Professor Jones. 'And you went straight off with it to the marquee. That's the last I saw of it.'

'And the statue?'

'I thought you'd want to see it straight away, sir, so I got Peggy to take it down to you in the marquee. But I gather that by then you'd already left for the Church Hall to look up some references about the plaster thing.'

'So what happened to the statue? And where's Peggy?'

A pale, timid girl steps forward. 'I'm Peggy, Professor Jones,' she admits. 'When I got to the marquee and found you weren't there, I put the statue in a tray on its own, with a big notice saying *Professor Jones to see - urgentest* and then I went back up to the dig.'

'So what happened to it?' demands Professor Jones.

Nobody answers. Nobody knows, except Bony Jay, and he's not saying. Apart from anything else, they wouldn't believe him if he did.

Professor Jones knows exactly what to do in a situation like this: he goes straight to the man at the top. He buttonholes Chief Inspector Morris, and forces him to listen to the whole story. The bemused policeman hears him out, and makes a serious effort not to throttle Professor Jones with his bare hands.

'There was a serious suspected arson last night and a fortune in gold and silver has gone missing, and you're worried about a chip of old plaster and a garden gnome?' he asks, fairly calmly, he feels, in the circumstances.

Professor Jones' eyes bulge alarmingly, and he looks more than ever like the Mad Professor that he isn't. He really isn't. Well, not usually.

'The plaster chip was - shall we say - of doubtful provenance,' he admits. 'It was almost certainly a modern intrusion, although how it got there I cannot begin to imagine. But the statue! From the description,' says Professor Jones, his voice soaring with excitement and frustration, 'I believe that it could actually have been a Lar!'

'A Lar,' says Chief Inspector Morris. 'Well, fancy that. A Lar. I wonder if you can even begin to imagine, sir, just how interesting I find that piece of information? Can you perhaps understand how important I think it is, on a scale, say, of one to a hundred thousand, that while I am investigating a serious arson attack and a major theft, one of you clowns has gone and lost his Lar?' He pauses for breath. 'And what, for pity's sake, is a Lar anyway? No, no, don't tell me. I really, really do not want to know.' He turns on his heel and stalks off.

Half an hour later, he is back. 'Ah, Professor Jones, if I might have a moment? I wonder if you would very kindly tell me what a Lar is?'

Chief Inspector Morris has, of course, just been interviewing Andy of Bee-Safe Security Consultants, and Andy has told him about the little stone statue which he saw under the tarpaulin covering the treasure pit. 'And then after the robbery, it was gone too. I think they must of took it as well as all the gold. But it was just a little stone man, a bit like a garden gnome, sort of. It didn't look like anything special.'

A subdued Chief Inspector Morris explains all this to Professor Jones.

'So were there two of them?' the policeman asks. 'Two little stone men? Or was your one that went missing from the marquee

102

the same one as the one that went missing from under the tarp? And if so, how did it get there?'

'*Two* Lares?' says Professor Jones. 'Very unlikely, Chief Inspector. Finds of Lares - if that's what it was, of course - are really very rare.'

'You mean, there weren't ever many of them made, or you don't find them very often?'

'The latter,' says Professor Jones, and slips seamlessly into lecture mode. 'In Ancient Rome, and Roman Britain, too, and indeed all over the Roman Empire, the Lares and Penates represented the household gods, the ancestors, the genius of the house, and so on, although of course the genius of the house usually took the form of a snake.'

'Of course,' echoes Chief Inspector Morris.

'The Lares and Penates were kept in the home, generally in stone shrines known as Lararia, which were usually placed next to the hearth in the kitchen. They were at the very heart of the home and the family. If the family moved away, the very last things they would ever leave behind were the Lares and Penates, and this means, of course, that we very rarely find them. Except in Pompeii, of course, and Herculaneum, places like that - where people didn't have the chance to get away.' He pauses to consider this sombrely for a moment. 'I suppose that if a Roman paterfamilias were planning to move his family temporarily from their usual residence, he might leave behind one, or even a few, of his Lares to watch over the building in his absence. He would almost certainly take the Penates with him, of course.'

'Of course,' says Chief Inspector Morris, utterly bemused by this rich stream of information, and unwisely soliciting still more. 'So what are Penates?'

'They presided over the household's food supplies,' replies Professor Jones. 'So there wouldn't be much point in leaving them behind in an empty house.'

'No, of course not,' says Chief Inspector Morris. 'So we can be pretty sure that this was a Lar, not a - not a - Penat? And that's good, is it?'

'Good? Good?' says Professor Jones, puzzled. 'I don't know about good. It is merely a fact. Or probably a fact. We may never know,' he adds wistfully, before dropping back into lecture mode.

'The whole subject is an endlessly fascinating one. So many cultures have these little spirits - piskies in Cornish tin-mines, elves, fairies at the bottom of the garden, garden gnomes even, and brownies, of course - they are probably the closest equivalent to the Lares and Penates - kindly, benevolent little creatures who help around the house.'

The Chief Inspector's thoughts fly to his seven year old daughter Melissa, who has just joined the Brownies. Kindly, benevolent little creature who helps around the house does not describe her. Noisy, idle, destructive, spoiled little madam comes rather nearer the mark.

'Of course, beliefs change over the centuries,' continues Professor Jones blithely. 'And sometimes with them the attributes of the spirits.' *You said it*, thinks Chief Inspector Morris. 'I have a pet theory that perhaps demons, and gargoyles, and suchlike fanciful creations might have had their origins in the old belief in Lares. Wouldn't you agree?'

Demons and gargoyles, thinks the Chief Inspector, and he pictures Melissa's face whenever she doesn't get her own way. 'Yes,' he says sadly. 'That sounds about right to me.'

'Of course, a large house like this villa would probably have had quite a number of Lares and Penates,' continues Professor Jones. Chief Inspector Morris shudders. Lots of the little beggars! His Melissa is an only child, but she often says that she wants some little brothers and sisters. Having encountered some of her friends who do have siblings, he suspects that what she wants them for is target practice. He shakes his head sadly, and mentally corrects himself. Melissa doesn't have friends. Children today don't have little playmates. They have *accomplices.*

CHAPTER XXI

Meanwhile Vera has managed to gain admission to the Church Hall, on the pretext of helping the WI ladies with the tea and coffee. She avoids them, however, and makes for Mr Horton, who she knows is the County Archaeologist, because he once gave a talk to her class at Crowborough High School. Vera thinks that being the County Archaeologist probably makes him the most important person here, except perhaps for the Mad Professor from the TV, and to approach Professor Jones is just too intimidating. Mr Horton is not intimidating at all.

'Please, sir,' says Vera, giving his sleeve a little tug. 'Can I ask you something about the digging?'

Mr Horton is a kindly man, and quite likes children, although they do rather frighten him en masse.

'Yes, of course,' he replies, and they sit down side by side on a dusty bench. 'What is it you would like to know?'

'Please, what will happen to all the things they find, sir? I mean afterwards, when the cameras and everything have gone?' asks Vera. 'I don't suppose they put them back again?'

Mr Horton gives a little chuckle. 'Oh no,' he replies. 'Everything will be studied and catalogued, and eventually it will all go to a museum - possibly the County Museum at Berchester, if I have any say in things. You will be able to see it all there.'

'Even human bones?' asks Vera, trembling.

'Well, we haven't actually found any human bones yet,' says Mr Horton. *These kids!* he thinks indulgently. *It's always the skeletons they go for.*

'But if you do?'

'Any human remains have to be examined by the Coroner first, to make sure they aren't recent, and then they will go to a laboratory for analysis,' says Mr Horton.

Vera is appalled. 'But what about their families?' she asks. 'I mean, they buried them. They wouldn't want them dug up again, and taken away.'

'I'm talking about very old bones here,' says Mr Horton kindly. 'We wouldn't remove legally buried bones from recent times.'

'I don't think it matters how old they are,' says Vera stubbornly. 'I think they should be left where they were put by the people who cared about them.'

Mr Horton smiles kindly at her. 'Well, it's a point of view,' he admits. 'Lots of people do think like that about old burials.'

'And -?'

'I'm afraid that won't happen,' says Mr Horton. 'Lots of other people don't think like that.'

'Thank you for talking to me,' says Vera politely, and turns away. There is no hope there for Vera Alauda. The Lares will just have to come up with a Plan.

Jim Southerton can't bear it any longer. He waits until Mr Horton has finished talking to Vera, and buttonholes him firmly.

'You do realise, don't you,' he says, 'that you've got this TV lot over a barrel?' Mr Horton stares at him, uncomprehending. 'You must have heard what they say at the beginning of every one of their dreary programmes,' continues Jim, who is not a big fan of archaeology, even this dumbed-down, souped-up television version. 'They always have 'only two days' to dig the site. Well, there was yesterday, when I guess things went more or less to plan; and now there's today - when they can't even get near the place, let alone dig it or film it.'

'But surely they'll just wait until the police have finished and let them back in again, and then do their second day?' says Mr Horton, puzzled. 'The Chief Inspector said it wouldn't be more than a couple of days at most, and then his men would all be gone.'

Jim shakes his head. 'These TV people work to an incredibly tight schedule,' he explains patiently. 'With all that expensive gear - camera, computers, not to mention lab time and editing facilities - plus all the people they need - every person and every bit of kit will have been allocated months in advance to go straight on to the next project. They can't possibly wreck their schedule for the rest of the series by staying on here after today.'

Mr Horton gazes at him like a lightly stunned owl. Can this be true? It can. It can! He nods sagely.

106

'I do know from my own experience,' he says earnestly, 'that if you miss your allotted time-window with the County Hall photocopier, you can sometimes wait all day. You have to go to the back of the queue.' (He is rather proud of the expression 'time-window' which he picked up at a meeting from one of the young management consultants in Public Relations, and he likes to use it whenever he can, which sadly is not very often. He thinks it sounds very modern, almost *racy*. Mr Horton is aware that he is neither modern nor racy, and sometimes this depresses him). 'Won't they just put Rooks Ridge to the back of the queue?' he asks diffidently.

'Well, they won't scrap it, that's for sure,' says Jim. 'But even if they can squeeze in a bit more digging and filming when they've shot the rest of the series - well, you can see the possibilities, can't you?' Mr Horton gazes at him wide-eyed, as pupil to master. 'For starters, I'm sure their contract with the landowner will specify yesterday and today, not yesterday and some day in about three months' time. You might want to talk to my uncle about that.' Light begins to dawn. Mr Horton beams at Jim. 'And even if my uncle does agree to let them back in again at some time in the future, what happens to the site between now and then? Didn't you have any plans …?'

'I was going to approach a few of the local amateur archaeology groups,' says Mr Horton slowly. 'We don't have any funding, but -'

'I bet you could get the High School involved too,' Jim prompts him. 'It would make a good project for them. You could get the kids doing the unskilled work, washing pots and so on. I'm sure pot-washing must be somewhere in the National Curriculum - just about everything else is, even if they don't seem to include History these days.' Mr Horton nods eagerly. His friend Mr Gibbon the History Master will surely be able to help him there. 'And as for funding,' continues Jim, 'it's just possible that my Editor on the Crowborough Herald might be interested. A dig like this wouldn't usually cut the mustard, but what with the TV involvement and the fire and the treasure, not to mention the school children, and that fluffy chick, of course - well, you never know.'

'Involve the press?' says Mr Horton anxiously. He is rather frightened of the media.

'And of course, you could allow a bit of filming,' Jim goes on. Mr Horton flinches at the word. 'My photographer Spike could handle all that for you -' and sell it on to IBBC, Jim thinks, but doesn't feel he has to mention that. He'll make sure Ronnie gets a copy of anything good, and that'll keep him more than happy.

'And then there's my uncle,' says Jim. 'He's as rich as - rich as - whoever that bloke was in Greek mythology who was very very rich.'

'Croesus.'

'Thank you,' says Jim, writing down the name.

'Don't you want to know how old he was?' asks Mr Horton, with a twinkle.

'As rich as Croesus brackets age unknown close brackets,' Jim continues, acknowledging this hit with a swift grin. 'I bet if you asked Uncle he might well cough up some cash, especially if you can get the School involved in some way. He never had kids himself - poor old boy, his wife died when she was only about twenty-five, and he never married again. So he does a lot for children's charities, and especially anything with a local connection.'

'Would you perhaps be very kind and introduce me to him?' asks Mr Horton, who is old-fashioned enough to have good manners, and would not dream of simply button-holing the old man.

'Any time you like,' says Jim. 'I wouldn't mind giving him a new interest. I worry about him a lot. He spends far too much time on his own these days, brooding up at the old shrine. He scattered my Aunt Rose's ashes in the little spring there, you know. Very sad.'

Mr Horton's eyes widen.

'Old shrine? Spring?'

'Well, I guess it's some sort of a shrine, or maybe a holy well, or something,' says Jim. 'It's up in the hills, half a mile or so above the villa. It's where the stream starts, the one that runs around the eastern side of the villa.'

Mr Horton discovers that he has forgotten how to breathe.

'The spring comes up in a little pool, all lined with stone,' continues Jim, unaware that his companion is on the point of expiring for lack of oxygen. 'It's on Uncle's land, so I don't suppose anyone else even knows it's there.' He looks at Mr Horton with some concern. 'Are you all right?'

Mr Horton stares at him, looking perfectly demented, and suddenly regains the use of his lungs.

'A shrine! An old shrine! Please, please, you haven't told the television people ...?'

'Certainly not,' says Jim. 'Anyway, it wouldn't be included in their contract with my uncle - I know that's only for Rooks Ridge and the five-acre wheat field.' Mr Horton breathes a heartfelt sigh. 'Would you like to go up and have a look at it?' asks Jim kindly.

Mr Horton nods dumbly, and Jim smiles at him indulgently. 'Let's go and find my uncle.'

'And what would you do with the old shrine if I show you where it is, young man?' asks Hob, in a voice that does not bode well. 'Rip it out with a JCB?'

'Never, never!' cries Mr Horton, tears in his eyes. 'I would *study* it!'

'Dig it up? Pull it to pieces?'

'No, sir!' cries Mr Horton. 'I would *respect* it!'

Old Hob pats him on the hand. 'No need to get worked up, my boy. Certainly I'll take you up there.'

'When? Oh, when?'

'How about now?'

CHAPTER XXII

Bony Jay is a frustrated man. Petro promised to get him one of the gold coins from the hoard - but how is he to collect it? No one from *Ready Steady Dig!* is allowed anywhere near the excavation site, and the day after tomorrow they are all due at their next location. The programme's irritating mantra runs through his head - he has *only two days* ... Of course he could try sneaking up there tonight - but what explanation could he give if he were caught going up there? Worse, what explanation could he give if caught coming back down ... if he were to be found in possession of one of the missing coins! The consequences would be appalling. He could come back later, of course, but the chances of being recognised are huge, and besides, this is an archaeological site. People *dig*. He has to get to the coin before someone else finds it.

Bony becomes aware that a small girl is staring fixedly at him. He sighs, and reaches for his special autograph pen, then realises that she is offering him a cup of the awful coffee that the WI ladies have been pedalling all day.

'No thank you,' he says, then he does a double-take. It's his sister Verity. Another double-take. No it's not. Verity isn't twelve years old and hasn't been for a very long time now. He remembers Petro's exposition of the previous evening, and realises that this must be Petro's Domina Vera.

Vera hasn't been able to get up to the villa site, which is closely guarded by large numbers of policemen, and the next best thing she can do is linger in the Church Hall and at least try to find out what is happening, and what is going to happen. Helping the WI ladies is a good excuse for hanging around, eavesdropping on anyone and everyone. So far she hasn't found out much, apart from her chat with Mr Horton, which confirmed her worst fears about the fate of Vera Alauda's bones if they are eventually unearthed, as she knows they must be. The only other thing she knows is that no one is allowed anywhere near the villa yet. This man, who is, after all, the presenter of *Ready Steady Dig!* may well be able to tell her how long this will be. After some thought, she arms herself with a cup of coffee as a pretext for approaching him.

'Actually yes, I will, thank you,' says Bony, taking the coffee.

'Milk? Sugar?' asks Vera automatically, although she is carrying neither.

'No thank you,' says Bony, and leans down conspiratorially. 'I wonder if we could go somewhere a bit quieter. I'd really like to talk to you.'

Vera scowls at him. 'No,' she says baldly.

'We could go for a ride in my car,' suggests Bony, who for all his show-biz sophistication is basically a bit naïve. More naïve than a modern twelve year old, anyway.

'No!' says Vera, more firmly this time. 'And I don't want any sweets, either.'

Bony Jay looks at her, bewildered. 'I haven't got any,' he says. 'Look, your name is Vera, isn't it?'

'You could have found that out easily,' says Vera, backing away a little.

'What?'

'You're going to tell me that you know my parents and they want me to go with you,' says Vera, who pays attention in class and knows all about Stranger Danger.

'I've never met your parents,' says Bony. 'I just want to have a little chat, where no one can hear us. It will be our secret,' continues Bony, not appreciating how deep is the hole he is innocently digging, but with the increasing feeling that he is missing something important.

'I'll scream,' says Vera, narrowing her eyes. She is not particularly frightened: after all, she is in the midst of a crowd that includes a number of policemen and WI ladies, so the threat level from this particular Stranger must be pretty low.

'Why?' asks Bony, utterly bewildered.

'Is there a problem here?' asks Jim Southerton, who has been watching Vera for the past few minutes with increasing concern. He smiles at her reassuringly. 'Is everything all right?'

'No,' says Vera firmly. 'This man offered me sweets to go for a ride in his car with him.'

The penny drops. Bony gives a strangled cry of horror.

'Did he now,' says Jim Southerton levelly.

'No! No!' wails Bony. 'She misunderstood me! I never said anything about sweets, all I want to do is to talk to her in private!'

'Do you now,' says Jim in a voice that bodes no good.

This is awful. Bony sees his career flashing before his eyes, until desperation brings inspiration. He turns to Vera.

'I need to talk to you about Petro!' he cries.

'Who's Petro?' asks Jim.

Vera looks at Bony, and light dawns. It occurs to her that he looks a lot like the photograph of her Great Uncle Jack, who fell at Tobruk.

'Right,' she says. 'Do you think we could go for a ride in your car? It doesn't matter about the sweets.'

Jim Southerton makes it clear that he won't allow Vera to do any such thing, and shows an infuriating inclination to linger, looking at Bony with an *I've got your number* expression that is galling in the extreme.

Bony and Vera are rescued by the arrival of Hob, who announces that he and Mr Horton are going to have a look at the you-know-what, and is Jim coming with them? Jim hesitates, but he doesn't seriously think that Bony is a child abductor (his four marriages and a number of less formal arrangements, all with ladies of mature years, are common knowledge in press circles), but he has a nose for a story, and he can tell that something here is a bit off-kilter. At the same time, he does want to be there when Mr Horton first sets eyes on the spring and the shrine. Jim has taken rather a fancy to Mr Horton, and doesn't want to forego any of the advantages that could accrue to him as an on-the-spot benefactor. With a final minatory glance at Bony Jay, he departs with his uncle and the archaeologist.

Bony breathes a heartfelt sigh of relief.

'How do you know about Petro?' Vera demands, and he explains about their last evening's encounter in the marquee, and how Petro recognised him as one of the Family.

'So you could be my-' Vera hesitates, and does a bit of mental arithmetic. 'My Grandfather?'

Bony winces.

'No,' he says firmly. 'I think the relationship is a lot more distant than that, and I don't mean Great Grandfather. I'm a Trueman, and you're a - what did Petro say? - a Rookwood? So our family lines probably split centuries ago, maybe even right at the very beginning. Petro told me that Caius Verus Pugnax Corvo had four sons. Anyway, it's not important. We're Family, according to Petro, and that's all that matters.'

'Yes,' Vera agrees. 'And what's really important now is for us to stop the excavation before they get to the graves.'

'Ah,' says Bony. 'The geophysics people said there are what look like graves all along the farm track, didn't they? That's why they put Trench Four down there - is that where you mean?'

'Yes,' says Vera. 'We've got to stop them digging there.'

'Why?' asks Bony, genuinely puzzled. 'Is there more treasure buried with them?'

'Treasure! No!' cries Vera. 'They're graves! Our *Family's* graves!'

Bony looks blank.

'One of them is Vera Alauda,' continues Vera. 'She was the daughter of Caius Verus Pugnax Corvo, and she looked just like me, and her name means Lark in Latin, and she was killed by barbarian raiders when they burned down the villa, and it's not *right* to dig her up and send her to a laboratory and put her in a museum. It's just not *right*.'

Bony thinks about it, and it does seem a bit off. He wouldn't want anyone digging up his Granny, so why should he let them dig up his Great, Great, a hundred times Great Granny, especially when she looked just like his sister? He is very fond of his sister. Suddenly it occurs to him how very much he doesn't like the archaeologists, in fact almost as much as they don't like him.

'I'll help if I can,' he says. 'But I don't see how.'

'Surely you could stop them,' says Vera hopefully. 'I mean, you're in charge of the TV programme.'

'I wish,' says Bony sadly. 'No, I'm just the presenter. No one ever listens to me, not the archaeologists anyway. Look, I'll help if I can, but that's not what's really important right now - I mean, really *urgent* right now.'

'So what is?'

'The treasure,' says Bony. 'I know it's been stolen, but there's a chance that Petro may have got a bit of it out before it was all taken.'

'What makes you think that?' asks Vera suspiciously.

'Because he said he would,' says Bony. 'And I took him back up to the ridge from the marquee, and he managed to hide under the tarpaulin without being spotted. But that's all I know. He was going to bring one of the coins to me this morning, only of course I can't get up there now to see if he managed it.'

'Why was Petro going to bring you one of the coins?' demands Vera, and there is a distinctly hostile note now in her voice.

'Well, because I asked him to,' admits Bony. 'I could really, really do with the money, and a coin like that would sell for - well, I don't know what, but it would have to be a lot.'

'Petro never offered to give me any of the treasure,' says Vera.

'Did you ever ask him?' asks Bony.

'Well, no.'

'There you are then,' says Bony. 'The treasure belongs to the Family, and I'm guessing that if someone in the Family says they need it, then the Lares will hand it over. I think they probably have to.'

'Yes, I expect they do,' says Vera thoughtfully.

'I wonder if the Lares have any idea who emptied the treasure pit last night?' says Bony. 'They were there all the time, after all. They must know something about what happened. It could even have been them who took it all!'

'I don't see how,' says Vera, who has, however, been thinking along those lines herself. She knows the Lares had a plan to do just that. 'The two big plates, and the jug - how could they possibly have moved them? And even if they did somehow, how could they have done it without being seen?'

'I don't see how anyone could have done it without being seen,' Bony says gloomily.

'So it can't have been them,' says Vera rather speciously, realising that if the Lares do somehow have the treasure, she doesn't particularly want Bony Jay to know about it. Not when they may be under an obligation to hand it over to him just for the asking.

115

'No,' says Bony, thinking like mad. 'But I'd still like to talk to them about it. If they have got it ...! And anyway, I want to get my coin. I wish there was some way to get up there to the villa without the police seeing us.'

'Well, there probably is,' says Vera, who is pretty keen to get back up there herself, and certainly doesn't want Bony going up on his own. 'I've done it before, although that was when there were only two policemen. But we might be able to, if we're careful.'

'How?'

'If we go up along the west side of the hedge, you know, on the edge of the wheat field,' answers Vera. 'I don't suppose they'll be guarding that. The fire and the stealing and everything, well, that all happened on the other side of the hedge. That's where they'll be investigating. I suppose they might see us, but we could always make up an excuse.'

'Such as?'

'I could say I lost my dog,' says Vera. 'That's sort of how I met Petro in the first place.'

'Do you have a dog?'

'He's my Step-Dad's,' says Vera. 'His name's Rags. He's a terrier. He's always running away, especially when there's rabbits.'

'Lots of rabbits at the villa,' Bony points out. 'This sounds like a plan.'

'Yes,' says Vera doubtfully. 'I'm not sure, though - if we were caught -'

'Don't worry about it,' says Bony, with increasing confidence. 'With the lost dog story, I'm sure I can talk our way out of it if they do catch us. Rags, was it? Terrier? I ought to have the details straight. And anyway, even if they do get us, what can they do to us?'

'If we've got the treasure?'

'Ah. Yes, I think we'd have to leave any treasure behind,' says Bony sadly. 'Even my gold coin. Unless you'd like to carry it for me?' Vera gives him a look. 'No, maybe not. But at least we could find out if the Lares know what happened last night, and if Petro's got my coin for me. But even if he has, I don't think I can risk bringing it away.'

That's all Vera needs to hear.

'Let's go now,' she says. 'Where's your car?'

CHAPTER XXIII

Vera and Bony make their way cautiously up the western slope towards Rooks Ridge, lightly concealed by the hedgerow that runs parallel to the farm track, along the edge of the five-acre former wheat field. They manage a fair compromise between being seen and being seen to be furtive, both of which would undoubtedly mean being sent briskly on their way by the police, with little hope of a second more successful attempt. Fortunately they are both of them small and the hedge is dense, while the chattering of the stream on the other side of the farm track helps to cover any slight sounds as they make their way carefully up the hill.

At the edge of Rooks Ridge, they pause and take stock. There are two policemen down on the gate to the site, and two more, in what look like spaceman suits, are up on the ridge, engaged in close examination of the treasure pit, while further off a whole gaggle of spacemen are sifting through the burnt-out wreckage of the commissary wagon. So far, so good. All Vera and Bony have to do is keep in cover, and not make too much noise.

At the top of the slope, Vera locates a rabbit hole, and calls Petro's name very softly. The tunnel magnifies the sound of her voice, and in less than a minute all six Lares are there. Adrogantio steps forward.

'Salve, Domine,' he says formally to Bony Jay. 'We your faithful Lares welcome you to Villa Corvo. I am Adrogantio, and these are Lapidilla, Grumio, Cibus and Mopsus. Petro you have already met.'

'Er, hello,' says Bony. 'Um, Petro? What about my gold coin? Did you manage to get it for me?'

'I got it for you and hid it, Domine,' says Petro, bowing to him.

'So where is it now?'

For answer, Petro points at the floor of the burrow. 'Buried just under the surface there,' he says. Bony digs a little with his fingers where Petro indicates, and his hand closes over a heavy gold coin. He rubs it on his sleeve to clean it, and it gleams with the promise of a debt-free future. But dare he take it with him?

'I think you ought to leave it there for the time being,' says Vera firmly. 'We still have to get back down the hill, and we could easily be spotted.' Reluctantly Bony re-buries his treasure.

'Besides, there is much to be done,' announces Adrogantio. 'Domina Vera, when will the digging start again?'

'Yes,' says Petro, 'those men who were digging up the graves - when will they come back, and how can we stop them digging there?'

'I'm afraid the news isn't good,' says Vera. The Lares regard her anxiously. 'The excavation has stopped for the moment, and the TV people will be going away tomorrow - they have to go on to their next dig. But the County Archaeologist is going to carry on here when they've gone, and he told me that if they find human bones, they will dig them up and take them away. And they won't ever bring them back.'

Lapidilla gives a little cry of anguish, and the others look solemn.

'What can we do?' asks Mopsus pathetically, wringing his hands. 'What can we do?'

'There's nothing you can do, they know exactly where the graves are,' says Bony. 'They pin-pointed them with the ground-penetrating radar, and that's why they put Trench Four exactly where they did. Ron Horton stopped them going deeper, but he knows the graves are there, and as soon as he's finished with his Anglo-Saxon layer he'll dig on down until he finds them.'

'He thinks he knows where the graves are,' says Petro slowly. 'That ground-penetrating radar thing - will the TV people take it away with them?'

'Yes, we use it on all the programmes,' says Bony. 'In fact it's already gone on to the next site.'

'So Magister Horton won't be able to check the results?' says Petro, thinking fiercely. 'If he notices anything ... *odd?*'

'What, Petro?' asks Vera. 'What have you thought of?'

'It's just an idea,' says Petro slowly. 'We'll need Drippy's help, of course, and -'

'*Drippy*?' says Bony, and Vera explains the nymph of the valley and stream, insofar as this is possible without the aid of paper and coloured crayons.

'So let's go and find her,' continues Petro. 'You said you'd take us up to the shrine, Domina Vera, and with your help, Dominus Osseus, we could go now.'

'With my help?' says Bony.

'Yes, we can't get there by ourselves, it's too far, and Domina Vera can't carry us all.'

'We can bathe in the spring again!' says Lapidilla joyfully. 'We ought to do that, to speed the enterprise!'

'A very good idea,' says Adrogantio judiciously.

'All of us, of course,' says Lapidilla quietly. There is a little silence.

'Yes, of course,' says Petro. 'Fidelio should come too.'

Fidelio the Stone Lar, Petro explains, lies buried under the hedgerow, at the head of Vera Alauda's grave, and Vera is delegated to fetch him, taking Petro with her in her top pocket to pin-point the exact spot.

It is not an easy task: she creeps back down the hedge-line, and carefully pushes through almost to the other side, keeping as low down as possible. While Petro keeps an eye on the three groups of policemen, Vera digs into the loose soil with her hands where he indicates, and within a few minutes her fingers touch solid stone.

The Stone Lar is a young man, hardly more than a boy, tall and slender, with a thin, serious face. His sightless eyes seem nevertheless to stare longingly, and his lips are parted as if at any second he could speak - or cry out in anguish. Vera gazes at him with pity that makes the tears well in her eyes. *He is stone...*

'Come, Domina Vera,' says Petro urgently. 'We should not stay here.'

Vera pulls herself together, and crawls backwards out of the hedge, cradling Fidelio gently in her hands. Once on the other side of the hedge, she hurries back up to the ridge, where Bony and the other Lares are waiting. She sets Fidelio down on the grass before them. Lapidilla and Mopsus touch him gently, and Lapidilla kisses his unresponsive cheek. Petro, Grumio and Cibus look embarrassed; Adrogantio doesn't look at all.

'Come,' says Adrogantio. 'We should be going.'

'Which way?' asks Bony. 'We mustn't be seen. Professor Jones made a heck of a fuss about losing just one Lar. I really, really do not want to be caught with seven of you.'

'The way is quite secret, up through the woods,' says Adrogantio. 'If you will take me on your shoulder, Domine, I shall direct you.'

Bony lifts him into place on his right shoulder, and Adrogantio take a firm grip on his ear to steady himself. Bony tries not to wince.

While Bony is distracted, settling Adrogantio and picking up Grumio, Cibus and Mopsus, Vera kneels and swiftly scoops up the gold coin that he has just re-buried in the mouth of the rabbit hole, and slips it into her pocket. Petro raises his eyebrows, but says nothing. She picks him up, together with Lapidilla and Fidelio. They are surprisingly heavy, she finds, but then, they are made of stone. She follows Bony through the trees and onto a narrow path up the hill behind the villa.

It is a pretty path, going steeply uphill through groves of hazel and alder, and after a few yards it meets the little stream and wanders alongside it. Sunlight gleams through the leaves, shadows dapple the ground, and the air is golden and full of birdsong. Vera feels her heart lighten with every step she takes, as if the path leads to a place of peace and joy. It seems familiar too - she somehow knows when each bend is coming up, and when to expect the smooth, mossy bank where they stop and rest for a while from the steep climb. Soon they are moving on again, quietly through the shadows, their feet silent on the hard-packed earth. The air smells green and cool, and the constant sound of tumbling water follows them as they climb. It is as well they are quiet, because it means that they hear the people moving slowly up the path ahead, and have no difficulty taking cover to avoid being seen, but close enough to hear what they say.

CHAPTER XXIV

Jim Southerton lends his uncle a supporting arm as they climb the last few yards to the shrine and its bubbling spring. Mr Horton, eager though he is, stays politely in the rear, his heart thumping with expectation and excitement. A shrine! A sacred spring! He can still hardly believe it, and steels himself for disappointment.

But he is not to be disappointed. At last he sees up ahead of them, cutting down through the trees, a shaft of sunlight that falls softly upon a little pool, all lined with stone. Hob and Jim stand back to let him approach, and he gazes in sheer delight at the softly bubbling water in the centre of the pool. The stone basin is full to the brim with clear water, which trickles steadily over the edge and down a mossy, ferny bank into a little gully and on down the slope to become the stream that flows past Rooks Ridge. Somewhere on the villa site, the academic half of his brain knows that there will be the pipes and drains that would have carried the water into the buildings and out again to rejoin the stream; but it is the other half of his brain that is thinking for him now. Mr Horton gazes in rapturous wonder at the sparkling water, the overhanging ferns, the mossy stones, and knows that he has found the loveliest place he will ever see in all his life.

'Thank you,' he says quietly, tearing his gaze away at last, and looking at the old man, who is smiling at his evident pleasure. A wild rose has scattered its pale petals in the spring, and the water carries them softly over the brim and down to float away on the stream. 'Thank you for bringing me here.'

'My wife loved this place,' says Hob simply. 'You know, we were neither of us fanciful people, but we both agreed we often felt a friendly presence here. I still do sometimes.'

Mr Horton looks up, and for a moment he thinks he sees the face of a young woman staring intently at him between the branches of the wild rose bush. She has long, shimmering golden hair, in which a large quantity of foliage and flowers have been artfully entwined. He blinks, and the face is gone, but not the feeling he has of a presence. This is quite enough to make any respectable academic a little uneasy; but what makes him a *lot*

121

uneasy is the very definite feeling he has that the presence is focussed on him.

'Yes,' he says uncertainly, 'I can understand that.'

They gaze in silence for a while at the spring and the pool.

'So,' says Hob, all sentiment suddenly set aside. 'What do you make of the place, young man? How old is it?'

Mr Horton carefully examines the stones that line the pool - they are dressed Cotswold limestone, water-worn and mossy, clearly ancient.

'It could certainly be Roman,' he says. 'I'm pretty sure that this would have been the villa's main water-supply. In fact, that's probably why they built the villa where they did - so that they would have access to a constant source of running water.'

'And would it have been a sacred site?' asks Jim.

'Oh, certainly,' says Mr Horton. 'Springs like this would have a guardian nymph.' He looks nervously behind him at the wild rose bush, but there is nothing there now but leaves and flowers and branches. 'We may even find a dedication carved somewhere on the stones, and there will certainly be offerings in the pool.'

They look down into the water. It is crystal clear, but a fine sediment covers the bottom. Mr Horton looks to Hob for permission, then rolls up his sleeves and reaches into the water. He sifts the sediment carefully with his hands, and comes up with a small piece of twisted metal.

'Yes!' he says, examining it carefully. 'This is a brooch, Roman certainly, fourth or fifth century at a guess - I'm afraid it's not really my period. See where it has been deliberately broken before being thrown in as an offering.' They examine the little bronze piece with some reverence.

'The last person to handle this,' says Mr Horton solemnly, 'was probably a young Roman girl, who gave it to the nymph of the spring, hoping for - who knows what?' He puts it carefully back in the water, and it sinks into the sediment once more.

'Don't you want to take it away?' asks Hob, looking at him curiously.

'Not just yet,' replies the archaeologist. 'One day I would like to make a proper examination of the pool, but only after we have finished work on the villa, I think. It would be a mistake to open up too many sites at the same time - these things need to be done slowly, and carefully, not dug out as quickly as possible just to see what's there. After all, the shrine has been here for centuries, and it will still be here in a few months, or even a few years. Eventually, it would be interesting to dredge the pool, with your permission, of course, sir. But just for now I think the brooch, and everything else, should stay where it is.'

'Safer that way,' agrees Jim. 'No one but us even knows the shrine exists, after all.'

Mr Horton nods. 'Yes, and I'm sure there will be many other offering pieces here, and they all have a value to collectors. As soon as they are brought out and made public, they will be vulnerable to theft.'

'Look what happened on Rooks Ridge last night,' agrees Hob. He turns to Mr Horton. 'You're quite right, my boy, you leave everything here for now. And when the time comes to lift them, we'll do better by them than those idiots did with the treasure hoard.'

CHAPTER XXV

Vera, Bony and the Lares wait, concealed in the undergrowth, until at last Hob, Jim Southerton and Mr Horton take their leave of the shrine and walk off slowly down the path. The sound of their footfalls fades away, and the watchers emerge cautiously from their hiding place. They approach the pool, and gaze down into the crystal waters. Even Bony seems affected by the quiet beauty of the place, and the Lares are silent as they are set down carefully on the mossy rim. Vera lifts up the Stone Lar, and places him gently in the water. As the soft sediment settles slowly around his inert form, she half expects to see him move, but nothing happens.

'Don't wish him back again, Domina,' says Lapidilla softly. 'Please, don't wish him back.'

Vera starts, and looks at her guiltily. 'But Lapidilla, it's so sad! Surely - '

'He is stone, Domina. He feels no sadness now, just as his beloved Vera Alauda no longer feels her fear and pain. She was his whole life, and she is gone for ever. Why would you wish him back?'

There is no answer to that, and Vera knows it. 'Could I?' she asks. 'Could I bring him back?'

'Perhaps. As one of the Family, if you called him I think perhaps he might come,' says Lapidilla. 'But I think you will not do it. I think you will let him be.'

Vera bows her head, and reaches into the pool to touch the Stone Lar gently. 'Yes,' she says softly. 'Rest in peace, Fidelio.'

Satisfied, Lapidilla sits down on the edge of the stone basin, and slides softly into the water, where she floats serenely, the skirts of her stola billowing around her like the petals of a flower.

'We should leave him here for now, I think,' says Petro. 'At least until we know the graves are safe. Drippy will look after him for us.'

'Yes,' says Vera. 'You heard Mr Horton say he won't be excavating up here until he's finished at the villa, and that could be months, or even years. Fidelio will be much safer here than back down there, where he could be found and dug up and taken away.'

Somehow, too, she thinks he will like it here, Stone Lar though he be. Besides, if they leave him up here, she won't be tempted to try to wake him.

She sits down beside the pool, where Lapidilla is coaxing Mopsus to come into the water: he is clearly nervous, and holds on to the edge for a while before letting go and dog-paddling out into the centre where the spring bubbles up. Grumio goes next, wincing and grumbling at the chill, which makes Petro roll his eyes. Adrogantio follows, sitting down on the edge and sliding in decorously without a splash. Cibus and Petro exchange glances, then suddenly Cibus shoves Petro hard in the small of the back. This move is clearly not unexpected, however, for Petro manages to grab Cibus by the arm as he falls, and the two of them tumble in together, and surface spluttering and laughing. Lapidilla smiles at them indulgently, while Mopsus looks anxious and Grumio and Adrogantio scowl. For a while the Lares float or splash around, while Vera and Bony watch, until Vera suddenly becomes aware that there is a third person on the bank beside her.

She turns her head to see that the nymph Stillaria has appeared, elegantly draped around a slender willow tree, gazing heavenwards with a dreamy expression on her face.

'Love! O love! O cruel, cruel love!' she cries, and vanishes just as Bony turns around at the sound of her voice.

'Who was that?' he asks. 'Did you see anyone?'

Vera smiles at him. 'That was Drippy,' she explains. 'Stillaria. I told you about her, she's the nymph of the stream and the valley. This is her shrine.'

Petro paddles to the side of the pool.

'I wonder what that was all about,' he says darkly. 'As if I couldn't guess.'

Cibus joins him, and they tread water. 'Sounds to me as if our Drippy's gone and fallen for a mortal man again,' he says. 'I wonder which one of them it was?'

'Well, it won't be the old man,' says Petro, hauling himself out of the water. 'He's been coming up here for years, she'd have fallen for him ages ago if it was him. So it'll be either the tall one with the notebook or the short one with the little round glasses.'

'My money's on the little round glasses,' says Cibus. 'Drippy could never resist spectacles.'

126

'Did I just see Stillaria?' asks Adrogantio, joining him at the side of the pool.

'Yup,' says Petro. 'Cibus thinks she's in love again. Probably the short one with the glasses.'

Adrogantio rolls his eyes. Petro reaches down to help Lapidilla out of the water, and the rest of the Lares follow, and settle themselves on the mossy rim of the pool.

'There'll be trouble, you mark my words,' says Grumio darkly.

Petro agrees.

'It's never good news when a nymph falls in love with a mortal.'

They all turn, and gaze thoughtfully at a young sapling growing beside the pool. It is bent gracefully over, its branches almost touching the water.

'Hill walker, wasn't he?' says Adrogantio. 'Small man, spectacles, knobby knees, big boots, hairy socks? I ask you, what did he expect, wandering up here on his own looking like that?'

'Well, I don't suppose he expected Drippy,' Petro points out. 'Mind you, I think he probably felt it was worth it.' He pats the little tree on a bumpy protrusion that in some lights might be thought to resemble a back-pack.

'I don't think she'll have much joy with this new one, mind,' says Adrogantio. 'I doubt she's his type,' he adds delicately.

'Ah,' says Petro. 'No, probably not.'

'Since when did a little thing like that ever stop our Drippy?' asks Cibus cheerfully.

'True enough,' Petro concedes. 'Nymphs do tend to be very single-minded. And a bit slow on the uptake.'

'A few twigs short of a thicket,' agrees Cibus.

'Exactly,' agrees Petro. 'Remember that Narcissus bloke? Somewhere in Greece, wasn't it? Sad, that.'

'Oh, I don't know,' says Cibus. 'It's not as if he had much of a life before it happened. I expect he's happy enough.'

'For a bunch of daffodils,' says Grumio darkly.

'We'll just have to find ways to keep her occupied,' says Petro. 'My plan for saving the graves from being dug up is going to need both her and the Genius Loci.'

'Good luck with that, then,' says Grumio glumly. 'You'll never get him to help.'

'Contrary old so and so,' agrees Cibus.

'Don't worry,' says Petro. 'I know just how to handle him. He'll be a piece of cake.'

'So what is your plan?' Adrogantio demands. 'How can you stop them digging where the graves are?'

'Well,' says Petro, 'first we're going to need a bit of that old greenish pot - you know, that really rubbish stuff that Breca of Hrafnsburh used to make. There should be plenty of it around, Breca's pots were always cracking and breaking.'

'Why does it have to be that pottery?' Cibus asks.

'Because for some reason the guy in the little round glasses seems to think it's something special,' answers Petro. 'It's what's stopped him digging straight down to the graves so far. As soon as he spotted that bit of pot, he sent that big machine away and wouldn't let anyone dig any more. So I want a bit more of it to distract him, and to stop him thinking too much about anything else.

'Now, while I was in that big tent I definitely saw a bit of it somewhere, when I was looking for Micandillia's ear.'

'But of course you can't remember exactly where,' says Grumio.

'No, but we'll find it,' says Petro firmly. 'The Anglo-Saxon settlement was mostly in the five-acre field, so all we need to do is locate the finds from that area, and there's bound to be a bit of Breca's stuff amongst them.'

'That's where Domina Vera and those people in the matching tunics and leggings were picking up all the stones and things,' says Lapidilla. 'Do you know what happened to them, Domina?'

'If there were any of Breca's pots there,' says Grumio. 'There probably weren't.'

But Vera can't help. She already knows that all the finds from the excavation, including those from the Field Walkers' Challenge, were taken from the marquee down to the Church Hall by Mr Horton and Professor Jones earlier in the day, and are now being packed up to be sent on their way for further study. They are unreachable.

'Told you we wouldn't be able to get at them,' says Grumio with gloomy satisfaction.

'Well, we'll just have to find some more,' says Petro firmly. 'There must be lots more of Breca's stuff lying around in the field. There's probably a few bits of it around the villa too - we could try the spoil heaps. There's a good moon tonight - surely if we all look we'll manage to find at least one piece?'

'We'll be lucky,' says Grumio.

'Yes, we will if we try,' says Lapidilla brightly. 'What do you want it for, Petro?'

'Well, it's not absolutely vital to my plan, but I think it could help,' says Petro. 'We know that Drippy's flame just loves the stuff, and he's the one who's going to be in charge of all the digging now that the television people are going away. I want to use it for a decoy, a distraction, but first I need the Genius Loci and Drippy to do their bit - it won't work at all without them.'

'So you need to find some special pottery?' asks Vera, trying to keep up.

'Yes,' says Petro. 'It's that heavy, crumbly greenish stuff. There's most likely to be some in the field, so as soon as the policemen have gone, we'll have a look - we should have a bit of time, shouldn't we, Domina, before they start up the digging again?'

'I don't know,' says Vera.

'Probably,' says Bony. 'I don't think Ron Horton's exactly a live wire. He'll take a while to get things started. After all, he's a civil servant. They always do things as slowly as possible, in fact I think it's probably a rule.'

'So there's no hurry now, with the TV people going, and the new dig not starting straight away,' says Petro. 'That's good. It may take a bit of doing to get Drippy to co-operate, what with her new flame - it does tend to be one thing at a time with nymphs.'

'They don't really do double-tasking,' agrees Cibus.

'It's time we went back to the villa,' says Adrogantio.

'Yes, I need to find the Genius Loci,' says Petro.

'You've mentioned him before,' says Vera. 'Who is he? What is he?'

Petro explains the Genius Loci.

'So he's six inches high and a thousand feet tall?' says Bony, by now punch-drunk with unlikely information. 'And that was a nymph just now, that I didn't actually see, and she's fallen in love with *Mr Horton*?'

'Yes, it is a bit unlikely, isn't it?' says Lapidilla sympathetically. 'Never mind, Domine. At least she hasn't picked on you.'

'Time to go,' says Petro. 'Adro's right, it'll be getting dark on the path under all those trees if we don't get a move on.' He looks at Bony, and looks at Vera. 'You go on ahead, Domine,' he says to Bony. 'I just need a word with Drippy, and I don't think she's going to come out while you're here.'

Bony nods eagerly. 'I think I'd really rather she didn't,' he says, with a puzzled glance at the little drooping tree. Surely they couldn't have meant …? In the fading light, it does look awfully like a hiker with a rucksack. He helps Adrogantio up on to his shoulder, gathers up Grumio, Cibus and Mopsus, and scuttles down to the path with rather a hunted look. He's had a few very dodgy moments himself with fans, but this …!

'I'm just going to make an offering to the success of your plan,' says Vera to Petro, as soon as Bony is safely on his way. She extracts the gold coin from her pocket.

'I thought that might be what you wanted it for,' says Petro, grinning at her.

'What else?' says Vera simply. 'Do I just drop it in?'

'You could say something like *Meum accipi donum, Stillaria*' says Petro. 'I mean, I know she speaks English, but I think it probably works better in Latin.'

'*My accept gift?*' queries Vera, whose Latin has come on by leaps and bounds in the last few weeks.

'It's more poetic that way,' say Petro apologetically. 'In Latin, anyway. Go on, just do it.'

Vera tosses the coin into the centre of the pool, and watches as it drops, winking and glittering through the water, and the sediments settle softly over it.

'*Meum accipi donum, Stillaria,*' she says solemnly.

'Oh, who is he! Oh, who is this mortal man! who has pierced my poor heart! with the fiery arrows of love!' cries Drippy, materialising suddenly, draped around her willow tree again. 'Thank you very much for the lovely offering, Domina Vera,' she adds politely. 'Oh, who is he! Oh, who -'

'Not now, Drippy,' says Petro sternly. 'I've got a job for you.'

'But my heart is smitten!' cries Drippy.

'Look, you've accepted the offering, so just shut up a minute about Magister Horton, will you?'

'Horton! Horton! Horton!' cries Drippy in ecstasy. 'O blessed name! I shall strew his path with flowers! and all the birds of the air shall sing his praises!'

'Not while he's digging, please,' says Petro.

'It really wouldn't be a good idea, Drippy, dear,' says Lapidilla firmly. 'People would be bound to notice, and we don't want that.'

'Horton! Horton! Horton!' cries Drippy single-mindedly.

'Give it a rest, Drippy, there's a good nymph,' says Petro. 'And leave the poor man alone. He's not even your type.'

'My type!'

'Trust me on this,' says Petro. 'The tall guy with the little notebook would have more of a chance with him than you. *Dominus Osseus* would have more of a chance.'

There is a brief pause while the nymph works it out.

'Oh, woe is me! Woe! Woe! Woe!'

'Stillaria,' says Vera firmly. 'We really have to be going soon, and Petro needs to talk to you first.'

'Sensibly,' adds Lapidilla, rather sternly.

'O misery! misery! misery!'

'How would it be if I brought you a picture of him?' asks Vera desperately. It will be getting dark soon, and Drippy shows no signs of abating.

'A picture!'

'Yes, I promise, I'll get you a picture of him,' says Vera.

'O joy! O rapture!'

'Oh, shut up,' says Petro. 'Now listen, you daft nymph, I'm going to need you to do a bit of tidying up and tending down near the villa in a few days time. I'm going to get the Genius Loci to do some earth-moving-'

'No!' cries Lapidilla. 'Not the graves! Petro, you can't disturb the graves!'

'No, Petro,' agrees Vera. 'You really can't move the graves, it wouldn't be right.'

'I'm not going to,' says Petro patiently. 'The very last thing I'm going to do is move the graves.'

131

CHAPTER XXVI

Vera carries Petro and Lapidilla back down to Rooks Ridge, where she finds that Bony Jay has already left. (It has occurred to Bony that he really does not want to be seen by Jim Southerton alone with Vera in a remote spot, so he has taken a swift departure). The other Lares are waiting at the entrance to one of the rabbit holes under the hedge, out of sight of the police and fire investigators who are still working away on the ridge and down by the burnt-out commissary wagon.

'Last night, the treasure -' Vera begins, but Adrogantio interrupts her.

'Alas, we have failed you,' he says sadly, shaking his head as if he cannot believe that such a thing could have happened. 'We have failed in the task laid upon us by Caius Verus Pugnax Corvo.'

Vera's hopes plummet.

'I really hoped you'd got it all,' she says.

Adrograntio shakes his head. 'We tried,' he says. 'But the great gold plates, the wine flask - how could we Lares move such things?'

'Dominus Osseus took me back up to the ridge and helped me to hide under the tarpaulin,' says Petro, 'and once the moon had set I managed to get away with the coin for him without being spotted, but it was touch and go. Then I went and I found the others. We had a plan, and it needed all of us. Only it didn't work.' He shakes his head sadly.

'When I heard about the fire, I really hoped - that box of matches I gave you - ' Vera looks at Grumio, who shakes his head.

'We thought of that, Domina,' he says gloomily. 'But there's nothing up here that would burn.'

'And the big tent and the chariots were too far away for us Lares to get to,' adds Petro.

'And anyway, Lapidilla wouldn't let us,' says Cibus.

'It would have been very destructive and quite unnecessary,' says Lapidilla firmly. 'We didn't *need* a diversion. All we needed to do was to put the guards to sleep for a few minutes.'

'Could you do that?' asks Vera.

'Easy-peasy,' says Petro.

133

'So why didn't you - ?'

'We were going to. But we wanted to do it at first light, so we'd be able to see what we were doing,' Cibus explains.

'We thought we had all night,' says Petro. 'But the thieves came in the dark, and beat us to it.'

'You saw what happened?' Vera asks.

'Yes, Domina,' replies Adrogantio. 'When the fire started in the kitchen chariot, the guards all ran down the hill, and then two men appeared on the ridge, so we stayed in hiding. We didn't realise they were going to steal the treasure.'

'Did you get a good look at them?' asks Vera. 'Was it my Stepfather and his mates?'

'No, Domina,' says Adrogantio. 'They came later. By the time they arrived, the treasure was all gone.'

'So the first two men, the ones who stole the treasure - who were they? What did they look like?'

'We do not know their names, Domina, but we have seen them twice before,' says Adrogantio. 'Both times they were with a third man. You saw them too. They were here in the crowd on the morning after you found us, and they were here again yesterday morning too.'

'All three of them were in the wheat field yesterday,' says Petro, 'helping to pick up all the rubbish.'

'You mean the Field Walkers' Challenge!' says Vera, excited now. 'Can you remember what colour they were wearing?'

'Black, I think,' says Petro, and Cibus nods. Grumio shrugs. He can't remember.

'I'm sorry, Domina, I'm not sure,' says Lapidilla. 'A dark colour, I think.'

'Black or dark blue,' says Adrogantio.

'Mopsus, what do you think?' asks Vera.

'I don't know!' says Mopsus, and bursts into tears.

'Mopsus didn't see them,' says Lapidilla. 'He was down in the tunnel. You were looking after Salliendillius and Micandillia, weren't you, dear?' Mopsus nods damply, and gives a big sniff.

Grumio snorts. 'Hiding, more like,' he says.

'But you think they wore black, Petro, Cibus?' asks Molly, ignoring him. Petro and Cibus nod.

'Probably black,' agrees Adrogantio.

'I might be able to find out which team had the black tracksuits,' says Vera. 'You don't remember any more about them?'

'They were the ones who collected the least rubbish,' says Petro.

'Definitely,' Cibus agrees. 'They weren't really trying. They hardly looked at all - they spent the whole time looking around, trying to see what was happening on the rest of the site.'

'They weren't there to collect the rubbish,' agrees Adrogantio. 'They were there to see what they could steal later.'

'That means they probably came last in the competition,' says Vera thoughtfully. 'That should help to identify them. Well done, Lares!'

'But we have failed in our trust,' says Adrogantio sadly.

'You did your best.'

'But it was not enough.'

'Now that we can find out who took the treasure,' says Vera firmly, 'I'm sure there must be a way of getting it back. Don't give up hope - I'm going to go and tell the policemen what we know.'

'How will you do that, Domina?' asks Petro. 'You won't tell them about us?'

'No, I won't do that,' says Vera, thinking hard. 'They wouldn't believe me anyway. But I'm sure there must be a way.'

CHAPTER XXVII

It is six pm, and Chief Inspector Morris's day has just got a whole lot better. Mr Black, Mr Grey and Mr White have been apprehended and some of the treasure has been recovered.

The Chief Inspector had been in the middle of interviewing the first of the Field Walkers when one of his men, Detective Constable Meakin, interrupted him to deliver a rather grubby scrap of paper.
'A little girl brought it,' said DC Meakin, handing it over. 'She said it was very important, sir, so I looked at it, and I think you ought to look at it too, sir.'
Chief Inspector Morris put on his reading glasses, and scanned the note.

THE MEN WHO STOLE THE TRESHER WERE AT ROOKS RIDGE ON THE DAY AFTER IT WAS DISCUVERED. THEIR WERE THREE OF THEM THEN AND THAT FOTOGROFER TOOK PICHERS OF THEM BUT IT WAS ONLY TWO OF THEM THAT STOLE THE TRESHER AND I THINK THE OTHER ONE HE PROBLY STARTED THE FIRE. ENYWAY THEY WERE ALL IN THE FIELD WALKERS CHALLINGE YESTEDAY AND THEY HAD BLACK TRACKSOOTS ON, I THINK IT WAS BLACK ONLY IT CUD OF BIN DARK BLUE AND THEY PROBLY CAME LAST BECOS THEY WER'ENT REELLY TRYING BECOS THEY WERE LOOKING TO SEE WHAT THEY CUD COME BACK AND STEAL AND AFTERWOODS TOO OF THEM DID THAT AND THE OTHER ONE DID THE FIRE. I THINK SO ANYWAY.
  YOU'RS SINCERELY FROM YOUR TRUE FREIND
  A NONNY MOUSE

Vera's Latin, Geometry and Home Economics schoolwork may have improved immeasurably with the help of the Lares, but they haven't been able to make much impression on her grammar and spelling.

'The little girl said someone gave her the note and asked her to deliver it,' said DC Meakin, 'but I think she wrote it herself.'

'I think so too,' said Chief Inspector Morris. 'I detect the subtle signs of a modern education. Is she still here?'

'No, sir, she ran off,' replied DC Meakin. 'But she's been around here all day, someone's bound to know who she is.'

'Let's not worry about Little Miss Mouse for now,' said Chief Inspector Morris. 'Get me those photos the Chief Constable got for us from Sir Oriole's nephew, will you? The ones of all the people who were up at the villa site the day after it was discovered. And get me that tall dark woman who was in charge of the Field Walkers' Challenge.'

After that it was easy. Trinni told him that the wooden spoon in the Field Walkers' Challenge had gone to the Black Team, who had given their names as Mr Brown, Mr Green and Mr Pink. Chief Inspector Morris showed her Spike's photos, and she immediately picked out Mr Black, Mr Grey and Mr White. The three men were at the Church Hall, waiting to be interviewed, along with all the other field walkers, and Chief Inspector Morris wasted no time in summoning them one by one for interrogation.

All of them claimed to have spent the previous night in each other's company, playing three-card brag from midnight to dawn, and insisted that their wives would back this up; but Chief Inspector Morris reckoned he already had enough for a search warrant. In less than an hour, the presence of a stolen saloon car with false number plates only two doors down from Mr Black's house, some empty petrol cans and a glass cutter in Mr Grey's garden shed, and two gold plates and a silver wine jug in Mr White's attic were casting considerable doubt upon their alibi. All three were arrested, and they are now at Crowborough Police Station, saying nothing and awaiting the arrival of Mr Unwin the Duty Solicitor.

Chief Inspector Morris is confident that a more thorough search of the homes and gardens of Messrs Black, Grey and White will soon reveal the rest of the treasure. He dismisses his men from their work on the villa site, and the fire investigators likewise decide that it's time to pack it in for the day.

Chief Inspector Morris goes home to his tea a happy man.

CHAPTER XXVIII

Darrell Grindley is very much less happy with life in general, and with matters archaeological in particular. True, he and his mates have been released by the police without charge, but that hasn't stopped Darrell's wife, Vera's Mum, giving him a hard time about the whole Rooks Ridge incident. She has been doing this, on and off, ever since he slunk home from Crowborough Police Station late in the afternoon, and by eight o' clock he has had enough of it. He grabs his cigarettes and makes for the front door.

Vera arrives home just as he is leaving.

'Where the hell have you been all day?' growls Darrell, not because he has the slightest interest in Vera's activities or whereabouts, but simply to be as disagreeable as possible to anyone who happens to get in his way.

'I helped the WI ladies at the Church Hall with the teas and coffees for the archaeology people,' replies Vera, not untruthfully but somewhat disingenuously. Darrell says something very rude about the WI, the Church, and archaeology.

'They've all gone now,' says Vera. 'And the police.' She hopes this may put Darrell in a slightly better frame of mind.

'Good riddance to the pack of them,' says Darrell, and pushes past Vera out of the house. Half-way down the garden path, the penny drops. 'Here, Vee,' he calls out. 'Is that gone for the day, or gone for good?'

'For good, I think,' replies Vera. 'Well, the TV archaeology people, certainly: they're going to another dig somewhere up north. And the police have all gone from the villa site. Only there's some new archaeology people that will be coming soon from the County Council,' she adds, suddenly remembering Arthur and his metal detector.

'How soon?' asks Darrell, accessing the same memory.

'I don't know,' answers Vera. 'But I don't expect there's anything left to find,' she adds rather desperately.

'No? So why're they coming, then?' demands Darrell, reasonably enough.

'I mean any good stuff,' says Vera, floundering.

'Yeah, right,' says Darrell, and continues on to next door for a conference with Arthur.

Arthur opens a couple of cans of lager, and slumps on the ratty old sofa in the squalid living room of Number Seven, Harnstone Close. Darrell takes a long pull at his drink and wipes his mouth on his sleeve before confiding in Arthur that the archaeologists and the police have now decamped.

'So how about tonight then?' he asks. 'You saw all that stuff in the pit. Where there's that much treasure, there could be more. What we got to lose?'

Arthur thinks about it. 'And we could always say we was going back for that Dorm Corers thing again,' he says slowly. 'That's if we was to get caught up there.'

'Clever bloke, that lawyer,' says Darrell. They think about how clever their solicitor is. What he has done once, he could do again for them at need, and the risk is therefore minimal. 'Our Vera has got this bird book,' says Darrell. 'We could take that with us.'

'That'll fool them,' agrees Arthur. 'Good thinking, mate.'

Darrell goes off to fetch Vera's *Field Guide to the Birds of Britain and Europe*, which she surrenders rather reluctantly and with some bewilderment, not having been privy to the contents of Mr Unwin the Duty Solicitor's letter to Chief Inspector Morris. Darrell picks up a torch, a warm jacket and his wellies, and returns to Arthur's house to await the coming of night.

Just after midnight, Darrell, Arthur and Big Mac set off for Rooks Ridge, well fortified by an evening's solid drinking, during which they have been sustained by increasingly wild fantasies of what they will do with all the money from the treasure that they are now drunkenly convinced they will find. Darrell has a spade and a sack, Arthur has his metal detector, and Big Mac carries the bird book at arm's length. He has not had a book of any kind in his hands since being permanently excluded from Crowborough High School some ten years ago, and he regards it with a mixture of distaste and a sort of primitive awe.

The moon has not yet risen, and they stumble noisily along in the gathering dark, out of Crowborough towards the site access gate at the foot of the ridge. It takes them some time to negotiate this obstacle, since the police have rather touchingly left it padlocked, and adorned with a notice that says 'No Entry.' All three of them climb onto it and fall off onto the other side, only to find that they have left the spade, the sack, the metal detector and the bird book by the side of the road. They climb and fall back over again, and Darrell, the least drunk of the three by a very small margin, solves this complex logistical problem with the brilliant stratagem of dropping their encumbrances over the gate before climbing back again. This finally accomplished, they gather up all the bits and pieces, and set off up the hill.

'I reckon we orter try the five-acre first,' says Arthur. 'Stands to reason, they already found the treasure what was in the viller. I mean, if you was burying treasure, you wouldn't do it twice in one place, would yer?'

Darrell and Big Mac consider this argument carefully.

'An' I mean,' says Arthur, 'if I was burying treasure, I wouldn't bury it in a house, would I? An' a viller's a house, sort of. If it was me, I'd bury it in a field.'

'Easier to dig up in a field,' Darrell announces sagely. 'Much easier, the reason being, is, there's no floors.'

'Field it is,' says Arthur.

Big Mac offers no opinion. He is used to wiser heads than his prevailing, and, with an IQ that falls somewhere around the lower end of the woolly worm range, almost every head in the world that isn't either comatose or dead is immeasurably wiser than Big Mac's.

They make for the hedge, and push through it into the field. The moon has not yet risen, and by now the night is very, very dark. A fox screams, and Arthur jumps.

'Spooky, ain't it?' he says shakily, clutching his chest. They stand in the lee of the hedge, looking out, as far as they can in the dark, over the expanse of the five-acre field, where a ghostly ground-mist is rising.

'Boo!' says Big Mac, who has a primitive sense of humour. Arthur clips his brother round the ear, something that only Arthur can do without very painful consequences.

'Shut it, you great lummock,' mutters Darrell, who is also feeling a bit nervous. 'Come on, then, let's get on with it.'

Arthur crouches to tend to his metal detector, and stiffens suddenly at the sound of a voice that definitely isn't Darrell's or Big Mac's. It is a very tiny voice, and it seems to come from quite a long way off, somewhere across the dark, misty field and a bit downhill; but he is in no doubt that he heard it.

'Who was that?' he quavers.

'What?' says Darrell uneasily. 'I didn't hear nothin'.'

'There it is again!' says Arthur, standing up and peering out nervously into the darkness. 'And there's something moving out there!' he whispers. 'Look, something grey - and there's another one! And another!'

Then Darrell hears it as well: a tiny voice, this time from slightly uphill.

"Ere, stop messing about,' says Big Mac, who heard it too. He is fearless against just about anything on two legs, or four for that matter, but he really isn't too keen on tiny disembodied voices, not on a very dark and misty night.

'Them archaeologits said there was a graveyard,' says Darrell slowly. 'Somewhere over this way.'

'Shutupshutupshutup!' whispers Arthur, starting to panic. 'I don't want to hear no talk about graveyards!'

'Well, they did,' says Darrell, peering around nervously. An owl hoots, and they all clutch each other in sudden terror.

And then the moon comes out. Across the five-acre field, strung out in a line and coming slowly towards them through the mist are six small grey figures.

Arthur screams and leaps backwards, knocking Darrell over, who brings down Big Mac as he falls. They roll around on the ground for a bit in panic, then all three manage to struggle to their feet and take to their heels, leaving behind them the spade, the sack, the metal detector, Vera's bird book, and a single wellington boot.

'Whew!' says Petro, watching from the middle of the five-acre as they stumble off down the hill at speed. 'That was a bit of luck! I wonder what scared them off?'

As dawn approaches, the Lares are becoming despondent. They have been searching the field for hours, and it is a big field, for a Lar at least. Not a scrap of Breca of Hrafnsburh's pottery have they found, and they are beginning to despair of ever doing so.

'Wouldn't any old bit of pot do?' asks Cibus wearily.

'I don't know,' admits Petro. 'I mean, I don't know what it is about Breca's pots that Magister Horton thinks is so wonderful. As far as I'm concerned, they were all complete rubbish. I don't know how Breca ever conned the mistress into buying them once, let alone going on ordering from him for years and years.'

'I think she liked to support local craftsmen,' says Lapidilla.

'Even if they were useless,' agrees Cibus.

'Wasn't there some sort of buy-local campaign by the Hrafnsburh Wifsgemot?' asks Mopsus.

'Only because Breca's wife was president, or something,' says Cibus cynically. 'Look, Petro, can't we knock it off for the night? My back's killing me.'

'We could try again in the morning,' says Adrogantio. It is not in his nature to give up and admit defeat, but he is as fed up as the rest of them.

'I suppose so,' says Petro gloomily. 'We've got plenty of time to search, now that the TV people are going away. Here, watch it, can't you, Grumio?'

Grumio has tripped over something, and Petro falls over him. They sort themselves out, and Petro looks to see what tripped Grumio in the first place.

It is a large shard of crumbly greenish pottery.

CHAPTER XXIX

It is Sunday morning. Under normal circumstances, this is when Bony and the archaeologists prepare a presentation on the results of the dig, for locals and for any press people who can find nothing more exciting to do on a Sunday afternoon. This time it is different. There wasn't much digging and there aren't many results; but there are an awful lot of press people here already.

Chief Constable Bunny has, after due consideration, allowed the recovered gold plates and silver jug to be brought to the Church Hall in their transparent evidence bags, and is now toying with the possibility of allowing them to be taken out of their bags for photographic purposes. Since they have of course already been thoroughly finger-printed and swabbed for DNA or anything else the thieves might have left behind, he has only refused so far in order to tease the press contingent, something that he always enjoys on the very rare occasions when he gets the chance. Besides, annoying the press is something that he regards as a public duty.

The morning of Day Three is also, under normal circumstances, the time when, as per contract with the landowner, the student diggers return the site to its original state, on the surface at least. Trenches are filled in, and turf is replaced (most of the grass will die, of course, in a few days' time, but by then *Ready Steady Dig!* will be gone). Trystram Wentworth and Bony Jay, monitored with hawk-eyes by someone from IBBC's legal team, would normally be busy extracting from the landowner unguarded declarations of pleasure and satisfaction at the whole process of television archaeology in regard to his or her property. These are meticulously recorded on camera, against the day when the turf dies off or someone breaks an ankle after the earth has settled unevenly in the trenches. Occasionally some of this footage is also usable in the programme, and Trinni and Troy are adept at tracking down photogenic relatives of the landowner to take part in the session, with a preference for winsome moppets who can be coached into producing cute soundbites.

Today is rather different. Hob has no discernible infants in his immediate, nor indeed his extended family, in fact the only

145

relative that Trinni and Troy have been able to trace is Jim Southerton. Jim, as they both agree, is both photogenic and *very* cute, but he is not winsome, nor does he respond well to coaching. As for Hob himself, Trinni thinks he has some potential in the *comic old buffer* category, which is always a hit with the viewers, while Troy favours *daft pensioner amusingly baffled by the wonders of modern archaeological science.* However, after a very few abortive takes, it becomes clear that Hob is having none of it; he deliberately sabotages every attempt at a recorded interview which might be usable for either legal or televisual purposes. Hob is clearly feeling very pleased with himself, something which causes some unease to Trystram, Trinni and Troy; they would be still more uneasy if they knew the reason.

When Hob, Jim Southerton and Mr Horton came down from the shrine the previous evening, to Jim's surprise the old man insisted on taking both him and the archaeologist back to his tiny, almost unbearably picturesque cottage for the evening. Other than Jim himself, very few people had crossed the threshold of *Jackdaws' Roost* in the previous fifty years, and almost all of them had been either metre readers or the cleaning lady.

Mr Horton was still in a happy daze as Hob ushered him into a comfortable, book-lined study and instructed Jim to make tea and sandwiches.

'Sit down, sit down, my boy,' said Hob, indicating a leather covered armchair. 'I wonder if I may call you Ronald?'

'Yes, of course, sir,' said Mr Horton, flattered and happy, as well he should be, taking his seat and resisting a sudden mad urge to say 'And may I call you Uncle?'

Hob settled himself behind a massive knee-hole desk of obvious antiquity, and twinkled engagingly at his guest. Like his nephew, Hob had taken a liking to Mr Horton. He found the County Archaeologist modest, diffident and well-mannered, all of which qualities he thoroughly approved. He could see, too, that Mr Horton loved his work and did his level best with whatever limited resources he could lay his hands on, and above all cared about what he did. To a man for whom life-worth-living had come to a shuddering halt some fifty years ago, this was something very precious. Hob found himself wanting to look after Mr Horton, and make him happy.

'Now: tell me what you would like to see happen at Rooks Ridge,' he said, as soon as his guest was comfortably settled. 'If you could have anything you wanted.'

Mr Horton smiled shyly. 'What I would really like to see? Do you mean if I won the lottery, or something?'

'Do you play the lottery?'

'No, sir.'

'Thought not,' said Hob. 'Yes, that's what I mean - if you could do anything you wanted up there, money no object.'

'Well -' Mr Horton thought for a moment, but a moment was all he needed. This was a long-cherished fantasy, carefully nurtured through all the difficult times, to sustain him in those all too frequent dispiriting moments when he knew he would never have the funding or manpower or even the encouragement to do the job he loved as he longed to do it. 'I would like to conduct a thorough, well-funded excavation, over a number of seasons, and with enough staff to keep the whole place always open to the public, so that they could watch the dig, and see how it should be done, and there would be a Visitors Centre, where we could display the finds and study them and explain them, and run courses, and do experimental archaeology, all sorts of things like building techniques, and metal-work and wood-work and leather-work and agriculture and medicine and cooking, and it would be especially good for children, because children are the future and they need to know about the past, to care about it and cherish it, and preserve it,' he said, in one long breath. Hob gave him an encouraging nod. 'And it has to be long-term, sir, not like this television stuff, dig today, gone tomorrow. Now that I've met them I know that most of them are really nice people and I'm sure they do their best in their own way, but they don't care, sir, not about this place, not like I do. They're off again tomorrow, off somewhere else, and I don't suppose any of them will ever come back, or even want to, and they won't remember it once they've finished their programme, because for them the programme is the only thing that really matters, not the place. But Rooks Ridge will still be here, and they've only scratched the surface. I want to do more than that. I want to know about the people who were here before us, like the Roman girl who broke her little brooch for an offering, and dropped it in the pool with her hopes and her dreams -'

Over his head, Hob met Jim's eyes as he stood in the doorway with the tea-tray.

'Well,' said Hob quietly. 'It's taken me fifty years, but I think I've found what I want to do with the rest of my life. Thank you, my boy. Now, come and sit down, young James, and let's see how we can go about it.'

They talked about it all, long into the night.

'The shrine, young man - what would you do with that?' asked Hob, somewhere around midnight, when the sandwiches were long gone and the remains of a takeaway pizza were congealing on the massive oak desk. Hob had never had pizza before, and he was never, ever going to have it again.

Mr Horton took a sip of his J2O. He had refused all offers of alcohol, because he knew that this was the most important conversation that he would ever have in his whole life.

'That's a difficult one, sir,' he said carefully. 'Of course, I would eventually want to investigate it from the archaeological point of view.' He hesitated. 'But it's a special place, isn't it, sir? Almost - almost a holy place, I think. The stonework looks Roman, but of course the spring was there long before the Romans came, and it's still there now, long after they've gone. When - if - we dredge the sediments, I'm sure there will be offerings from as far back as people go in this place. And I don't suppose that stopped with the Romans.' He looked shyly at Hob. 'You will probably think I'm being very foolish, sir, but I kept thinking, all the way back, about what I could take up there myself to leave in the spring. It would have to be something very beautiful, and very precious, the most precious thing in the world, I think, but I don't know what.'

'One day you'll think of something, my boy,' said Hob quietly, remembering the soft April evening fifty years ago when he had scattered the ashes of his wife, the most precious thing in the world, in the waters of the pool. 'But not for a long time yet, I hope.'

Mr Horton did not quite understand this, but he did understand that he wasn't really meant to. 'So anyway, sir, I should like it to stay as a shrine - not for a religion, or anything like that, just somewhere that people could go when they needed to.'

'A retreat,' said Jim.

'Yes, a quiet place. Just a quiet place.'

Hob smiled at them both. 'There isn't enough quiet in the world these days,' he said. 'That would be a pretty good legacy, wouldn't you say? When I'm gone, I'll leave people a place where they can be quiet.'

An hour or so later, they were getting down to brass tacks.

'So until we can appoint someone better, you'll take care of the general management, young James - the administration, and the press relations, and all that nonsense,' said Hob. 'Should suit you down to the ground.'

'Yes, Uncle,' said Jim meekly.

'And Ronald will manage everything else, and keep you in order too.'

'I hope so, Uncle,' said Jim demurely.

Hob gave him a minatory look, and added, 'I'll get on to Unwin first thing in the morning, get him to put it all in lawyers' language. He's a clever man, Unwin, a bit slippery, mind you, but that's no bad thing in a lawyer, and he's got imagination, too, I'll say that for him.'

'Vision,' said Jim.

'No, I wouldn't exactly call it vision,' said Hob, and told them about the Dawn Chorus letter, details of which he had heard in a telephone call from an exasperated Chief Constable Bunny.

'We must definitely have Unwin on board,' said Jim, making a note to interview Darrell and his mates for the paper. He would enjoy teasing them with ornithological questions, and the only difficulty would resisting the expression *gaol birds* when writing it up. He would just have to be strong.

'Of course, I shall have to speak to my superiors at County Hall,' said Mr Horton anxiously.

'Don't you worry about that, my boy,' said Hob. 'I'll have a word with the Chairman.'

'I expect you went to school with his father, didn't you, Uncle?' said Jim.

'No,' said Hob. 'Grandfather,' he admitted. 'I'll call him in the morning. And now it's high time I was off to my bed.'

'Yes of course, sir, I really must be going,' said Mr Horton. 'I can't thank you enough -'

'So don't even try,' said Hob kindly. 'Now, off you go, off you go. We shall meet again in the morning. Ten o'clock, they told me I'm to be at the Church Hall. Well, it's Matins from 9.15 to 10.15, so they'll get me at 10.20, like it or not. You can see yourself out.'

Mr Horton closed the cottage door behind him, and wandered in a daze down the garden path and through the rickety gate. All his hopes and dreams had come true tonight. He collected his modest little car from outside the Church Hall, and drove carefully away along the Crowborough to Berchester road. So rapt was he in happy reverie that he did not even notice the three stumbling figures hurrying along the road towards the shelter of Numbers Six and Seven Harnstone Close, one of them wearing but a single wellington boot.

CHAPTER XXX

It is nearly lunchtime on Sunday before members of the public are allowed in to the Church Hall, Vera amongst them. The first thing that catches her eyes is the dazzling display of two enormous gold plates and a slender silver jug from the treasure pit. Everyone is crowding around to examine them, leaving all the rest of the villa finds looking rather forlorn. Professor Jones is perfectly resigned to this. He is honest enough to admit that, archaeologist he may be, but he is himself far more interested in thousands of pounds worth of ancient gold and silver than a heap of broken potsherds and roof tiles.

The Chief Constable takes centre stage to recount the recovery of the treasure. It's not very often that he gets a chance like this to appear on television with such spectacular props and such a good-news story. It is perhaps a tad disappointing that the bulk of the hoard has not yet come to light, but Chief Inspector Morris has assured him that it is only a matter of time and diligent searching. The Chief Constable concludes his little speech and departs from the platform, and Professor Jones takes over. He talks at some length about the plates and jug and their decorations, with a swiftly but expertly assembled PowerPoint presentation. The three pieces all have a fairly standard classical motif, but with one little quirk that Professor Jones speculates might be a reference to the family who once owned them: each has a central figure with a bird perched on its wrist. They certainly aren't hawks, as one might expect: they looks more like crows. Vera smiles at this, and catches Bony's eye.

When Professor Jones has finished his presentation, which also covers the lay-out and possible history of the villa site, he surrenders the stage to Mr Horton. Trystram Wentworth frowns. This is not in his running order for the afternoon, even if Mr Horton does seem to be expecting it, since he gets to his feet clutching a small sheaf of notes. Hob joins him on stage, which is not in Trystram's script either, and Mr Horton introduces his benefactor to the press by his title and all four names, something which Hob has strongly resisted, but which Jim has threatened to do anyway if Mr Horton does not.

As Mr Horton outlines the plans for the future of the villa site, there is a furious scribbling and taking of flash photographs amongst the newspaper people, and Trystram does his best to appear pleased about this very thorough up-staging of *Ready Steady Dig!* at its own press conference. Vera takes it all in with mingled delight and apprehension. Mr Horton's plans for the villa site sound wonderful - the Visitors' Centre! the courses! the activities for children! It's what comes before all that which worries her. It was one thing to disrupt *Ready Steady Dig!* for *only two days,* or one day as it turned out. Mr Horton is going to be digging at the villa for months, even years. *Ready Steady Dig!* were only ever going to scratch the surface of the site. Mr Horton, on the other hand, sounds very *thorough.*

The County Archaeologist finishes his presentation to an enthusiastic round of applause, especially from the local contingent, and Trystram Wentworth leaps to his feet before anyone else can spring any surprises.

'I am sure we are all absolutely delighted to hear about these exciting plans,' he says, smiling his tight little smile. 'We on *Ready Steady Dig!* will look forward to learning more about them when we come back for our second day of excavations.'

There is a brief pause. Mr Horton looks like a rabbit caught in headlights.

'I don't think so,' says Jim Southerton, loudly and firmly.

Trystram Wentworth looks at him with a bright, false smile. 'Excuse me?'

'Your second day was yesterday,' says Jim.

'We couldn't dig yesterday,' says Trystram.

'That's your problem,' Jim retorts. 'Friday and Saturday, that's what my uncle agreed. Not Friday and any other day of your choice.'

Trystram Wentworth turns to the IBBC's legal-eagle, a cadaverous man with a dead white face that looks like a mask - the sort of mask you might wear if you took Halloween really, really seriously. 'Mr Crail, can that possibly be correct?' asks Trystram, but he looks as if he knows full well that it isn't. Mr Crail gets to his feet. He is very very tall, and seems to rise up in slow motion.

'No,' he says simply, having reached cruising height. "That is not correct.' He carefully positions a pair of half-spectacles on his beak of a nose, and stoops to look at Jim over the top of them. 'You will find, young man, that under the terms of IBBC's contract with the landowner, Mr Wentworth is absolutely within his rights to return to the site for a second day to complete the excavation.' Jim starts to protest, and Mr Crail raises a thin white hand to silence him. 'We always make sure that all likely and unlikely contingencies will be covered in our contract with the landowner,' he continues with an air of superiority that makes almost everyone in the hall want to rush off and find something to throw at him, such as a very sharp spear. 'Adverse weather conditions, staff sickness, strikes - that sort of thing.' He gives a thin smile that reveals a lot of little pointy teeth, like a rat's. 'And legal problems, of course, as for example being shut down temporarily by a police investigation.'

'I don't believe it,' says Jim stoutly. 'What's the exact wording in the contract? About the two days, I mean?'

'Two days,' says Hob, scowling horribly at Mr Crail, 'of which the first shall be Friday, 31st July.'

'Well, that's clear enough,' says Jim. 'If the first day is Friday 31st July, then the second one must be Saturday 1st August.'

'No,' said Mr Crail. 'That is nowhere stated.'

'But it's implied!' says Jim hotly.

'It may be implied,' says Mr Crail smugly, 'but nowhere is it actually stated. What is stated is that IBBC shall have two days to excavate, the first day being Friday 31st July. The other date is unspecified, and can therefore be at any time of IBBC's choosing.'

Trystram Wentworth stands up, and surveys the Hall with triumph.

'We shall be back on site the day after tomorrow,' he announces. 'There has been severe flooding in the north of the country, so we're going to have to postpone work on our programme up there until the end of the series.

'Thank you for your attention, ladies and gentlemen. This presentation and press conference is now closed.'

There is a light smattering of applause from some of the local contingent in the Hall. Professor Jones tries to look both keen and conciliatory. Hob and Jim look stony. Mr Horton buries his face in his hands.

153

The Chief Constable signals to one of his aides to re-package the Corvo treasure in its evidence bags, and supervises its removal from the Hall, while the press and public all file out, with the exception of the WI ladies, who have no intention of missing anything, and have provided themselves with an unanswerable argument for being allowed to stay: a gorgeous array of home-made cakes, scones, jam and clotted cream. Trystram Wentworth would himself be perfectly happy to send them and their cream teas packing, but one glance at his workforce tells him that coming between two dozen hungry students and a magnificent spread such as this would be a vain, and possibly even a dangerous move, particularly as they have all been forced to subsist for two whole days now on Mrs Hamble's horrible cooking. The WI ladies further make it clear that they are going to stay to serve the feast personally: if they go, so does the food. Trystram gives in, and glowers impatiently as students, archaeologists, support staff and camera crew descend like locusts.

Only Mr Horton fails to join the stampede: he stands apart, a rather hopeless little figure, twisting his hands together in silent misery. Hob and Jim have been firmly ushered out by Trinni and Troy, but the two researchers are uncertain of Mr Horton's status - is he still a consultant to the programme? They leave him be for the moment, pending clarification from Trystram, who is now engaged in mutual congratulations with Mr Crail.

Vera, who has once again managed to attach herself to the WI ladies, pours a cup of tea and boldly takes it to Mr Horton, who stares at it blankly as if he has never seen such a thing before in his life.

'Please, sir, I do think your plans sound wonderful,' says Vera, feeling sorry for the solitary little man. 'Especially the things for the children.'

Mr Horton gives a wan smile. 'Yes,' he says simply. 'It will be wonderful. And after all, it's only one more day.' He accepts the tea, and takes a restoring sip. 'Thank you, this is very welcome. They can't do too much damage in just one day, can they?'

'I hope not,' says Vera. 'Please, what will happen about the graves?'

Before he can reply, Trystram Wentworth calls everyone to order.

'Listen up, everybody. Tomorrow, Monday, will be your statutory rest day,' he announces. 'You can stick around or go home, whatever you choose, but work will start again first thing on Tuesday. That will be at 6am -' this is greeted with a chorus of groans '- and I shall expect everybody to be there on the dot. No exceptions. We shall be working through right up until midnight, as we are perfectly entitled to do -' more groans '- using arc lamps when it gets dark.

'Professor Jones, Mr Jay, Mr Horton, a word with you all, please.'

Professor Jones and Bony Jay swiftly refill their plates with cakes and scones, and follow Trystram to a far corner of the Hall, with Mr Horton trailing unhappily in their wake. Vera follows, determined to hear the worst.

'I want Trench Four underway first thing,' Trystram announces. 'And by that I mean I want those graves opened and stripped. Any problems with that?' He glares at Mr Horton.

Mr Horton does his best. 'We know there could possibly be an Anglo-Saxon layer -'

'I don't want to hear about Anglo-Saxon,' says Trystram firmly. 'You had all day Friday to sort that out.'

'It's not something you *sort out*!' says Mr Horton miserably. 'Professor Jones -' He looks hopelessly at his colleague.

'Sorry, Horton,' says Professor Jones. 'I have to say that I think we've pretty much established that the piece of Berumware was just a single aberrant find. I saw no other signs of Anglo-Saxon occupation - did you?'

Mr Horton is an honest man. 'No,' he admits. 'There was nothing but that one piece.'

'And the grave cuts at either end of the trench,' says Professor Jones, 'which I think are likely to be Roman.'

'Yes,' says Mr Horton.

'Right, then,' says Trystram briskly. 'First thing on Tuesday, that's 6am, you start taking that trench down to the level of the graves. And this time I want to see *bones*!'

Vera stares at Trystram, appalled. She even feels a bit shaky, and sits down next to one of the dozen or so big covered screens

155

on which are displayed details of the *Ready Steady Dig!* activities. This one is the *Meet The Team* screen, and it has photographs of everyone involved in the programme, from Professor Jones right down to the student diggers. Vera looks at the faces, vaguely wondering if any of these people might possibly be persuaded to help her in some way. But how? What can any of them do? She finds she is looking at a not very flattering photograph of Mr Horton, and that reminds her of her promise to Drippy. Surreptitiously, Vera removes the photograph and slips it into her pocket. She is not at all sure that it is a good idea to give it to Drippy, but she promised, after all, and it might just help to persuade the nymph to do whatever it is that Petro needs as part of his plan to save the graves. She slips out of the Hall, and makes for Rooks Ridge.

Mr Horton has had enough. He slips away unnoticed from the Hall, and hesitates outside, thinking miserably of the day after tomorrow. On the opposite side of the street, Jim Southerton sees him from where he is sitting at one of the tables outside the Pig and Whistle, and waves to him to come and have a drink, but Mr Horton looks straight through him, clearly lost in unhappy thought. Suddenly he straightens up, and an intent look crosses his nondescript features. He turns abruptly on his heel, and sets off at a good pace down the street in the direction of the site. Jim watches him go, and wonders whether to follow. He finishes his drink, hesitates for a while himself, and then sets off in Mr Horton's footsteps.

CHAPTER XXXI

'There's good news and there's bad news,' Vera announces when the Lares have all emerged cautiously from the hypocaust and are sitting on the grass in front of her, looking much more hopeful than she can feel at that moment.

'Tell us the good news, Domina Vera,' Lapidilla eagerly.

'Tell us the bad,' says Grumio.

'The good news,' says Vera, 'is that the two gold plates and the silver wine jug have been recovered from the men who stole them.' The Lares cheer at this, and Lapidilla and Mopsus hug each other. 'I saw them at the Church Hall just now. The trouble is, the Chief Constable has had them taken away again, to the police station, I suppose. There's absolutely no way we can get them back from there. I'm sorry, Adrogantio, I know you think we have to get them back, but I just don't see how we can do it.'

'That was the good news, was it?' asks Grumio disagreeably.

'Yes,' says Vera firmly. 'At least they've been recovered, and they haven't been melted down, or anything like that. They still exist, and they're safe, even if we can't get them back.'

'Yet,' says Adrogantio stubbornly.

'The police haven't found the rest of the treasure yet, but I'm sure they will soon,' says Vera reassuringly. The Lares exchange startled glances.

'But Domina Vera -' says Petro, but Vera interrupts him.

'Anyway, the bad news,' she says. 'It's just too awful! The TV people are coming back again the day after tomorrow. They're allowed one more day after all, and that'll be enough, because the very first thing they're going to do is to dig up the graves!'

The Lares gaze at her, appalled, and then they all look at Petro.

'So what's your plan, Petro?' demands Adrogantio. 'You said you had a plan, and we found you your bit of pot, so now what are you going to do with it?'

'*I* found you your bit of pot,' mutters Grumio.

'The day after tomorrow ... It's not much time,' says Petro, looking worried. 'I mean, I think it could still work, and I'm sure I can get the Genius Loci to do his bit it tomorrow, but it needs Drippy as well, and I'm not at all sure about her. And I wasn't expecting anyone to come along and look at it the very next day, especially not that closely - I thought there would be plenty of time for things to settle down afterwards.'

'Petro,' says Vera. 'I really do think it might help if you told us all exactly what you are planning to do.'

'No time, no time,' says Petro, shaking his head in an abstracted way. 'I've got to go and find Drippy first. Will you take me up to the shrine, Domina?'

'Yes, of course, if you think that will help,' says Vera.

'I can't get there without you,' says Petro, 'and it doesn't look as if Drippy will be coming down here any time soon, not if she's still mooning around up there over the little man with the glasses. I suppose it might be a good idea to take her another offering.'

'Will this do?' asks Vera. She takes out the photograph of Mr Horton from the *Ready Steady Dig!* notice board. The Lares examine it with great interest. 'It's called a photograph,' says Vera.

'He's very ugly,' says Grumio.

'Not ugly,' says Lapidilla. 'more - well - *plain*.'

'Drippy obviously doesn't think so,' Petro points out. 'I'm not sure, Domina … yes, yes I think perhaps it could help. And you did say you'd take her a picture of the wretched man, so there's not much choice, really.'

'Fine,' says Vera. 'Shall we go?'

CHAPTER XXXII

Mr Horton walks quickly up the steep woodland path towards the shrine, trying to shake off the uneasy feeling that he has had for some minutes now, that someone is watching him. The place looks somehow different, too. It takes him a while to work it out, but eventually he notices that there are primroses and bluebells growing in profusion where yesterday he is fairly sure there weren't any at all. Anyway, it's August, he thinks uneasily. Primroses and bluebells shouldn't flower in August, should they? He wonders vaguely if this is something to do with global warming, but surely that means they should all have flowered around Christmas time, not in high summer? And then he notices the birdsong, so many birds that their sound is almost alarming, and they are flying all around him, almost as if they are keeping pace with him. He stops, and sure enough, they settle in the trees that line the path, all singing at him like crazy. This is very, very strange. Mr Horton is no naturalist, but he is quite sure that birds don't normally do this, and he is pretty certain about the primroses and bluebells too. Nervously he continues on his way towards the shrine, pursued by a singing, chattering, chirping flock.

Several times along the way he considers turning round and going back, but somehow the idea of turning round makes him even more nervous. He has a definite feeling that if he did he might see something still more unsettling than an unnatural abundance of birds and out-of-season flowers. Besides, he wants to get to the shrine, to recapture what he felt yesterday, and he wants to make an offering too, to the success of his project and the confounding of *Ready Steady Dig!* He knows that this is a very foolish thing for a rational man of science even to think of doing, but he's going to do it anyway. In his pocket he has the most exciting of all of his pieces of mid 8th century pottery. He often carries it with him, as a sort of talisman for the difficult times, and today he is glad he did, because it will make a perfect offering for the shrine. It is a large, greenish-coloured shard, which unusually carries an incised decoration, rather unevenly done and apparently representing part of a deformed pigeon, or possibly a crow. Or it could be a sheep. He can still remember the thrill of finding it, and the memory of that day, which was a very happy one, gives him the courage to continue along the path to the shrine.

A few hundred yards behind him, Jim Southerton is untroubled by any ornithological excess, but he does notice that the path appears to be lined with and awful lot of fading primroses and bluebells that certainly weren't there yesterday.

With Petro standing in the pocket of her jacket, Vera walks quickly up the path that leads to the shrine. At the low mossy bank where they all rested the previous day, she stops for a few moments to get her breath, for the way is quite steep, and she has been hurrying.

'Petro, tell me about your plan,' she says, but he shakes his head and says nothing. He looks desperately worried. Eventually Vera gives up, gets to her feet again rather wearily, and walks on towards what she remembers as the last bend in the path before the shrine. She rounds the bend: and the path disappears into an impenetrable wall of brambles, ten feet or more high, and stretching away on either side as far as she can see. In front of the bramble barrier, looking utterly demented, is Jim Southerton. Vera claps a hand over her pocket, but Petro has already ducked down out of sight.

'Thank goodness!' says Jim shakily, stumbling towards her. He grabs her by both arms. 'Look, we need to get help - is there anyone else with you?' Vera shakes her head. 'You'll have to do it then, I've got to stay here - you must go and get help.'

'Why? What sort of help?' asks Vera, looking past him at the towering barrier of brambles.

'That hedge! It shouldn't be here! It wasn't here yesterday. And Ronnie Horton has disappeared, I was behind him on the path, only a hundred yards or so back, and when I came round the bend he was gone and there was this hedge that wasn't here yesterday.'

'Do you think he's on the other side of it?' Vera asks.

'Yes, yes, I think he must be. I called out to him, but he didn't answer, and I can't get through it - you must go and get help!' says Jim desperately. He turns back to the bramble hedge, and starts tearing at it with his bare hands. Vera winces in sympathy as

Jim's hands begin to bleed, then she becomes aware that Petro is kicking her in the ribs, trying to get her attention.

'Pick me up! Pick me up!' whispers Petro urgently. 'Turn away and hold me to your ear like one of those mobile 'phone things.'

'Sssh!' says Vera. 'Let me find out what's wrong first.'

'I *know* what's wrong! Trust me on this! We have to talk *now*.'

Vera pushes him back down into her pocket, and calls out to Jim.

'I've got a mobile, I'll 'phone my Step-Dad!'

'A mobile!' Jim turns with hope in his eyes. 'Give it me, quick!'

'No, no,' cries Vera hastily, backing away from him. 'I'll do it, I'll call him.' She thinks fast. 'The battery's nearly flat, you wouldn't have time to explain who you are and why you've got my 'phone, and everything.' She moves down the path a little way and extracts Petro from her pocket. With her back to Jim she pretends to dial, and then half-turns and holds Petro up to the ear that Jim can't see.

'Right, what is it?' she whispers. 'Where did the hedge come from?'

'Drippy, of course, drat her,' says Petro crossly. 'This is all we need. I just know she's got that poor wretch of an archaeologist trapped in there. Goodness knows what she's doing to him this very minute.'

'What can you do?' asks Vera. 'I don't want her to hurt him.'

'I don't think hurting him is what she has in mind,' says Petro. 'It's what happens to him afterwards that's bothering me. If he disappears, like that hiker did years ago, there'll be all hell let loose. We have to get him back.'

'But how? Can you do something about that hedge? Can you get through it?'

'Not a chance,' says Petro. 'But I know someone who can.'

'Who?'

'You'll see,' says Petro. 'Now, the easiest way to go about this would be to get that one over there to go to sleep.' He indicates Jim, who is tearing frantically at the hedge again.

'Sleep!' cries Vera. 'He's trying to rip the hedge out single-handed! He's hardly going to drop off to sleep!'

'Trust me,' says Petro. 'Just get him to stop for a minute. Make him sit down under that big oak tree over there. That ought to do it.'

'But he won't fall asleep, even if I can get him to stop and sit down!'

'Just do it, please?' says Petro. 'Now! It's our best chance of summoning up - Oh, just *do* it!'

Vera puts Petro back in her pocket, and approaches Jim tentatively.

'Mr Southerton? Please stop, you're not doing any good,' she says.

'Is your Step-Dad bringing help?' asks Jim breathlessly.

'Yes, yes,' says Vera. 'He's bringing his friends, and he's got a pair of seccateurs, and, and a chain saw!' she adds inventively. 'You've really hurt your hands. I know first aid, if you'll come and sit down for a moment.'

Jim hesitates, but he knows by now that he can do no good alone against the monstrous hedge. He sits down where Vera indicates, beneath a big oak tree that looks oddly out of place in the hazel and alder woodland.

'*Dormi!*' whispers Petro from Vera's pocket, and Jim slumps against the trunk in a profound slumber. 'Gotcha! Now we just have to wait.'

'What are we waiting for?' asks Vera anxiously, after several minutes of nothing happening at all.

'You'll see,' says Petro. 'You're just about to learn why mortal men should never fall asleep under oak trees at undern-time.'

'What time?' says Vera curiously. 'It's just gone half past two.'

'Yes, that should be about right,' says Petro, though he sounds rather anxious. 'Undern-time has tended to move on down the years - it used to be about ten o' clock in the morning, but it has kept getting later and later. I just hope ... *Ah!*'

An enormous and very beautiful pure white stag leaps onto the path opposite where Jim is sleeping, and disappears again into the trees on the other side, and now faint strains of music can be heard, as if from a little flute, far off in the trees from which the stag appeared.

'*Yes!*' says Petro. 'I thought that would fetch him out.' He turns to face the sound of piping, which seems to be getting closer, and calls out. '*Salve*, Quercillus!'

The piping stops. Vera follows Petro's gaze, and sees a small stocky creature emerging from the trees. Emerging is the word, and so is creature. He looks somewhat like a man, but his skin and hair are browny-green in colour, and he is dressed in what looks like an old-fashioned bathing-suit made of oak leaves and lichen. At a distance it is quite difficult to make him out: unless you look very hard, he could be just a trick of the dappled light, but as he approaches he seems to become clearer, until by the time he reaches the path there is no doubt at all that he is there, and solid. He steps onto the path, and glares at Petro. Vera he ignores, or perhaps he doesn't even notice her.

'Oh, it's you, Petro,' says the creature in a whispery voice that sounds like the wind in the leaves of a very large tree. 'By the way, I'm not Quercillus any more; I'm calling myself Aikin these days. I think it sounds a lot more modern.'

'Well, yes,' says Petro. 'I suppose mediaeval is a lot more modern than Roman.'

'Got to move with the times.'

'Hard to do anything else, really,' agrees Petro.

'Quercillus is so last millennium, don't you think?'

'Absolutely.'

'Whereas Aikin -'

'Is more modern, right.'

'More of a snap to it.'

'Right, right.'

'I did think about not having a name at all, just using a symbol,' says the creature. 'An oak leaf. Or an acorn, maybe. That would be appropriate, I thought.'

'How about a nut?'

The creature formerly known as Quercillus appears to consider this carefully, head on one side.

'Nah,' he says eventually. 'I think I'll just stick to Aikin for now. Easier to pronounce.'

'There is that.'

'Anyway -' He looks around, puzzled. 'You know, I could have sworn I felt - *Ha!*' He spots Jim, still sleeping beneath the big oak tree. 'I thought so! Well, well, well, it's been a very long time since a mortal strayed up here and went to sleep under my tree. People these days are always in such a rush. Let's have a look at him -'

'Let's just leave him where he is, Aikin,' says Petro firmly. 'You can't have him. I'll wake him up again if you try. I need to talk to you.'

'Spoilsport,' says Aikin petulantly. 'What do you want? Why should I help you?'

'Because Drippy's been playing silly nymphs again, and I want you to put a stop to it before it goes too far. You know you're just about the only one she'll listen to.'

'Ha!' says Aikin. 'What's she done this time, as if I couldn't guess? *Who's* she done this time, I suppose I should say.'

'He's the County Archaeologist for Bersetshire,' says Petro, 'and we want him back.' The Lar points accusingly at the towering bramble hedge.

'You have to hand it to Drippy,' says Aikin, walking up and down, examining the hedge with a professional eye. 'She does a really good Impenetrable Barrier when she puts her mind to it.'

'Yes, yes, it's state of the art,' says Petro. 'The point is, can you get through it and sort her out?'

'I could,' says Aikin. 'If I wanted to.'

'So -?'

'What's in it for me?'

'We'd be very grateful,' says Vera winningly. Aikin appears to notice her for the first time.

'This is Domina Vera,' says Petro. 'She's one of the Corvos from Rooks Ridge.'

Vera smiles at Aikin, who scowls at her.

'Hello,' she says politely. 'Are you a nymph too?'

Aikin adopts an even more disagreeable expression. 'That's dryad, *if* you don't mind, thank you so *very* much,' he says. '*Nymph!*' he adds in a scathing voice. 'I ask you. Young mortals today!'

'I'm sorry,' says Vera, 'I didn't mean to be rude.'

'He makes our Grumio look like a little ray of sunshine, doesn't he?' says Petro. 'Now come on, Aikin, don't mess us about. Are you going to help us or not?'

'Are you going to let me have that mortal?'

'What, do a swap, you mean? Him for the archaeologist? No, certainly not,' says Petro. 'We want the full set. They're a pair. Or they probably will be one day.'

'Oh, like that is it?' says Aikin disagreeably. 'Well, he wouldn't be much use to The Lady, then.'

'No use at all,' says Petro firmly. 'You'll have to go back and tell her you were mistaken, or he woke up again before you could get here, or something.'

'Oh all right,' says Aikin. 'I'll go and sort Drippy out, but you've got to do me a favour in return.'

'What is it?' asks Petro cautiously.

'You're really thick with the Genius Loci, aren't you?' asks Aikin. 'Tell him we could do with a bit more rain up here, will you? All this global warming, it's really getting to my roots, you know? This year's tree-rings won't be a patch on last year's, and last year's weren't up to much. Just get him to send us a really good downpour, say every week or so until further notice.'

'Consider it done,' says Petro. 'And - *Juno's electric pepper-mill!* Aikin, you're a genius!'

'What? What did I say?'

'Never mind, never mind, it's just that you've given me an idea,' says Petro. 'Now, go and sort out that daft nymph, will you? We really need to get back to the villa.'

The dryad raises a hand in farewell, and melts into the trees.

'Sorry about all that,' says Petro. 'I mean, with the names. He's always changing his name, and it's all a bit pointless really, because he hardly ever meets anyone. And anyway, all his names mean the same thing.'

'Oak tree? Little oak tree?'

'That's right. Last month he was Chenette, until he decided that sounded a bit sissy, so he decided to call himself Derwen-fach. That lasted for almost a week, and then he went back to Quercillus again. All dryads are a bit that way - very self-absorbed, and absolutely obsessed by their names. You just have to humour them if you want to get anything done. I just hope he can get Drippy to see sense - I really do not want to be up here when it gets dark.'

CHAPTER XXXIII

Mr Horton reaches the shrine over the spring, wading the last few yards through a deep drift of pink rose petals. He looks down, and is not entirely surprised to see two faces reflected in a wobbly sort of way in the gently bubbling water.

'Hello,' he says nervously, turning to see Drippy the nymph just behind him, draped around her tree.

'Salve! Welcome!' cries Drippy in an ecstasy of adoration.

'I'm sorry if I startled you,' says Mr Horton apologetically. 'I didn't know any other people even knew about this place.' Drippy beams at him in a distinctly drippy way. 'I just came up here to leave an offering in the spring,' continues Mr Horton nervously. 'I expect that sounds very silly.'

'No!' cries Drippy. 'What offering?' she asks, being a nymph who has her priorities.

'It's this -' Mr Horton reaches into his pocket and pulls out the piece of mid 8th century local pottery, and holds it out for her to look at. Drippy stares at it with some bewilderment.

'It's Berumware,' says Mr Horton earnestly. 'And a particularly fine piece, too, the best I've ever seen, anyway. I found it myself, you know. I'm writing a paper on Berumware, that's mid 8th century local pottery, there's quite a lot of it around here, we think it was probably manufactured in the Crowborough area, even in Crowborough itself, but you don't often find pieces as big or as good as this one. See,' he continues, warming to his subject as Drippy looks on, bemused, 'it actually has an incised design on it, that's really, really unusual. I think it may be a pigeon, well, part of a pigeon, anyway, or it could be a crow, what do you think?' He hands it to Drippy, and watches anxiously as she examines it, ready to catch the precious thing if she should drop it. 'Some people have said they think it looks more like a sheep, and I suppose it could be, if you turn it upside down, or it might be a sheep lying on its back, of course, but I still think it's a bird of some sort, wouldn't you agree? I'm pretty sure that's a beak, that pointy bit there. Anyway, I can tell you, it's really unusual to find decorated Berumware, sometimes you do get marks, but most of them are just scratches, I think, either contemporary damage or later, it's quite hard to tell - there's a whole chapter in my paper devoted to the subject of decorated Berumware. This is my prize piece. Do you like it?'

Drippy stares at him. She is used to all sorts of reactions from the mortal men to whom she occasionally reveals herself; but none of them has ever given her a comprehensive lecture on mid 8th century local pottery.

'Are you interested in archaeology?' asks Mr Horton. 'I'm the County Archaeologist for Bersetshire, that's not nearly as grand a job as it sounds, mind you, because we just don't have the funding to actually do anything very much in the way of actual archaeology, but last night the most wonderful thing happened, this old man, his name is Hob, well, really he's Sir Oriole Ravenscroft-Corbie-Hob, only he doesn't like to be called that, and anyway, he owns all the land round here, and he has offered to fund a proper excavation down at Rooks Ridge - I expect you know Rooks Ridge? - with all the money and equipment and people we need, it's going to be so wonderful, I can still hardly believe I'm not dreaming, and I'm going to be in charge, and his nephew, he's called Jim, Jim Southerton, I really like him, I think we are soul-mates, you know? - that probably sounds a bit strange, but I really really like him, and we are going to be working together on this project, and it's going to be so wonderful, especially working with Jim, he likes to be called Jim, he told me, and he has promised never to call me Ron, my name's Ronald, you see, Ronald Horton, but I really don't like being called Ron, I prefer Ronnie, I think it sounds more friendly, more like - well, more like someone who gets invited to lots of parties and doesn't always end up in the kitchen, I always seem to end up in the kitchen, not that I get invited to very many parties, but anyway there's these people from the television, *Ready Steady Dig!* the programme's called, it's quite dreadful what they do, and they've been doing it to Rooks Ridge, and they're going to do it again the day after tomorrow, and there doesn't seem to be any way we can stop them.'

Drippy continues to stare at him with a glazed expression which he takes for encouragement. Mr Horton doesn't have many people to talk to in his rather lonely life, and when he does, as he himself is the first to admit, he can sometimes get a little bit carried away.

'Still I don't suppose they can do too much more harm in just one more day, can they?' he says. 'But I thought I'd come up here and make a sort of offering, and Hob said it should be the most precious thing in the world, so I brought this.' He takes the shard of Berumware from Drippy's unresisting fingers, and looks at it fondly, and looks at the pool. 'I expect it sounds a bit silly, well, when you put it like that it *is* a bit silly, I know, but I'm going to do it anyway.' He takes a deep breath, shuts his eyes, and drops his treasure into the bubbling waters.

'Do you think I should, well, say something?' he asks, still with his eyes shut.

'No!' cries Drippy, and backs away, her hands outstretched as if to fend him off. 'Farewell!' She slips behind the wild rose bush, and vanishes.

Mr Horton opens his eyes, and sees that she has gone. 'Goodbye!' he calls out. 'It was so nice meeting you.' What a very nice girl, he thinks. It's not often he gets to meet anyone who is really interested in archaeology.

He sits beside the pool for a while longer, staring down into the crystal waters, dreaming of the future, and feeling unaccountably happy. He is completely unaware of the presence of a short stocky creature dressed in oak leaves and lichen, watching him from the cover of a hazel with a bemused expression on its face. After a minute or so the creature shakes its head in apparent bewilderment, and fades back into the woods.

Mr Horton rouses himself, and sees that it is starting to grow dusky under the cover of the trees. Time to get back to his responsibilities, he thinks with a sigh, and steps down onto the path, from which the drift of rose petals has now completely vanished.

He walks down the path, and quickens his step at the sound of voices up ahead.

CHAPTER XXXIV

'Better wake him up again, I suppose,' says Petro, looking at the still sleeping form of Jim Southerton under the big oak tree. 'I hope Aikin gets a move on - we don't want to be up here when it gets dark.'

'Do you really think he'll be able to persuade Drippy to leave Mr Horton alone?' asks Vera anxiously. 'It would be just so awful if -'

'Hello there!'

Petro dives back down into Vera's pocket just in time as Mr Horton comes trotting along the path, completely unimpeded by the high bramble hedge, which isn't there any more.

'Fancy seeing you up here!' says Mr Horton. 'Didn't we meet just now, down at the Church Hall, and - good gracious, it's Jim!' He stares at Jim, who continues to sleep soundly. 'Whatever is he doing there?'

'He's asleep,' says Vera.

'How odd,' says Mr Horton, still staring at Jim. 'I've just been up at the spring. I met such a nice girl up there, she was really interested in archaeology. You don't get that very often with young people these days.'

'*Suscita!*' says a tiny voice from Vera's jacket pocket, and Jim's eyes fly open.

'Ronnie!' he yells. He leaps to his feet and seizes a startled Mr Horton in a bear hug. 'Ronnie, you're all right! You're here! I thought -' Jim releases Mr Horton, and looks round wildly at the path to the shrine. 'The hedge! Where's the hedge?'

'What hedge?' asks Mr Horton, still reeling from the shock of being embraced by Jim Southerton.

'There! There was this huge hedge of brambles, all across the path, and I knew you were in there but I couldn't get to you! And I scratched my hands nearly to pieces trying to tear it down, but I couldn't get through!'

'*Manus sanate!*' says Petro hastily.

Mr Horton looks at Jim's hands with some concern. They show not a mark. Jim looks at them too.

171

'I was *bleeding!*' he says, bewildered. 'I was bleeding like anything, and there was this little girl - yes, here she is, you tell him, there was a hedge and I was really bleeding -'

He tails off at Vera's expression.

'You were asleep,' she says, crossing her fingers behind her back.

'You called your Step-Dad on your mobile to get help, and he was going to bring his seccateurs!' says Jim wildly. 'And a chain saw!'

'I haven't got a mobile,' says Vera. 'But Darrell has got some seccateurs, except I think they're broken,' she adds helpfully. 'I don't think my Mum would let him have a chain saw.'

'You were asleep when I got here,' says Mr Horton. 'I think you must just have had a bad dream.' Jim shakes his head in bewilderment. 'You were lucky nothing worse happened,' says Mr Horton, with a twinkle. 'It's very dangerous, going to sleep under an oak tree at undern-time.'

'What?'

'Look what happened to Thomas the Rhymer,' says Mr Horton, teasing. 'It's always happening in Middle English poetry. The hero goes to sleep under a tree, and the next thing he knows he's been carried off to serve seven years with the Queen of Fair Elfland.'

'But I don't understand how I could have fallen asleep,' says Jim helplessly. 'I don't even remember sitting down!'

'Well, the alternative is that I really was trapped behind a thick briar hedge that isn't there now, and that this little girl called for help on a mobile telephone that she hasn't got,' Mr Horton points out. He knows he ought to be feeling really sympathetic and concerned, but for some reason the memory of having been hugged by Jim Southerton keeps making him want to smile. 'Would you like to come home with me and have a nice cup of tea?'

'No,' says Jim. 'I'd like to come home with you and have a very, very large scotch.'

They set off down the path together, completely forgetting Vera's existence.

As they disappear around the bend in the path, Petro pokes his head out of Vera's pocket.

'Well, that went pretty well,' he says. 'We ought just to go on up to Drippy's spring, so you can make your offering, Domina Vera, and I can ask her to come down to the villa tomorrow morning.'

Vera makes for the spring, where they find the dryad still looking faintly bemused.

'Well done, Aikin!' says Petro, as Vera sets him down on the rim of the pool. 'Thanks a million. We owe you.'

The dryad shakes his head. 'I didn't have to do a thing,' he admits. 'He did it all himself.'

'What? How?' asks Petro.

'Well, I'm not sure I understood most of it, but he ended up making an offering that was a bit of an old pot,' says the dryad. 'I don't think she liked it much.'

'Was it greenish coloured, a bit crumbly?' asks Petro.

'Yes, yes it was.'

'He must have wanted something really really badly,' says Petro.

'I think he just didn't really notice her,' says the dryad, shaking his head in puzzlement. 'Hard to imagine, isn't it, someone being as totally self-absorbed as that?'

'Extraordinary,' says Petro.

'But you will still talk to the Genius Loci about the rain, won't you, Petro?' the dryad asks, in faintly hostile tones. 'You did promise.'

'Of course I will, Aikin,' answers Petro, 'provided you promise to get Drippy to come down to Rooks Ridge tomorrow at first light.'

'Consider it done,' says the dryad. 'Oh, by the way, I've decided to call myself Robort from now on.'

'Robert?'

'No, Roborrrt, as in *Quercus Robor*,' says the dryad. 'Good, don't you think?'

'That's a new one,' says Petro. 'I like it.'

The dryad raises a hand in acknowledgement, and melts away into the trees.

'Oh, hello, Drippy!' says Petro, and Vera see that the nymph has materialised, and that somehow she looks a good deal less drippy than usual.

'What do you want?' she demands somewhat crossly, standing arms akimbo and glaring at them.

'Domina Vera has brought you an offering,' says Petro.

'Yes, Stillaria, you remember I promised I would bring you a picture of Mr Horton, and so -' Vera holds out the photograph of the County Archaeologist.

Drippy gives a delicate little shudder. 'Thank you very much,' she says politely. 'Just drop it in the spring.'

'But it will get all wet!' says Vera. 'It's a photograph, it will be spoiled!'

Drippy looks at her, and looks at the photograph.

'Just drop it in the spring,' she says again. She departs in a cloud of rose petals, and this time she is flouncing, not dancing.

'That went down well,' says Petro, as Vera lets go of the photograph, which flutters onto the surface of the bubbling water and gradually sinks, disintegrating gently as it does so. 'I don't think you need to bother doing the words this time.'

They make their way slowly back down the path.

'So are there fairies in the woods too, Petro?' asks Vera, looking from side to side in the hope of catching a glimpse of one.

'Fairies? No, there's no such thing as fairies, they're just a myth,' answers Petro. 'Nymphs and dryads, yes, only people call them elves nowadays, or the Fair Folk, although I can't think why they bother giving them names when they mostly don't believe in them. Elves - or nymphs and dryads - are under the dominion of The Lady. That was her stag you saw just now. He always turns up when anything interesting is going to happen. His name's Graham. So if you ever see Graham again, it's probably quite a good idea not to be there. And especially if you happen see one path that suddenly splits into three paths, and you have to choose which one to take, now that's *really* bad news. If that happens, just make sure you don't take the bonny bonny road that winds amongst the ferny braes. That is the road to Fair Elfland, and I promise you, Fair Elfland is somewhere you really, really do not want to go.'

'Why not, Petro?'

'Because that's where The Lady is Queen, not that I'll hear a word said against her, mind, I think she does a wonderful job, but would you really want to spend seven years with a woman who can't think of a better name than Graham for a pure white stag?'

'Er, no,' says Vera, suspecting he is leaving a few things out, but taking the point anyway, and making a note to pay extra special care in the event of the sudden appearance of threefold paths in the woods.

CHAPTER XXXV

Next morning sees Petro up and about well before first light, ready to put in to action his plans for protecting the graves of Septimus Verus Pugnax Corvo and Vera Alauda. In just twenty-four hours, *Ready Steady Dig!* will be back, and it will be too late. Twenty-four hours is really nowhere near long enough for what he has in mind, but he can see no other option but to try.

He looks about for the Genius Loci, and soon locates him, stamping around the villa site, glowering at the excavations that have disfigured his territory.

Petro invests a few minutes sympathetically deploring the activities of the archaeologists, and speculating that the Genius Loci would really, really enjoy doing anything that might seriously upset them.

The little man cocks a cynical eye at Petro.

'Come on, Shorty, spit it out,' he says dryly. 'What is it you're after?'

Petro explains his plans at some length. 'But of course, I don't suppose for a moment you'd be able to manage it,' he remarks casually.

'Oh no?' says the Genius Loci. 'Just you watch me.'

He stalks down the hill and stares intently at Trench Four, the grave trench. It lies across the slope, and if it gets very much deeper, it will cut into Septimus Verus Pugnax Corvo's grave at the end next to the track, and Vera Alauda's at the other end, almost under the hedge. It is ten feet long by four feet wide, and so far the JCB and Mr Horton between them have taken it down to about two feet.

'You might want to move that little red thing,' says the Genius Loci, pointing to the finds label in the bottom of the trench that marks the spot where Mr Horton found his piece of Berumware. 'I can't do anything with that.'

Petro hops in and gathers it up, carefully noting its exact position in the trench. If this really works...

Petro clambers out again, and the Genius Loci stares very hard at the trench, then at the ground that lies up-slope of it. He places both his palms together, and then brings them apart sharply.

'*Humus dissili!*' he cries.

There is a sound like ripping cardboard, and two four foot long cracks open up, extensions to the two short edges of the trench. The Genius Loci does the reverse hand-clap gesture again.

'*Rimae coniungete!*' he shouts. There is another ripping cardboard sound, and a third crack, ten feet long, joins up the other two.

'Ready for this?' asks the Genius Loci, who is clearly getting into his stride and enjoying himself very much. 'I wouldn't want to be standing too close, if I was you.'

Petro moves a little further off, and holds his breath. The Genius Loci bends one knee and moves his arms like a discus-thrower throwing two at once.

'*Humus ruere!*' he yells triumphantly.

There is a sound like rushing water, and the cut-out section of ground up-slope of Trench Four begins to move. Earth and stones tumble down the hillside, slowly filling up Trench Four and leaving behind a new ten foot long, four foot wide depression, about two feet deep. The turf rides smoothly along on top of the little avalanche, every blade of grass, every leaf, every flower ending up exactly four feet down-slope from where it started.

'That do you?' asks the Genius Loci smugly.

Petro grins. 'That'll do nicely.'

He hops into the new trench, puts down the red finds label in the same position as it was in the original Trench Four, and carefully places the small piece of Berumware which Grumio found by tripping over it. He half-buries it, with the greenish side upwards, in the very middle of the new trench, just where Mr Horton is bound to spot it. That should take care of any suspicions that he may have about the position of Trench Four. The chances of him noticing that it has somehow moved four feet up hill are pretty small in any case, and with a new piece of his beloved Berumware to distract him, they will surely be nil. And since, as Bony Jay assured them yesterday, the geophysics equipment has already been taken away to the next *Ready Steady Dig!* location, no-one will be able to use it to double-check the position of the graves, even if any serious doubts do arise. The only big give-away is, of course, the position of the spoil heap, and Petro is almost willing to bet that Mr Horton won't even remember exactly where that was in relation to the original Trench Four. But somebody else might …

The Genius Loci sees Petro glance at it.

'Want me to shift that too?' he asks casually.

'Would you? Can you make it go up hill?'

The Genius Loci gives him a *look*. He does the double-discus throwing movement again, and shouts '*Agger ascendere!*' There is the rushing water noise, and the spoil heap pours up the slope to reposition itself in exactly the same relation to the new trench as it was to the old.

'That was terrific,' says Petro.

'You might want to get that daft nymph to tuck the flowers and grasses in, and give them a bit of a pep-talk,' says the Genius Loci. 'Make sure they don't die off, or anything. I may have been a bit rough with them. I don't really do perishables.'

'The dryad promised she'd be down later,' says Petro. 'By the way, he's calling himself Robort now. Or he was yesterday.'

The Genius Loci rolls his eyes.

'I thought he'd settled on Darach-og?'

'Nah, that was in May,' says Petro. 'He went through a bit of a Celtic phase in the run-up to Beltane.'

'So now it's Robert?'

'Roborrrt. Like in *Quercus Robor,*' says Petro. 'I think he's trying to get back to his roots.'

The Genius Loci does another eye-roll. He surveys the re-arranged landscape with a professional eye.

'I daresay a bit of a shower wouldn't come amiss, just to tidy things up a bit, and maybe sluice down where the heap of earth was?' he suggests.

'If you really wouldn't mind…'

'*Ex caelo plue imber!*' shouts the Genius Loci. He jumps up and down and waves his arms about vigorously. Big fat drops of rain begin pattering down. The Genius Loci points to the sky, and then does an expansive 'Let's be having you' gesture. '*Fulgur! Tonitrus!*' he yells.

'Here, steady on,' says Petro, glancing up nervously as a shaft of lightning splits the heavens, followed almost instantly by a crash of thunder. 'There's no need to get carried away.'

The rain falls steadily for half an hour, and at the end of it the bottom of the new trench is nicely muddy and the grass where the spoil heap originally stood is washed clean of loose soil, while beneath the relocated turf, Vera Alauda and Septimus Verus Pugnax Corvo sleep soundly, if rather damply, once more.

Drippy arrives at 5.30am, still looking distinctly put out and a good deal less drippy than usual. She looks at the re-located Trench Four, and her eyes narrow with suspicion.

'My grasses!' she cries. 'What's happened to my poor grasses?'

'Ah, yes,' says Petro, 'sorry about that, but I had to get the Genius Loci to move them a bit.'

'Move them!' Drippy falls to her knees, and strokes the nearest bit of turf. 'How could you, Petro! Hurting my poor, poor grasses!'

'Well, I wouldn't have done it if it wasn't really, really important,' says Petro apologetically. 'It's all the fault of those archaeologists.'

'Them!' cries Drippy. 'I might have guessed! They're all the same, archaeologists! No heart! No soul! The only thing they care about is *pots!*'

'So I just wondered if you wouldn't mind sort of settling it all back in again, giving it a bit of tlc, you know?'

Drippy glares at him, and rises gracefully to her feet. She dances several times round the re-located turf, waving her arms about and singing even more tunelessly and rather more forcefully than usual. When she finally comes to a standstill, the grass certainly looks a bit greener, and one or two new flowers have opened.

'There,' says Drippy. 'Now don't touch them again.'

'No, Stillaria,' says Petro meekly. 'Ah, there was just one other thing.'

'What?'

'Well, it's Vera Alauda's grave, you see,' he says. 'The archaeologists might still find it again, even though the Genius Loci has shifted the trench, so I thought if maybe there was a little tree or a bush or something growing on it, say about here -' he indicates where he knows the head of the grave lies '- then maybe they wouldn't. I don't suppose you could ...?'

'Of course I *could*,' says Drippy, 'if I wanted to.' She narrows her eyes. 'Do you think it would upset him? I mean, them?'

'Oh yes,' says Petro earnestly. 'I'm sure it would completely ruin his day.'

'Good,' says Drippy. She goes over to the hedge and searches briefly in the leaf-litter. 'Hawthorn, will that do?'

'Perfect,' says Petro.

The nymph picks up a small, shrivelled, reddish brown haw, and brings it back to the head of the grave. She raises the seed to her lips and breathes on it softly, then sets it down carefully, parting the grasses to make a little depression to receive it. She bends down and breathes on it again, and it suddenly splits open, and a pale, fragile stem appears with two small green leaves at its tip. Then a thin white rootlet breaks through the other end of the seed, twisting and burrowing its way down into the ground. The little plant sways gently as it slowly begins to grow, a millimetre at a time, reaching up towards Drippy, who stands over it, gazing down at it intently. A second pair of leaves bursts from the delicate stem, and then a third.

'You're quite sure it will really upset him?' asks Drippy.

'Absolutely.'

The little plant seems to gather its strength, and suddenly puts on a spurt of growth. Now it is nearly a foot high, and three pure white blossoms open, then drop their petals and begin to swell at the base to produce a cluster of crimson haws. The leaves of the little tree turn a dark red-gold before falling, dry and rustling, to the ground, and then new buds swell, and new leaves burst forth in a bright spring green. More blossom, more haws, more autumn leaves, and suddenly it is spring again, and the tree is nearly three feet high.

'There,' says Drippy, standing back to admire her handiwork. 'It should fill out nicely in a few hours. And if anyone *should* come along and try to pull it up - well, all I'm going to say is that they'll be really, really sorry they tried.'

'Drippy, you're a marvel,' says Petro. 'I just knew you could do it. It's perfect, just perfect.'

'I only do perfect,' says the nymph coldly, and dances away in a cloud of gauzy draperies.

It is 5am the following morning, and in an hour's time *Ready Steady Dig!* will be returning to Rooks Ridge for their second day of excavations. As a faint grey dawn comes up over the eastern wolds, Petro is giving the Genius Loci a last-minute briefing. He has been doing this for about an hour, and things are getting a little tense.

'It's very important not to get too carried away,' says Petro earnestly. 'I want to see some really good, sharp showers, but no more than ten minutes at a time, just enough to get them to down tools, but not enough so they give up for the day.'

'You have already told me that, Petro.'

'And it would be nice if the rain reached up as far as Robort's oak tree, you know, the one by the spring.'

'Yes, Petro, I got that.'

'I sort of promised him you would.'

'You did mention it, Petro.'

'And after all, fair do's, it was him who gave me the idea.'

'Yes, Petro, you said.'

'And I really don't want to see any thunder and lightning. That could make them stop digging altogether.'

'You have made that quite clear, Petro.'

'If they actually abandon the dig, especially right near the beginning, then that lawyer might be able to demand another day.'

'I think you already said that, Petro.'

'We just want to disrupt them as much as possible, so they can't get very much work done, without actually stopping them completely.'

'I have grasped that point, Petro.'

'So in between the showers, I want to see a few good sunny spells, to encourage them to think it's going to clear up completely any minute.'

'Yes, I do understand that, Petro.'

'And if you could just drop the temperature a bit, so they all get really chilled. That should slow them down.'

'I haven't forgotten, Petro.'

'But I don't want any wind - that could dry things out.'
'Petro?'
'Yes?'
'Go away.'
'But perhaps I should just remind you about -'
'Go away.'

CHAPTER XXXVI

It is 5.30am on Tuesday, and in the growing light of dawn Trystram Wentworth stands looking down into Trench Four.

Petro watches him narrowly from the shelter of the hedgerow. The Director bears all the signs of a man who is up to no good, and in any case he is one of the people who are most likely to notice that the trench has shifted position. He bends and peers intently down into it, then, with a quick glance over his shoulder, he steps in, stoops, and picks up the shard of Berumware that the Lares had worked so long and so hard to find. He examines it carefully, and his lips tighten. For a moment it looks as if he will put it in his pocket, but some vestiges of conscience restrain him. Instead he climbs out of the trench and places it in the spoil-heap, on the hedge side, where it will be hidden from any casual glance. Then he hurries back down to the site access gate as the programme's vehicles begin to arrive and park up. It is starting to rain.

By 6am the crew of *Ready Steady Dig!* are assembled below Rooks Ridge in a chill drizzle, mostly huddled in a colourful variety of anoraks and parkas, some clutching steaming mugs of coffee which they have managed to extract from Mrs Hamble, who has turned up in spite of many hysterical threats to resign and/or sue. She is refusing to cook anything at all that contains eggs, but otherwise appears to be functioning as per normal, that is to say she dispenses every last item as if it were meat and drink snatched from the mouths of her starving children.

Only Trystram appears to be in the least bit ready or steady this morning. He is dressed in a long pale leather coat, which makes him look like an SS officer in mufti, and he clearly cannot wait to get started.

'You'll do much better to hold off for a bit,' says Professor Jones. 'There's just no sense in everyone getting soaked to the skin with the day barely begun yet. Look, there's blue skies coming up over there. Give it fifteen minutes, and then we'll get going.'

'It's already easing off,' says Trystram. His blond hair is plastered to his skull by the downpour, and today's floppy silk cravat looks like a bit of chewed string. 'Ten minutes, and not a second longer.'

Nine minutes later the rain has indeed eased off, and the sky overhead is an encouraging blue. Trystram firmly propels Professor Jones and nine student diggers of his choice in the direction of Trench Four, and Mr Horton follows unbidden in their wake.

'Right, I want this taken down *now* to the level of the graves. How deep do you think that's going to be?' asks Trystram, in a voice that brooks no arguments.

'Another two feet should do it,' says Professor Jones. 'Three at most. And no, I'm not having that JCB back in here. It could be a lot less than two feet.'

'Cameras in half an hour, then?' says Trystram. It is not really a question. Professor Jones nods, and signals his diggers to get to work. Mr Horton watches anxiously as the trench deepens, but he can see no signs of archaeology being damaged by over-hasty excavation. In fact, he can see no signs of any archaeology at all.

Trystram Wentworth today is a man possessed. He dispatches the JCB up to the plateau, and soon Trench Five is being ripped open over the centre of the north wing, under the supervision of Micky, one of the four senior archaeologists. No sooner has Micky performed the frantic dance with accompanying shrieks that is the accepted signal to the driver of the digger that he has just smashed into some archaeology, than Trystram sends the JCB speeding on its way to the bottom of the slope to open Trench Six, where the geophysics suggests the villa's gatehouse may be located. Within minutes Nicci, another of the senior archaeologists, is also doing the hysterical 'Stop, stop, you've broken something' routine. Professor Jones and Mr Horton ricochet between the two new trenches and Trench Four, which is continuing to show not the slightest sign of anything even remotely interesting. By 6.30 it has reached four and a half feet deep, and the rain comes down again as the cameras arrive to set up.

Troy thumps on Bony Jay's dressing room door and calls him to get a move on, and he emerges from the caravan, yawning and resentful. He had rather counted on being able to fetch his gold coin, which he thinks still lies buried in the mouth of the rabbit burrow, before anyone else arrived on site at the scheduled hour of 6am; but when he looked out at 5.30 it was to see Trystram already stalking around the place. Thwarted, Bony went back to bed again, but he dare not be late for a camera-call: he is rather frightened of Trystram, and very much aware that his contract is up for renewal within the next couple of weeks. He knows he is a popular presenter of *Ready Steady Dig!* but the IBBC has many popular *young* presenters on its payroll, and Bony is becoming more and more aware these days that he is not one of them. His ego hugs the description *mature* like a security blanket; any day now, he fears he will hear himself described as *veteran*. All the more reason to get his hands on that coin; and now that the police have gone and everyone on site is being kept fully occupied by Obersturmfurer Trystram, surely some time today he will have his chance?

By 7am the rain has eased off again, Trench Four has reached five and a half feet with no sign of anything whatsoever to film, and Bony and the cameramen are getting bored. Professor Jones is a deeply puzzled man. He sends for the geophysics print-outs, and spreads them out on the bonnet of Bony's Range Rover. As the students keep on digging, Professor Jones beckons Mr Horton over to confer.

Mr Horton doesn't like to admit that he hasn't interpreted a geophysics plot since he was a student, but it is always nice to be asked for one's expertise, even when one doesn't have any.

'What do you think, Horton? These sure do look like graves to me, and the location's spot-on for Roman graves - all along the track-way, that is except for this one here, by the hedge line.'

'I suppose they could still be a bit deeper,' says Mr Horton, 'but the trench is - what? - at least five and a half feet already? That's got to be near any reasonable limit for late Roman graves.'

'And there should have been some sign of them anyway, all the way down,' points out Professor Jones. 'If it weren't for the geophys, I'd have to say we have been digging into the natural all morning.'

Mr Horton agrees. On the first day's dig, there were faint signs, down to the two foot level, of what could be grave cuts. Today there are no such signs at all. The conclusion is inescapable: they are digging through undisturbed natural soil. 'It's a mystery to me,' he says brightly. 'Look, it's starting to rain again.'

Bony points to the anomalies on the geophysics print-out. 'They have to be something,' he says reasonably. 'I mean, they're so regular, all along the track like that. And the trench takes in one end of the first one on the track, and the other end of the one on its own. There has to be *something* to see down there.'

'There isn't,' says Professor Jones curtly.

'So what do I say to camera?' asks Bony. Professor Jones shrugs. 'And more important, what do you say to Trystram?' adds Bony pointedly.

'I say we keep right on digging,' replies Professor Jones. 'He's not going to let us give up yet, and I'm not prepared to argue with him.'

They keep on digging as the rain begins to ease off.

CHAPTER XXXVII

Mr Horton wanders away. He can see what Professor Jones can also see perfectly well: geophys or no geophys, there is simply nothing there in Trench Four. He makes for Trenches Three and Five, up on the plateau, where two groups of student diggers, supervised by two of the senior archaeologists, a slender young man named Ricky and his stout, middle-aged colleague, Micky, have taken shelter in the trees beside the west wing of the villa. They huddle together with their hoods up, peering out miserably into the wet grey day, and watching Simon Jackson, the student digger who fleeced Trystram Wentworth over the mobile 'phone clips, who is on punishment detail at the old Trench One.

Trench One was shut down, recorded and filled in early on Day One, but one final task remains: it is Simon's dismal job to go over the whole area inch by inch with a metal detector before the turf is replaced, just in case anything has been missed in the spoil. Trystram has made it very clear that he can see no reason whatsoever why this task cannot be carried out even in monsoon conditions.

The rain eases up again, and the diggers make their muddy way back to Trenches Three and Five. In Trench Three Ricky looks on as the students trowel carefully away at the remains of the demolition rubble in the west wing of the villa, where the treasure pit was unearthed. Mr Horton, watching them, has to admit that they are working very skilfully, although rather more quickly than perhaps he would like to see.

He moves over to Trench Five, opened that morning and supervised by Micky. There is rubble here too, but much less of it. Probably the inhabitants of Crowborough have been coming here over the centuries to take away the dressed stone for reuse down in the town. Micky calls a halt and gives instructions for the detailed recording of the demolition layer before it is lifted, but no sooner has the process begun than the rain comes down again and sends everybody scurrying back to the shelter of the trees, all except the luckless Simon Jackson, who plods on over the increasingly muddy erstwhile Trench One.

From the shelter of the trees, Mr Horton looks back down to Trench Four, the lack-of-graves trench, and now he can barely see the heads of the diggers over the edge of it. Trystram is there, standing over them, clutching the geophysics print-outs, and it is pretty clear from his body language that he is not giving up yet. Professor Jones stands back, tight-lipped and clearly impatient at the waste of time and manpower. Bony Jay and the camera crew are all packed into Bony's Range Rover to keep dry. If this were any normal dig, Mr Horton thinks disapprovingly, everyone would have been sent home an hour or more ago. He looks up at the louring sky. This on-again off-again rain could go on all day, and probably will.

As skies brighten once more and the rain stops, Mr Horton makes his way down to Trench Six, which cuts across the trackway at the bottom of the slope. Three very wet students and a sodden senior archaeologist called Nicci are four feet down on what is clearly a wall line. It looks as if they have found the villa's gatehouse. Mr Horton watches with interest, and also with some concern: water is trickling into the trench from all sides, but especially from up-slope. At this rate, the diggers are going to need snorkels. The situation is absurd. Mr Horton gathers his courage, and strides purposefully across to Trench Four to have it out with Trystram, since it appears that no one else will.

Trench Four is also awash, although less so than Trench Six, being considerably up-slope. It is now at least six feet deep.

'This is ridiculous,' says Mr Horton bravely. 'No one should be expected to dig in these conditions. And anyway, there's nothing there!'

Trystram gives him a venomous look.

'There must be something! The geophysics is perfectly clear!'

'As you very well know, Trystram,' says Professor Jones calmly, wringing the rain water out of his beard, 'we often get interesting-looking geophys responses that turn out to be very disappointing in the ground.'

'I want to see some bones,' says Trystram stubbornly.

'Well you're not going to see any here,' says Professor Jones. 'Roman graves at this depth would be highly unusual. Look, get a metal detector up here, and if there are no responses, we close the trench down. How about that?'

'How can you expect to find bones with a metal detector?' demands Trystram. Professor Jones rolls his eyes.

'I don't, Trystram,' he says carefully. 'But if there are any metallic grave goods, I would expect those to register.'

'It would be quite unusual *not* to have any metal objects at all in a Roman grave,' says Mr Horton helpfully. 'Brooches, cloak pins, that sort of thing. Even a dagger or a knife.'

Trystram glowers. He stalks over to the Range Rover and pulls open the driver's side door.

'You!' he says sharply to Bony Jay. 'Make yourself useful. Go and get a metal detector, now.'

Bony's jaw drops. He knows that the Director does not like him very much, but he has never spoken to him in such a manner before. And to do so in front of the camera crew! Bony Jay is not a gofer. He is the celebrity presenter of the programme, and it's not his job to run around fetching bits of kit. He is as astonished as he is angry.

'Fetch it yourself,' he retorts.

Trystram goes white. Bony sees his career in TV archaeology flashing before his eyes, and surprises himself by thinking *So what?* He's hardly going to end up in the gutter, after all. He has his gold coin from the Corvo hoard, or he will have as soon as he gets a chance to go and fetch it; and he still has his chat show, where he interviews friendly, interesting people in a nice warm comfortable studio. He doesn't even like archaeology, for heaven's sake! He *hates* standing around in cold, wet, windy fields in the back of beyond, trying to sound enthusiastic about old bits of broken pot. He *hates* bedding down night after night in a draughty caravan miles from anywhere even remotely civilised. He hates having to subsist on Mrs Hamble's cooking, which is frankly horrible. And he *hates* the way the archaeologists treat him like an idiot just because he can't tell Roman tableware from a Homebase flower pot.

'I'm going to go back to my dressing room to put on some dry clothes,' he announces. 'And then I'm going to get a cup of coffee, and I'm going to stay in the dry until it really stops raining. And if any of you had the sense you were born with, you'd be doing the same.' He notes with a perverse satisfaction that everybody, even

Professor Jones, is struck dumb by his words. He turns to Mr Horton.

'Would you care to join me, Ron? I think I've got some chocolate digestives.'

'Thank you, Bony, that's very kind of you,' says Mr Horton, smiling shyly, and adds, 'I think that is probably the most sensible thing I've heard anybody say all day.'

Trystram Wentworth is shaken by the defection of his celebrity presenter, but he has no doubt the rebellion will soon be over: the state of Bony's personal finances is an open secret in television circles, and his contract is coming up for renewal very shortly. At this moment a runner arrives, sent by Nicci from Trench Six, to report something that might actually be worth filming. The villa's gatehouse has been identified and there are now clear wall lines, admittedly largely robbed out, and some good finds, including a couple of nice coins. Trystram rousts the camera crew and points them in the direction of Trench Six. He hesitates over sending for Bony Jay, then has a better idea, positively Machiavellian in its cunning. Nicci the archaeologist is young, personable and articulate, and he fancies her like mad, but he has never managed to get anywhere with her. Anywhere interesting, that is. That could just change if he gives her the opportunity to speak to camera in place of Bony Jay. Trystram strides off down the hill towards Trench Six in the wake of the camera crew, and as he does so the heavens open and the rain comes down in torrents.

Nicci is still young, and she is still articulate, especially about the folly of digging in these conditions. Personable, however, she is not. Trystram stares in dismay at the straggle-haired, mascara-streaked harridan who confronts him. Where are the flowing blonde locks, where the delectable cleavage? Hidden under a voluminous hooded parka, that's where, and certainly not available for filming.

'Where do you want us to set up?' asks the senior cameraman, looking in vain for Trench Six. Nicci points wordlessly at what looks like a pond. In the last few minutes, here on the low-lying ground, the run-off from the wolds has completely filled Trench

Six with muddy water. They all look at the pond, and look at Trystram.

'I think the rain's easing off again,' says someone very brave. Trystram gives a beast-like snarl, and strides away again to the shelter of the large marquee.

Trench Six is abandoned, and Professor Jones, having driven his diggers down to the six and a half foot level, is absolutely refusing to do any more work on Trench Four.

In the large marquee, Trystram takes stock. It is now 12 noon, and the sky is a glorious cloudless blue, perfect conditions for filming, if only there were something to film. He could abandon the day's digging, and hope that Mr Crail will be able to compel Hob to allow *Ready Steady Dig!* to return for a further day, but Mr Crail has already warned him that he is highly unlikely to be able to achieve this; and in any case, Trystram is heartily sick of Rooks Ridge and never wants to see the place again. He sends Nicci to Crowborough to see if she can get her hair done and acquire an umbrella to keep it camera-ready in case of further rain; and orders an early lunch break for everyone.

The Genius Loci surveys the scene with satisfaction: work has been abandoned for the time being, so he decides to lay off the rain for a while. Time enough to start up again when digging recommences.

With the site deserted, Petro scuttles down the hedge line to the Trench Four spoil heap. It takes him some time, and he gets very muddy in the process, but he manages eventually to locate the piece of Berumware that he had set as bait - unneeded, as it happened - for Mr Horton.

He considers it for a while, wondering what it is about this wretched stuff that so enchants the County Archaeologist. This particular piece has an incised decoration, although to call it decoration is to use the word in its loosest possible sense. It is extremely ugly, and looks like the result of a high-speed collision between a badger and an egg whisk. Petro wonders what to do with it. He has developed rather a liking for Mr Horton, and feels somehow protective towards the modest little man who, he knows, will eventually be taking over the site. This miserable piece of pot would undoubtedly give Mr Horton a great deal of innocent pleasure, and Petro doesn't want to deprive him of that. Eventually he moves out into the former wheat field, and places the piece of pot as prominently as he can, as close as he can remember to the spot where Grumio found it.

CHAPTER XXXVIII

In the large marquee a very nasty and entirely eggless lunch is consumed by all, and at 12.45 Trystram calls everyone together for their afternoon assignments. Trench Six is still full to the brim, and indeed is now the centre of a slowly spreading lake at the bottom of the hill, so that it is impossible even to see exactly where it lies. Trench Four is only half full of water, but further work there is likewise out of the question. Trystram orders everyone up to the plateau, where Micky and Ricky assure him that all is now ready to lift the demolition rubble from Trenches Three and Five. Professor Jones has high hopes of some mosaic flooring in at least one of these areas, since none has been found so far, which is unusual for a villa of the size and obvious status of this one. Trystram brightens at the mention of mosaic flooring, something which always goes down well with the viewers, and assigns everyone except the luckless Simon Jackson to rubble-shifting. The personable Nicci returns from *Hair Today*, looking delectably ready for the cameras and toting a large umbrella to ensure that she will stay that way. The sun is shining from a brilliant blue sky, and all looks set for a good afternoon's filming.

Trystram steps out of the marquee, and the heavens open.

Trystram will not hear of waiting out the rain. He marches everyone up to the plateau, and works begins on lifting the meticulously recorded rubble in Trenches Three and Five. With Trystram present, no one dares suggest retreating to the shelter of the trees. The Director puts up a large umbrella, and stands glowering over the sodden workers.

After a ten-minute soaking the rain stops again, and the speed of work picks up. Mr Horton and Professor Jones look on, constantly skipping from one trench to the other and back again, each hopeful of spotting something that will improve Trystram's mood. Ironically, it is in the old Trench One that sudden drama explodes, over the east wing where Simon Jackson has resumed his solitary penitential quartering of the ground.

His metal detector, which has been buzzing away quietly in the background all day, suddenly gives a high-pitched banshee wail, and several people jump, including Simon. He frowns at the machine, twiddles a few buttons, and makes another pass over the noisy spot. The shriek is, if anything, even louder. There is an ironic cheer from Trench Three.

'Somebody's buried a trowel again!' one of the student diggers calls out in mocking tones. Mr Horton smiles. Of course. After all, there can't be anything interesting left in Trench One. Simon shakes his head.

'It's a lot bigger than a trowel,' he says.

'A spade! Who's been and gone and lost a spade?' another of the student diggers responds, and someone sets off a chant - *'Spade! Spade! Spade!'*

Trystram Wentworth turns on them with a snarl.

'Be quiet, all of you, you're disrupting the filming with that noise! Get back to your work!'

'Spade,' says someone, quietly defiant, but everyone else shuts up. Trystram stalks over to Simon and his metal detector, which is still shrieking as he passes it back and forth over an area a foot or more square.

'What is that?' demands Trystram, as the rain begins to fall once more.

'Well, it probably is just the blade of a shovel,' Simon admits. 'Do you want me to check?'

'Well of course I want you to check!' snaps Trystram. 'What's the point of a metal detector if you're not going to check when it detects metal?' Honestly, these people! *Do you want me to check?* Trystram despairs sometimes, he really does.

Simon switches off the wailing machine, to everyone's relief, and fetches a trowel. Mr Horton comes closer to watch. He is quite looking forward to watching Trystram Wentworth's face when nothing more exciting emerges than a modern, mislaid digging implement.

Simon kneels down in the mud, and begins scraping away at the area where the response was most ear-splitting. Suddenly he freezes. Mr Horton leans a little closer, and sees the glint of gold that has caught his attention.

'Bloody hell,' says Simon, trowelling a bit more. He sits back on his heels, a stunned expression on his face. 'What is it you're supposed to say?' he asks in a voice that is filled with awe. *'I have looked upon the face of Maggie Henman?'*

'Something like that,' says a bemused Mr Horton, as the Corvo treasure begins to surface for the second time.

Adrogantio is a broken Lar. 'But it seemed such a good idea at the time!' he wails. 'They'd finished with the East Wing! How was I to know they'd go back there again? I thought it would be safe there.'

Lapidilla puts a comforting arm around his shoulders.

'It's not your fault, Adro,' she says kindly. 'We certainly all went along with it, and none of us had any better ideas about where to hide the treasure. *Did we?'* she asks in a level voice, turning to the other four Lares who are glaring at Adro, most unfairly, she feels. Petro and Cibus shrug. Grumio goes on glaring. Mopsus bursts into tears.

'Oh shut up, Mopsus,' says Petro with uncharacteristic sharpness. After all their efforts, all their ingenuity, the hoard has been unearthed a second time. From their hiding place in the hypocaust they can hear that Professor Jones is already on the 'phone to his colleague Professor Smith again. His next call will be to the Coroner, and then the police, who this time will certainly not leave the treasure lying here a moment longer than necessary.

There is nothing the Lares can do. The gold plates and the silver flask are already gone, and now the rest of the treasure, which they had rescued and hidden away in the nick of time, has been unearthed once again, and this time there will be no chance to recover it. After sixteen hundred years, they have utterly failed the Family. It's enough to turn a Lar to stone... Petro sees a hint of this on Lapidilla's face.

'Don't!' he says sharply. 'There must be *something* -'

'You know there isn't, Petro,' says Lapidilla quietly. 'We did our best, but now our task is over - the treasure is lost.'

Mopsus bursts into tears. Lapidilla reaches out a comforting hand, but he turns his back and walks slowly away into the gloom of the hypocaust.

"*Vale, frater.* Farewell,' says Cibus quietly, as they all watch him go, then turn to look at each other, as if each waiting for the rest to make a move.

'Not yet," says Petro in a shaky voice. "Not yet. We must speak to Domina Vera and Dominus Osseus before we - before we - They have a right to that, at least.'

'Yes, we must report that we have failed,' agrees Adrogantio sadly. 'After all these years, we have failed in our trust. There is nothing left for us now in this world.'

CHAPTER IXL

This time Trystram won't hear of the treasure being left in the ground, and Professor Jones can see no objection to lifting it in any case. After all, it is no longer lying in its archaeological context, so painstaking recording of each stage of the lifting process does seem rather pointless. The stuff must have been dumped here somehow on the night of the theft, or possibly some time since.

As the rain begins to ease off again, Professor Jones asks Mr Horton to make an independent record of each piece as it is taken up by a pulsating Nicci, who places it in a series of finds trays held aloft by Trystram exactly an inch below the level of her cleavage. The cameras record every golden moment, and a lot of delightfully pink ones.

When the metal detector finally confirms that everything has been recovered, Trystram leads the way as Professor Jones escorts the trays down to the marquee, closely followed by Mr Horton. It is a measure of Trystram's state of mind that he does not even notice that his entire workforce has downed tools and is following in their wake.

Mr Horton is both excited by the find and devastated by it. If only *Ready Steady Dig!* had missed it, then *his* dig would eventually have unearthed it. The lost opportunity of such a glorious find leaves him speechless with regret, but the scholar in him soon reasserts control. This is, after all, the most exciting find that Bersetshire has ever seen - well, the most valuable, anyway, in purely monetary terms, he amends conscientiously - and he knows what he must do. He looks at the goggling faces around the trays of gold and silver, and picks on the most seriously goggle-struck: Bony Jay looks utterly and completely devastated. Mr Horton finds a moment to be mildly puzzled about this, but it does not deflect him from his purpose.

'Um, Bony, I wonder if I might borrow your mobile telephone?' he asks diffidently. The stricken presenter hands it to him without a word. Mr Horton thinks for a moment, and changes his mind about calling the Chairman of the County Council. Instead he follows his heart and loses no more time in dialling Jim Southerton's number.

Jim and his uncle arrive together just after two o' clock in the afternoon, and with them is Mr Unwin the solicitor. Detective Chief Inspector Morris arrives seconds later at a hand-gallop, sweeping aside all in his path as he crosses the marquee to the large group gathered around the treasure-filled trays. He comes to a halt with a wild cry of anguish.

'You've dug it all up!'

'Oh, everything's just fine, don't you worry, Chief Inspector,' says Professor Jones cheerfully. 'The finds were no longer in their archaeological context, so I gave the ok to lift them.'

'Fingerprints!' says Chief Inspector Morris in a voice like a frog being throttled.

'Oh, that's all just fine too, there don't seem to be any marks at all from the handling, but we've given them a light cleaning anyway. Obviously in future no one will be touching them without gloves.' Professor Jones looks sternly at the members of his team, who all try to look as if they wouldn't dream of touching anything at all without their standard issue little white cotton gloves. 'Anybody got any on them?'

Mr Horton permits himself to feel just a tiny bit smug as he pulls just such a pair of gloves from one of the pockets of his anorak and slips them on. 'If you would like anything moved, Chief Inspector, I would be very happy -'

Chief Inspector Morris gives another dying frog croak.

'A light cleaning!' he moans. 'Get away from those trays, the lot of you! Now!' He turns to Mr Horton and takes a deep breath. Such has been his haste to get to Rooks Ridge, he has left his SOCO kit at home. 'Please may I borrow your gloves?'

Bony Jay watches in despair as the Corvo treasure is carted away through the falling rain by Detective Chief Inspector Morris, closely escorted by the Coroner's Officer, Constable Whicker, who arrived shortly after him and held a brief and apparently satisfactory conversation with Mr Unwin the solicitor.

'Wonder when we'll ever see all that lot again?' one of the students remarks with a sigh.

'Constable Whicker has assured me that it will be made available for further filming and scholarly assessment immediately after the Coroner's Inquest to determine its ownership,' announces Mr Unwin, in a voice that is clearly meant to carry to everyone in the marquee. He permits himself a little smile as he becomes the instant centre of attention.

'But who does it belong to?' asks another student hungrily. Bony Jay knows just how he feels.

'Generally speaking,' says Mr Unwin, 'when the owner of an archaeological find cannot be traced, any find will belong to the owner of the land on which it was discovered. In the case of Treasure Trove, however, special legislation applies. All Treasure Trove, which was treasure that was originally hidden with the intention of recovering it at a later date, and where the owner or his or her heirs cannot now be found, belongs to the Crown and, when discovered, is subject to an inquest at a Coroner's Court to establish the circumstances of its loss or deposition.'

'The circumstances are pretty obvious,' says Professor Jones. 'Someone, probably the owner of the villa, buried it some time around the middle of the fifth century, and never came back for it.'

'So does it belong to the owner of the land, or is it Treasure Trove?' asks Trystram Wentworth.

'In fact the Treasure Act of 1996 replaced the Common Law of Treasure Trove in England, Wales and Northern Ireland,' continues Mr Unwin, as if no one else had spoken. 'Scotland of course has different laws. The Treasure Act removed the need to prove that objects had been deliberately hidden with the intention of being recovered at a later date, as opposed to being accidentally lost, or being buried in a grave without any intention ever to recover them. This of course was one of the principal tests of the Common Law of Treasure Trove. The Treasure Act also sets out the definition of treasure, which is any object which is at least three hundred years old when it is found, and which is not a coin but has a metallic content of which ten per cent by weight is precious metal, or which is one of at least two coins from the same find area of which ten per cent by weight is precious metal, or which is one of at least ten coins from the same find area, or which does not fall within any of the foregoing specific categories but which would nonetheless have qualified as Treasure Trove under Common Law before the passing of the Treasure Act in 1996, provided that it is made substantially of gold or silver and was buried with the intention of recovery and its owner or his or her heirs cannot now be traced. I do hope that makes everything clear.'

Hob beams at Mr Unwin, like a proud parent at an endearingly precocious child.

'So is it or isn't it?' asks Trystram, rather crossly.

'As I thought I had already explained,' says Mr Unwin, 'all Treasure Trove, which is treasure originally hidden and where the owner or his or her heirs cannot now be found, belongs to the Crown, and it is my professional opinion that this is likely to be the case in this instance.' He pauses for effect. 'However, one understands that in general Her Majesty feels that she already has quite enough treasure of her own, and therefore it is usual for an institution such as a museum to acquire such finds so that they can be put on display to the general public.'

'They're going to go in the Rooks Ridge Museum and Visitors Centre,' says Hob.

Trystram looks around wildly.

'There's no such place!' he says uncertainly.

'Most certainly there is,' says Mr Unwin, with another of his little superior smiles. 'On paper only, of course, at this point in time, but preliminary planning consent is even now being sought.'

'Since when?' asks Trystram.

'Since my secretary completed the paperwork and had it couriered over to County Hall yesterday afternoon,' replies Mr Unwin.

'I still think the treasure belongs to you, Uncle,' says Jim Southerton.

'That is for the Coroner to determine,' says Mr Unwin, rather severely.

'But it doesn't matter anyway,' says Hob. 'Even if it does turn out that it is mine, it's still going to go to the Rooks Ridge Museum and Visitors Centre. And the gold plates and the silver jug will end up there too, of course.'

Bony stares at Hob in utter bewilderment. All that gold and silver could be his for the taking, and he's going to give it to a museum. A museum that doesn't even exist yet! Somehow, that just seems to make it worse. And why on earth, thinks Bony, didn't I ask Petro to grab me a whole handful of those coins while he was at it? The things I could have done with that sort of money! And little Vera, too, he thinks belatedly. He feels rather responsible for Vera, who looks so much like his sister Verity. She lives in a council house, for pity's sake! Just think what a gold coin or two could have done for her. It's enough to make a man weep. He turns away and wanders out of the marquee, lost in passionate regrets, and makes for his dressing room to enjoy his depression in solitude.

Vera is standing outside the caravan, looking anxious.

'Please, Mr Jay, sir,' she says as he approaches. 'There's a rumour in the town that the treasure has been found again. Oh, is it true?'

'Yes,' says Bony simply.

'Do you think the Lares know yet?' asks Vera.

'Probably.'

'Don't you think we ought to go and talk to them?'

Bony thinks about it. There's no one up on Rooks Ridge at the moment: everyone is still down in the marquee, marveling over the find and arguing about its disposition, so now would be a really good time to go and collect his coin from the rabbit burrow.

'Let's go,' he says, feeling fractionally better.

'I'm really worried about them,' says Vera anxiously. 'Their whole reason for still being here after sixteen hundred years was to look after the treasure for the Family. Petro told me that if the Family had died out, they would all have turned into back stone, like Fidelio did when Vera Alauda died. She was his whole life, so when she was killed he turned back into stone and he has never moved or spoken since. So what will happen to our Lares if the treasure is lost, and they haven't got a job any more?'

'You think they might all turn into stone?' asks Bony, feeling a little uncomfortable at the idea. He rather likes the Lares.

'Fidelio did,' says Vera simply.

'We should certainly go and talk to them,' says Bony, picking up on her anxiety.

'Yes,' says Vera. 'Do you think we ought to run?'

CHAPTER XL

'It's all gone,' says Petro, as Vera and Bony, panting from their headlong race up the slope to the ridge, collapse on the grass beside the hypocaust.

The Lares are all there except Mopsus. Adrogantio sits hunched up with his face buried in his hands, and Lapidilla has a comforting arm about his shoulders. Grumio and Cibus look stunned, and won't meet Vera's eyes.

'The treasure is gone,' says Petro again. 'We have failed you, Domines.'

'No!' cries Vera. 'Don't say that!'

'What I want to know,' says Bony, 'is how it got into the east wing in the first place. Who put it there?'

'We did, of course,' says Adrogantio.

'*You* did it!' cries Vera. 'But why didn't you tell me?'

'We thought you knew,' says Petro. 'You knew we had a plan. And when you came here after the treasure was taken, you said 'I hoped you'd got it all,' so we thought you realised that we'd managed to get some of it.'

'Yes,' says Cibus, 'We explained to you why we hadn't been able to take the plates and the jug - we'd planned to wait until first light, and put the guards to sleep, and drag the big stuff out, only the thieves got there while it was still dark, and they took the three big pieces. We assumed you knew we'd already got the small ones.'

'But how did you manage to do that?' demands Bony. 'How did you move all that stuff without being seen?'

'The rabbits dug a burrow for us into the side of the treasure pit,' says Cibus. 'Of course, it was too small for the plates and the wine jug, but we got almost everything else.'

'And you hid it all in the east wing?'

'Yes,' says Adrogantio sadly. 'It was my idea. I thought that the last place anyone would look was in the trench that they'd already dug out and shut down again.'

'Mind you, it was touch and go once or twice,' says Cibus, his sad face brightening a little as he recalls the Lares' success. 'The rabbits took ages to make a big enough hole for the treasure to go in - we were all lining up with it in the burrow behind them. But we did it! By the time the fire went up and the thieves arrived, there were only a couple of denarii and the heavy stuff left in the pit. All the rest was safe.'

'Did you have time to fill in the burrow leading away from the treasure pit?' asks Vera.

Cibus shakes his head. 'The police are bound to have found it,' says Vera.

Cibus gives a wry grin. 'What if they have?' he says. 'Do you think they'll arrest the rabbits?'

'We did our best,' says Petro sadly.

Adrogantio briefly raises his head. 'But it was not good enough,' he says.

'Listen,' says Bony urgently. 'The treasure's gone for now, yes, but it will be coming back.' He explains about the Rooks Ridge Museum and Visitors' Centre.

Petro shakes his head. 'But when it comes back, it won't belong to the Family,' he says. 'It won't be in our care.'

'You could still look after it,' says Vera.

'But we can't,' says Petro. 'Not if it no longer belongs to the descendents of Caius Verus Pugnax Corvo. He laid the charge upon us. We were his Lares and now we are yours, not the Lares of whoever owns the Museum. We have failed to keep it safe for you.'

'We have only stayed this long to say farewell to you, Domines, and ask you to forgive us for failing you," says Adrogantio. A terrible thought strikes Vera.

'Mopsus! Where's Mopsus?' she cries. The Lares gaze at her in silent misery. 'No! No!' cries Vera. 'Tell me, tell me he's all right!'

'He is stone, Domina,' says Adrogantio.

'No!'

'He could not bear to face you,' says Lapidilla softly. 'And he loved the Corvo hoard, he was never happier than when he was looking after it, and caring for it, and polishing it. Now it is gone, and he could not bear either the shame or the loss. He is stone.'

'And now we must go too,' says Adrogantio. *'Valete, Domines!'* He turns, and walks away into the rabbit burrow.

'*Valete, Domines*,' says Grumio gruffly, and follows his lead. Vera and Bony Jay watch in stunned dismay as Lapidilla follows without another word, and Petro and Cibus turn to go.

'Petro! Cibus! No!' cries Vera, and the two small figures hesitate. 'We *will* get it back! I promise you!'

'I think you know that will not happen,' says Petro, and Cibus bows his head in silent agreement. As they too turn to leave, it is Bony Jay who is struck by sudden inspiration.

'No!' he says. 'I am a true descendent of Caius Verus Pugnax Corvo, and I *order* you to stay!'

His words halt the two Lares in their tracks.

'Yes,' says Vera. 'We *order* you to stay.'

"Look, I have to get back to the marquee,' says Bony some time later, when he is reasonably sure that Petro and Cibus aren't going to turn to stone the moment his back is turned. 'Once all the excitement has died down, Trystram will be wanting to start filming again, and he'll throw a fit if I'm not there. I'll try and find out a bit more about the treasure too, while I'm there.'

'And about how we can get it back again,' says Vera firmly. 'I'll stay here for now.' The truth is that she, even more than Bony, is frightened to leave Petro and Cibus alone. 'We could go and visit the shrine again, if you like?' she suggests to them hopefully, and it is a measure of their depression that the two little figures do not even respond. 'Come back as soon as you can,' she says anxiously to Bony as he sets off down the slope from the ridge.

CHAPTER XLI

By the time Bony gets back to the marquee, Trystram has noticed that every one of his team is standing around gossiping about the treasure, and he wastes no time in giving out their afternoon's assignments. The archaeologists, students and camera crew depart. Bony is left alone with the Director.

'What would you like me to do, Trystram?' he asks. Trystram ignores his question.

'I thought little Nicci did remarkably well in her piece to camera just now, didn't you?' says Trystram. 'I'm having dinner with her tonight, to talk about some ideas I've been mulling over for a change in the format of the programme.' He pauses for effect. 'I've been thinking for quite some time that instead of one presenter who hasn't the faintest idea what he's talking about, maybe we could actually use some of the archaeologists. Like Nicci. And Ricky has camera-presence too, don't you think? Smart. Nice-looking. *Young.*' Bony stares at him blankly. 'Of course, your contract is just coming up for renewal, isn't it?' continues Trystram. 'There's a lucky thing. I must go and fetch my briefcase from the car, get a few notes down on paper.'

Why have I spent the last six years of my life working for this poisonous little toad? thinks Bony, and hears himself saying 'Don't bother. I resign. I won't be asking for a new contract. I'd rather work for *One Man and his Dog*. I'd rather be on *I'm a Celebrity, Get Me Out of Here*. I'd rather do a *cookery* programme.'

'I'm sure we will all be very sorry to lose you,' says Trystram, beaming. 'I shall watch your future career with interest. If you have one.'

He turns his back and heads for his car, which is parked on the other side of the flooded track.

'Trystram, wait!' shouts Bony. 'Stop! Stop! Stop!'

Well, it didn't take him *long to come to his senses,* thinks Trystram, smiling one of his tight little smiles. He does not stop, nor even pause. Ignoring his erstwhile presenter's increasingly urgent cries, he strides onwards and plunges straight into the flooded Trench Six.

'Well, I did try to warn him,' says Bony Jay.

Mr Horton, Jim Southerton and Spike the photographer have been watching the scene between Trystram Wentworth and Bony Jay with undisguised fascination, and in Mr Horton's case horrified sympathy as well. Jim is now scribbling frantically in his little notebook, while Spike takes a comprehensive series of shots of Trystram struggling to climb out of Trench Six. Mr Horton barely spares a glance for this entrancing sight. Instead he turns to Bony, his face contorted with anguished concern.

'Bony,' he says helplessly. 'Are you going to be all right?' This, after all, is the man who befriended him at the outset, and who has never once been rude, or dismissive, or unkind.

Bony looks at him. This, after all, is the only archaeologist who has ever treated him like a celebrity, and who has never once been rude, or dismissive, or unkind.

'I'll be fine, Ron,' he says, trying for Mr Horton's sake to sound as if he means it. 'Don't you worry about me.'

'Only it did occur to me,' says Mr Horton tentatively, 'that the Rooks Ridge Museum and Visitors' Centre is going to need a General Manager. You would still be able to do your Chattering Show as well, of course.'

Bony is transfixed.

'Would it involve standing for hours in the pouring rain every day?' he asks.

'No, it would be more of a desk job,' says Mr Horton. 'An indoor desk.'

'Would it involve living in a leaky caravan?'

'No, there's going to be an accommodation block for the people who come on our courses, with a suite for the General Manager.'

'Would it involve living on anything like Mrs Hamble's cooking?'

'No, we're going to have a proper restaurant. Hob has especially vetoed pizza. He was very *definite* about that.'

'How soon can I apply?'

'I believe the advertisement will be going in the papers tomorrow,' says Mr Horton. 'But you could come and meet Hob now, if you like.'

'Do you have any advice for me, Ron?' asks Bony, suddenly and uncharacteristically humble.

'No, I think you're just perfect for the job,' says Mr Horton.

'Stop calling him Ron,' growls Jim Southerton. 'And lose the pigtail.'

CHAPTER XLII

It is four o' clock in the afternoon, and Hob, Mr Horton, Jim Southerton and Bony Jay are watching from the top of Rooks Ridge as the last of the *Ready Steady Dig!* vehicles leave the site. Trystram has closed down the excavation, in the teeth of protests from the archaeologists, who have started to unearth not one but two potentially very exciting mosaics. He does not care about mosaics; he does care about getting back to his hotel for a hot bath. Anyway, he has plenty of material for the programme now - what's a couple of old tiled floors compared with hundreds of thousands of pounds worth of gold and silver? Stuff their mosaics and their bits of broken pot. Stuff Rooks Ridge. And especially stuff Bony Jay.

Bony Jay has been talking non-stop about his ideas for the Rooks Ridge Museum and Visitors' Centre ever since Mr Horton introduced him to Hob; he makes Mr Horton sound taciturn.

'…and Roman medicines and healing practices as well, because the Ancients knew so much more than we do about the virtues of herbs and natural remedies. We could maybe have a herb garden, growing all the plants that the Romans used in their medicine, and in their cooking too, of course.'

'Where?' asks Mr Horton anxiously. 'It would be wonderful, but something permanent like that would have to be where we know that we'd never want to dig.'

'That's easy,' says Bony, and he thinks of the Lares, who so passionately wanted to protect the Family's graves. 'It could go all along the edges of the track, where we thought there were graves, but then there turned out to be nothing at all. We know there's nothing there to dig, so we can plant the herbs beds there.'

'Brilliant,' says Mr Horton happily.

'Of course, we'll need plenty of car-parking,' says Bony Jay. 'That'll take up a lot of space.' Mr Horton looks anxious again.

'The flattest area is the five-acre field,' says Jim. 'Let's go and take a look.'

They move down from the ridge and into the erstwhile wheatfield, and stroll slowly along the hedge line.

'You know,' says Mr Horton, 'I'm afraid I just can't help thinking about the treasure, and how much I wish that *Ready Steady Dig!* had never come back, so that I could have been the one who found it. Does that sound silly?'

'Not in the least,' says Hob kindly.

'It's very unprofessional of me, I know,' says Mr Horton. 'But it would have been so - would have been so -' He has stopped dead, and is staring at the ground as if turned to stone.

'What?' says Jim.

'What?' says Bony Jay.

'There,' says Hob, following Mr Horton's gaze and pointing at the shard of Berumware replaced by Petro a few hours earlier. Mr Horton falls to his knees in the muddy plough soil, and lifts the precious object with trembling hands. He wipes it carefully with his handkerchief, and gazes at it in rapture.

'Berumware!' he cries. 'And it's *decorated!* It's actually got the pigeon-crow-reversed sheep motif! *The whole thing!*'

'Is he all right?' asks Bony. 'He looks as if he's having a seizure.'

'He's fine,' says Jim fondly. 'He's found something much better than gold and silver. I think you could say that he has looked upon the face of Aggie Melon.'

CHAPTER XLIII

When Hob, Jim and Mr Horton have finally taken their leave, Bony Jay races back up to Rooks Ridge. Vera, Petro and Cibus are still there.

'I've lost my job,' he announces, 'but it doesn't mean I'm just giving up.' He looks sternly at the Lares. *'I'm* not going to turn to stone, I'm going to get myself a new job. And you could too.'

Petro and Cibus stare at him blankly. There is no hope at all in their sad eyes.

'Hob is going to build the Rooks Ridge Museum and Visitors Centre, and I'm applying to be the General Manager,' continues Bony. 'So I'll be in charge of the treasure. It won't actually belong to me, of course -'

'You could steal it back!' cries Vera. Bony swallows hard. He hadn't anticipated *that* response.

'I really don't think -'

'You could!' insists Vera.

'That would be ok,' says Petro cautiously, and Cibus nods.

'No it would not,' says Bony, very firmly. This is a crazy idea, and he has to scotch it right now. Living in his horrible caravan has been bad enough, but he is pretty sure that living in one of Her Majesty's Prisons would be immeasurably worse. 'Anyway, I couldn't possibly steal from Hob.'

'Who's Hob?' asks Petro. 'Does he own the treasure now?'

'Well,' says Bony hesitantly, 'there was this solicitor down at the marquee, and he talked non-stop for about ten minutes about exactly that, and I'm still not really sure of the answer. I think it'll be up to the Coroner, when he holds his inquest, but as far as I could make out, it will belong either to the landowner or to the Queen, and if it's the Queen, she won't want to keep it.'

'Well, I expect it would need an awful lot of polishing, and she wouldn't really have the time,' says Vera. 'The landowner is Sir Oriole, of course. Hob, I should say, he won't let anyone call him by his real names.'

Petro gazes at Vera as if he has already turned to stone. 'Who did you say?' he asks in a very quiet voice.

215

'Hob. His real name is Sir Oriole Ravenscroft-Corbie-Hob,' answers Vera. 'He's that nice old man who's often up here. He lives just outside Crowborough, at a cottage called Jackdaws' Roost.'

Petro stares at Vera, transfixed, and Cibus' jaw drops.

'Oriole! Raven! Corbie! Jackdaw!' yells Petro, punching the air with his fist. 'We *thought* there was someone else in the Family round here!'

'What's an oriole?' asks Bony.

'What's a corbie?' asks Vera.

'An oriole is a member of the crow family,' says Petro. 'I've never seen one in Britannia, but we used to have them in Italy, and Masilia, and Gaul.'

'Corbie is a folk-name for a crow,' says Bony the New Age enthusiast. 'Ravens and jackdaws are a sort of crow too, aren't they?' They all look at each other, hardly daring to believe it.

'The Corvo treasure still belongs to a descendent of the Corvo family,' says Cibus, in a shaky voice that sounds most unlike him.

'And the Corvo treasure will be coming back to Rooks Ridge,' says Petro.

'Yes,' says Vera, and Petro and Cibus hug each other.

When everyone has got over the shock, it is Bony who voices the question Vera has been dreading.

'So what about the others? Is there any way we can get them back?'

'I don't know, Domine,' says Petro simply. 'You can try.'

'What do we do?' Vera asks.

'I don't know,' he replies. 'Perhaps if you called them?'

Vera kneels down close to the entrance to the rabbit burrow and calls softly to the Stone Lares.

'Adrogantio! Lapidilla! Grumio! Mopsus!'

Nothing happens.

'Mop*se*,' says Petro. 'You need the vocative case, not the nominative.'

'Do you really think that'll make a difference?' asks Bony, a touch sarcastically.

'Well, it might,' says Petro stoutly. 'Call them in Latin, Domina. Proper Latin, like we taught you.'

Vera takes a breath, and calls softly a second time.

'Adrogantio! Lapidilla! Grumio! Mopse! Revenite!'

Still nothing happens. Vera sits back on her heels, and looks up at Bony in despair.

'They won't come back,' she says, and feels the tears welling up. 'They won't come back.'

'Try again!' says Petro. 'Try, Domina Vera!' Vera shakes her head.

'It's no good, it's too late!' she cries. 'Adrogantio! Lapidilla! Grumio! Mopsus! *Please* come back!'

But there is no response, and Vera feels the tears running down her cheeks.

'Let me in there,' says Bony suddenly. 'You're doing it all wrong. You're being too soft on them.' He pushes Vera to one side, and kneels down at the mouth of the rabbit burrow. 'They're *our* Lares, and they'll do as they're told! *Lares Corvonorum, revenire imperamus!*' he says sternly. 'And I mean right now this minute!'

Petro regards him with awe.

'I didn't know you could speak Latin, Domine,' he says. Bony shrugs.

'Everybody used to do Latin when I was at school,' he says simply. 'They always told us it would be useful in later life, although I don't think this is quite what they had in mind.'

'Look!' says Vera softly, as a dazed-looking Adrogantio appears at the mouth of the rabbit burrow, with Lapidilla, Grumio and Mopsus behind him.

'The treasure still belongs to the Corvo Family!' Vera says quickly. 'It belongs to Hob, or it will do because the Queen won't want it even if it turns out to be hers, and Hob is a Corvo, and it will be coming back to Rooks Ridge soon, very soon.'

'Even the plates and the wine jug?' asks Adrogantio, ever one to look a gift horse in the mouth.

'Yes, Adro. Them too. All of it,' says Bony Jay.

CHAPTER XLIV

Next morning, Bony Jay makes his way back up to Rooks Ridge. Today he has to leave Crowborough, to return to London for his chat show, and he doesn't want to go without saying goodbye. Besides, he still hasn't had a chance to collect his coin from the rabbit burrow, and he's going to need it. The morning's post has already brought a depressing number of final demands, and the sooner he can turn the gold into pounds sterling the better.

From a distance he sees that the Lares are all there, sunning themselves on the grass as they watch the skylarks spiralling up into a clear blue sky. With them is a tiny old man in rough-looking clothes of browny-green. He looks remarkably like Hob, except that he is only six inches tall. Petro sits up and waves to Bony as he reaches the top of the slope.

'*Salve,* Dominus Osseus!' Petro calls out. 'This is the Genius Loci. The rain yesterday, that was all down to him.'

'Well done!' says Bony. 'It was really - really - *Argh!*'

He sits down abruptly on the grass. The little old man is not little at all, he is a huge man, big as the hills, tall as the heavens, and the browny-green is leaves and grass and earth and stone, and in his blue-grey eyes is the whole infinite, cloud-dappled, lark-haunted Cotswold sky. Then suddenly he is gone, and there are only the Lares sitting on the grass, staring at Bony with some concern.

'I told you people get upset,' says a bramble bush, or something deep within its leaves.

'You know,' says Bony Jay to the Lares, when he has got his breathing back under control, and his heart is beating at only twice its normal rate, 'now that there's no danger of you all being carted off and put in some distant museum, it would be really good if I could *find* you all. The day before my job interview would be favourite. That should clinch it for me. Mind you, Hob told me that as far as he's concerned it's already in the bag.'

Petro objects. 'If anyone is going to find us, don't you think it should be Magister Horton?'

'No,' says Bony. 'He doesn't need you like I do. Anyway, it's me that's Family, right?'

'But it would make him so happy,' says Lapidilla.

'He's got all the happiness he can handle right now,' says Bony firmly. 'He's just found his heart's desire. And if I'm not mistaken, he's just *about* to find his heart's desire as well.' Mind you, thinks Bony, that young reporter may be tall, dark and quite astonishingly handsome, but how can he ever hope to compete for attention with a bit of old pot with a pigeon/crow/dead-sheep motif? Perhaps he can pass the time comparing notes with Stillaria.

'What will happen if you do discover us, Domine?' asks Petro.

'Well, you'll all be put on display in the Rooks Ridge Museum and Visitors' Centre. You could have a proper Lararium again - Professor Jones told us all about those. The visitors would love it. And then at night when everyone's gone, you'd all have your old jobs back, just like when the Family still lived here.

'We're going to be doing courses on Roman medicines and cosmetics and things, Lapidilla, and making them too, to go in the Gift Shop.' Lapidilla claps her hands in delight. 'And Roman food.' Cibus beams. 'And there will be a state-of-the-art kitchen in the restaurant, of course.'

'Will there be *woks*?' asks Petro, his eyes shining.

'Yes, I promise,' says Bony Jay. 'And more cafetieres than you can shake a stick at.'

'Oh *wow*!'

'Grumio, you were Lar of the Chimney, weren't you?' asks Bony. 'There's going to be Roman metal-working and pottery-making, so there will be a furnace and a kiln. And there'll be a working model of a hypocaust. With *flues*.'

'Sounds ok,' says Grumio cautiously, very nearly cracking a smile.

'Mopsus, what was your job?' asks Bony.

'Please, Domine, I was Lar of the Broom,' says Mopsus shyly.

'He used to come out at night to make sure the house slaves had all done their work properly,' explains Lapidilla.

'Do it for them, more like,' says Grumio.

'I didn't mind,' says Mopsus. 'I really really like cleaning things, and tidying things, and polishing things. The children's bedrooms were the best. They never put *anything* away.' He smiles fondly at the memory of Roman teenagers.

'Perfect,' says Bony. 'There will be cleaning staff, of course, with a Head Cleaner - Vera's Mum thinks she might apply for that - and you could keep an eye on them for me. And you'll be able to polish the Corvo treasure every single night if you want.'

Mopsus bursts into tears of happiness.

'And I?' says Adrogantio.

'Ah yes,' says Bony, suddenly feeling unaccountably nervous. 'What was your job, Adro?'

'Job? Job?' says Adrogantio thoughtfully. 'I would call it more of an Executive Role,' he says. 'I was in charge.'

'Right,' says Bony. 'Well, of course, you know I'm going to be the General Manager -'

'That will be splendid,' says Adrogantio. 'I am sure we will work very well together. I shall shadow you at all times. Keep you up to the mark. Offer helpful and constructive criticism whenever required. And so forth.'

'That'll be good,' says Bony faintly.

'My door is always open,' says Adrogantio.

Ah well, thinks Bony, I never really thought I could get away with any more of the treasure. Which reminds me ...

'Petro, how about taking me back to that rabbit burrow now? To collect the you-know-what?'

Petro looks stricken, but Bony doesn't notice: he scoops him up and strides off towards the hedgerow where he believes his treasure awaits.

Vera arrives just in time to see Bony heading purposefully in the direction of the rabbit burrow.

'Oh dear. Oh no. Oh dear,' she says helplessly. 'He's taken Petro to go and get the gold coin, hasn't he?'

'Yes, Domina,' says Adrogantio.

'The coin that I took and put in Stillaria's spring.'

'Yes, Domina.'

'So it's not there any more, is it?'

'No, Domina.'

'He'll be *so* angry, won't he?' says Vera in a frightened whisper.

'No, Domina,' says Adrogantio.

'No?'

'No. He will be very contented,' says Adrogantio. Vera stares at him as if he has gone mad. 'Petro told me that you took the coin that he gave to Dominus Osseus,' continues the Lar. 'So I made an Executive Decision. I fetched another coin from the hoard, and buried it in the mouth of the rabbit burrow.'

In the distance, cries of *Yes! Yes! Yes!* can clearly be heard.

'I think that he has just found it.'

EPILOGUE

Beneath a sky of cloudless blue, the high green wolds slumber in the summer heat. A myriad bees murmur in the grasses, and a blackbird sings his heart out from a hedgerow heavy with creamy elder flowers, whose honey perfume drifts on the soft breeze.

At the foot of a barely perceptible mound beneath a solitary hawthorn bush, the six Lares stand quietly with heads bowed. The latest invaders have left at last, and the land is at peace again. The blackbird falls silent as Vera gently puts down the little statue, Fidelio the Stone Lar, and lays beside him a posy of bright meadow flowers.

'Sleep well, Vera Alauda,' she says softly. 'They are gone now, and Fidelio is here. Rest in peace.'

And as she turns to leave, a tiny valiant lark takes flight, and spirals upwards to the infinite blue, on wings of joyful song.

Acknowledgements

My very grateful thanks go to Dawn and Ted Molenkamp for all their help and support during my constant computer crises, from the Vanishing Page Numbers to the Ever-Opening CD Drawer; to Ted for designing the book covers and unlocking the mysteries of the pdf and the jpg at 300 dpi; to Lizzie Gates, Annett Hillebrand, Mairi Macdonald, Mary Perry, Coralie Steel and Nick Winter for advice, suggestions and support; and finally to Moyra Holland for introducing me to Latin at Stratford-upon-Avon Grammar School for Girls, and for organising the school trip to Chedworth Roman Villa that sparked my life-long interest in the archaeology of Roman Britain.

Any mistakes are, of course, entirely my own.

Coming soon from the same author …

GNOME OR MR NICE GUY

Terror stalks the little town of Crowborough and the Rooks Ridge Museum and Visitors Centre.
A violent serial killer is on the loose.
He strikes openly in broad daylight, and yet nobody ever sees him. His target?
Garden gnomes…

Printed in the United Kingdom
by Lightning Source UK Ltd.
135338UK00001B/94/P